Witch Haven Weddings - part one

K.E. O'Connor

K.E. O'Connor Books

You are cordially invited to the wedding of...
Indigo Ash and Olympus Duke

Chapter 1

"If anyone had bothered to ask me, I'd have told them a winter wedding in Witch Haven was bound to get weird." My curmudgeonly black cat familiar, Nugget, sat on the inn's warped wooden bar, washing his face with a paw.

"It'll be fine." My soon-to-be husband, Olympus Duke, placed an arm around my shoulders and gave me a gentle squeeze. "Dobbie is just running late."

I held in a sigh. The last thing we needed on the day before our wedding was for our celebrant to be unreliable. And I'd not mentioned it to Olympus, but the first time I'd met Dobbie Doubleday, his powerful cologne had hidden a whiff of whiskey, so I was concerned he'd been attacking the Christmas spirits this evening and had lost track of time.

Olympus pressed a kiss to my forehead. "Everything's under control. This is the only hiccup we've had to face in the run up to our wedding day."

"So far," Nugget muttered as he shuffled closer to the roaring open fire in one of the large hearths.

I checked the time. Dobbie was half an hour late for the ceremony's final run-through. "What about the wedding cake? Albert said there'd been an incident, and he was behind schedule."

"Most likely because Luna got involved with decorating it," Nugget said.

My plump, long-legged spider familiar, Hilda, descended from the ceiling on a string of silver webbing and landed on Nugget's head. "Don't jinx the wedding with your grousing comments. Everything will be perfect. A wedding on Christmas Day is romantic."

I leaned in close to Olympus, keeping my voice low. "Dobbie wasn't keen on performing the ceremony. He could have changed his mind and left Witch Haven without telling us."

"He wouldn't dare. I'll admit, I had to twist his arm to officiate, but he's on board. Indigo, we're doing this. Any second now, Dobbie will get here full of apologies. We'll run through the ceremony, and then we can relax."

I rolled my shoulders and looked around the warm, festively decorated inn. The preparations for our wedding had gone smoothly until now. The venue had been available, we'd gotten a great deal on flowers, and Luna's Uncle Albert had offered to make our wedding cake as his gift to us. And we were keeping the ceremony small, just close friends and a few of Olympus's family, so things wouldn't get complicated.

I had no family to attend the special day, so it was simple to come up with a guest list. And I figured a small, intimate wedding at Christmas would be a fun way to get hitched without causing drama.

But we weren't getting hitched until our wedding celebrant showed up and walked us through tomorrow's ceremony.

"I could always stand in." Monty, Olympus's cheeky leopard familiar, poked his head over the top of the bar where he'd been hunting for food. "I can be Dobbie. I've been at all your planning meetings, so I know how everything works."

"You'll trip over your paws, eat the flowers, and end up getting yourself married to Indigo," Nugget said.

Monty swished his enormous tail and growled. "I could do it! I'd even dress up. What will the celebrant wear? I'd look amazing in a robe. Do you have time to buy one for me?"

"Thanks for the offer," I said, "but everywhere is closing since it's Christmas Eve. There'll be no time to find you a robe."

"I could use a curtain. That would work. What else do I need?" Monty leapt over the bar in an elegant movement, almost squashing my other familiar, an adorable jet-black crow, called Russell. He squawked in protest and flapped away, settling in a safer position on the back of a chair.

I walked to the window and peered out. It was only four in the afternoon, but darkness had settled over Witch Haven, and a huge bank of yellow clouds suggested we were in for more snow.

When Olympus had suggested our wedding take place on Christmas Day, I'd hesitated. But he'd convinced me it was the easiest way to have a small wedding because most people would be busy with their families and wouldn't be able to get away.

That's what had convinced me since I wasn't a fan of crowds. And a Christmas wedding did sound romantic.

I may have lost most of my romantic bones as life tossed me around in its maelstrom of adventures, but I loved Olympus, and I wanted to be his wife. There was something magical about getting married at Christmas.

The door to the inn was shoved open, and I turned, hopeful Dobbie had arrived. Instead, my three closest friends, Luna Brimstone, Odessa Grimsbane, and Storm Winter, marched in, bundled in thick winter clothes and covered in a thick spattering of snow.

"Sorry we're late." Odessa unwrapped a bright orange knitted scarf from around her face and neck. "We've been helping Storm ward off those clouds. Have you seen them? Snow is coming. Lots of snow!"

Storm stamped her booted feet and kept her hands stuffed into her coat pockets. "There's only so much I can do to keep it at bay. You're in for a white wedding."

Luna looked around. "Did you wait for us before starting?"

"Dobbie hasn't arrived," I said.

"He's usually reliable," Olympus said. "There'll be a reason he's late."

"He most likely got lost in the bottom of a bottle of whiskey," Storm muttered as she brushed flakes of snow out of her dark hair.

I turned to Olympus. "You didn't mention he liked a drink when you suggested him as our wedding celebrant."

Olympus lifted his hands, his gaze calm. "He's a sociable guy and is always the first to get in a round of drinks. It won't be a problem."

"It will if he's passed out drunk somewhere and forgets the wedding," Nugget said.

"We'll go look for him," Hilda said. "He's staying at the bed-and-breakfast, isn't he?"

"I'll come with you," Storm said. "I still don't like the look of that cloud bank. I'll send up a magic warning to ensure it doesn't get too feisty." Most people considered Storm spiky, and she had her moments, but when she let you in, you were a friend for life, and she'd do anything to keep her friends safe, even battle looming mountains of snow with her incredible elemental magic.

"It won't take long." Hilda scuttled along the bar. "Let's move, Nugget. You too, Russell."

"Why must I go?" Nugget asked. "It's warm in here, and I was planning a nap behind the dishwasher on the heating pipe. It's the perfect snooze place."

"Because you want to make sure Indigo and Olympus have the perfect day tomorrow. They can't have that until Dobbie's here." Hilda thumped her spidery limbs against his ears. "You're only grumpy because you missed out on your afternoon snack."

"Monty stole it!" Nugget said. "That was my dried meat stick, and he nabbed it while my back was turned."

Monty lowered his head and whined. "I was hungry. Olympus never feeds me enough."

"Check the size of your gut and try that again," Olympus said.

"I'm a growing familiar. I need extra calories." Monty sucked in his stomach. "And I'm in prime physical shape."

"Primed for a heart attack if you keep stealing my food." Nugget jumped off the end of the bar, Hilda on his back. "Let's get this over with, then we can go home."

"I'm coming too," Monty said. "Maybe I'll convince Dobbie I can co-host the wedding. That would be amazing."

Olympus opened his mouth to protest, but I walked over and took hold of his hand, gently shaking my head. "Let him go. As soon as we get Dobbie here, the sooner everyone can get back to enjoying the Christmas spirit. Or napping and grousing, in Nugget's case."

Olympus nodded. "Monty, behave. Go straight to the bed-and-breakfast and bring Dobbie back. No getting distracted by anything."

Monty stood to attention. "I won't let you down." He barged past Storm and my familiars and shot out the door, letting in a blast of icy air.

"That cat has too much energy," Olympus grumbled.

"Make sure to give him a long run tomorrow morning so he burns off his extra energy," I said. "Hopefully, he'll sleep through the ceremony and only wake for the dinner."

Olympus kissed the back of my hand. "Tomorrow will be perfect. All the stress will be gone. And I'll be the happiest man alive once you're my wife."

"You two are sweet." Odessa grinned and nudged Luna. "I never thought I'd see the day when you convinced Indigo to marry you."

"It took some trying," Olympus said. "Six rejections before she accepted me."

"Three of those proposals were when you'd had too much to drink," I said. "I couldn't take them seriously. They were like your first proposal when we'd just met and you were under the influence of a spell that made you obsessed with me."

Olympus's cheeks flushed. "Everyone was acting strangely then. I wasn't the only one affected."

"You were the only one affected with an obsessive love." Odessa giggled. "It was adorable."

"I had to know your proposals were serious," I said. "And of course, I needed time to make sure our familiars got along."

"Monty loves everyone," Olympus said. "You were making excuses."

"You got there in the end. That's the main thing," Luna said. "And tomorrow, it all comes together."

"And you'll be next," Odessa said to her. "Got any werewolf wedding jitters?"

Luna grimaced. "Let's focus on Indigo and Olympus's special day. A werewolf-witch union is a whole other world of weird I'm not prepared to discuss."

"So many weddings." Odessa sighed and pressed a hand to her chest. "And it'll be so beautiful if we get more snow overnight."

"Just not too much snow," Olympus said. "I've got family arriving in the morning, and I don't want them to get stuck on the way here."

I'd met a few members of Olympus's family. They'd been cautiously welcoming, given my checkered past, but they were excited to see Olympus married, and there'd been several comments that he was only married to his work and how surprised they were that he'd found a woman who'd put up with him. I cared nothing for other people's opinions, only that we were happier together than apart.

The inn door cracked open again. Peony Cashmere, Olympus's former fiancée, poked her head around the side of the door. "Hey, I hope I'm not intruding. I was told you'd be here."

I gulped down my surprise at seeing her. "Peony! Come in." I looked up at Olympus, and he seemed equally stunned she was here.

He pulled himself together and hurried to the door. "I didn't know you were in the area. You don't have Bloom until next weekend, do you? Or have I made a mistake?"

"I'm not here for Bloom. Well, part of me is." Peony stepped inside and closed the door behind her, her pretty face bright from the cold. "I'm here for your wedding. If that's okay."

"Oh! I didn't think you were attending since you didn't RSVP." Olympus led Peony over to the group, closer to the warmth of the fire. She was short, pretty, and dark-haired. They'd separated not long after their daughter, Bloom, had gone missing. I'd met Peony many times since she shared custody of Bloom with Olympus, and after a few hesitant meetings, we'd warmed to each other. She was an excellent mother and genuinely happy Olympus had moved on with me.

"It was a last-minute decision," Peony said. "I was feeling weird about you getting married, but I couldn't miss seeing Bloom in her beautiful bridesmaid's dress. And I got you a gift." She thrust out a small, wrapped package.

Olympus took it and set it on the bar. "Thanks. And you're welcome. It won't be a big celebration, but we can easily fit you in."

"I'll only stay for the ceremony," she said. "I don't want to intrude. It's bad manners to show up unannounced."

"Bloom would love to have you here for the whole event," I said. "And there'll be plenty of food. We're keeping it informal, so you won't even have to dress up."

Peony's smile was a little strained as she turned her attention to Olympus and bit her bottom lip. "This is odd. You're getting married! I didn't think I'd feel like this."

A small knot formed in my gut. "How do you feel?"

Peony shrugged. "It's silly, but if things hadn't happened the way they had, it would have been me marrying Olympus."

Olympus cleared his throat. "Everything happens for a reason. And we were young when we got engaged."

"And then you lost our daughter," Peony said. "That was hard to forgive."

I stepped forward, my gaze narrowed. "Olympus wasn't to blame for that. You know what happened. It could as easily have happened when Bloom was with you."

Peony tensed then sighed. "Sorry. You're right. I've been doing a lot of thinking recently. Bloom is growing up so fast. You're getting married. And me... I feel lost. That's why I decided to come to the wedding. It's the final door closing. Once you're married, I can move on."

I held in my frustration. "Didn't that door close a long time ago? And you have moved on. You seem happy. You're dating."

Peony's laugh was a little too high-pitched to be natural. "Maybe this is an early midlife crisis. I don't know. But I didn't come here to cause trouble. I'm pleased you're getting married, and I want the best for both of you. Bloom loves spending time with you. She's always talking about your familiars, Indigo." She glanced around. "They'll be at the ceremony, won't they?"

"You can guarantee it," I said. "They've just left to see to some last-minute wedding business."

Peony nodded, her hands clasped together. "I... yeah. Good. So, congrats. I'm looking forward to tomorrow. I'll sit at the back and keep a low profile. I don't want this to get strange."

"It won't be strange," I said. "And sit where you like. Bloom will want you up the front so she can show you her dress."

Peony smiled, gratitude in her eyes. "Thanks, Indigo. I knew you'd understand."

No one spoke, and the tension grew. Was Peony happy we were getting married, or did she still have feelings for Olympus? She couldn't, not after all this time. Their romantic relationship was ancient history.

"If there's nothing else," Olympus cleared his throat, "I'll show you out. You'll want to settle in and rest before tomorrow. You're staying somewhere local?"

"I'm renting a room from Mystica." Peony nodded, looked around the group, and then let Olympus walk her to the door.

"That was strange," Luna said the second Peony left. "She seemed worried about something."

"Peony's always been eccentric. You don't think she'll cause trouble at the ceremony, do you?" Odessa asked.

I hesitated. "No, but it must be strange for her, seeing the man she'd planned to marry make things official with someone else."

"You should check the gift she gave you," Luna said. "Make sure it's not spiked with anything nasty."

"Like a bad hair spell or a jinxing spell on your wedding dress." Odessa laughed as she prodded the parcel. "Peony's not malicious, though, just kooky. I used to love her upcycling store."

I looked at the small, wrapped gift and frowned. "I'll let Olympus open it."

He returned to the group after saying goodbye to Peony at the door. "Don't worry. She won't be a problem."

"I'm not worried, but I understand her feeling strange. I'd feel the same way if I got an invitation to the wedding of the first guy I'd fallen in love with." I squeezed his elbow. "I'm surprised she even showed up. When we got silence after we sent the invitation, I figured she wasn't interested."

"We'll make sure she does nothing shady," Luna said. "I'll get Cole to watch her and sniff out any trouble."

"Thanks, but Peony doesn't need a werewolf guard," Olympus said. "She'll spend most of her time with Bloom, anyway. That's why she's here."

I was confident in my relationship with Olympus and knew Peony was no threat, but I'd keep an eye on her during tomorrow's ceremony, just in case.

Olympus checked the time and frowned. "Monty should be back by now. The bed-and-breakfast is five minutes from here. He must have gotten upended in a snowdrift again. I keep having to yank him out whenever he goes snow diving. He gets snow clogged in his fur and stuck between his toepads and panics. I'd better go rescue him."

"I'll come too. I need fresh air. And once we've dug Monty free, we can walk to the bed-and-breakfast and meet with the others. See just how sozzled Dobbie is."

"I'll grab my coat." Olympus walked through to the back room of the inn.

"We'll stay here," Luna said. "Wait around to see if any more last-minute guests arrive and want to stir up old memories."

"Any news on your uncle's cake?" I tugged on my thick winter coat and pulled a bobble hat down over my ears.

Luna inspected a damp spot on the floor. "It'll be perfection."

"It's not ready yet?"

She gave a little shrug and still wouldn't meet my gaze. "There was a tiny problem."

"How tiny are we talking?"

"I... I wanted to help, but you know my baking magic can be weird. Don't worry. Uncle Albert is fixing everything. You won't even know I touched it by tomorrow."

Her words did nothing to settle my growing nerves. "I look forward to seeing it. Hopefully in time for when everyone wants to eat a slice."

"I've never let you down. Now go. Find your wedding celebrant." Luna shooed me to the door so enthusiastically that I sensed all was not well with the cake.

After giving her some serious don't-screw-up-my-cake side-eye, I pulled open the door. A menacing-eyed doll glared at me. I jumped back and yelped.

Ursa Worm peered around the doll. "Whatever's the matter with you?"

"Ursa! Um... what's that?" I jabbed a finger at the creepy doll.

"Your wedding gift." Ursa stamped inside, uninvited, snow splattering off her boots and across the floor.

"You got Indigo a hexed killer doll as a wedding gift?" Luna wandered over and peered at the doll. "She's creepy."

"She's not hexed! Nor is she creepy."

"Is she a killer doll? Full of dark magic? Maybe she's got a curse on her?" Odessa stood a healthy distance away from the unwanted gift, frowning at the doll. We'd all had less than friendly dealings with Ursa's twisted doll collection. They tended to get stabby if you didn't have your guard up.

"Why do I bother? I spent weeks searching for the perfect doll for your wedding, and this is the thanks I get." Ursa turned to leave, the freaky doll clutched to her bony chest.

I glanced at Luna, and she shrugged. "Wait! Thanks, Ursa. I appreciate the effort. She's... unique." I'd repaired fences with Ursa a while back and didn't want to insult her by refusing the disturbing present.

Ursa turned away from the door and looked down at the doll. "You want her?"

"Of course! What's her name?" I gingerly took the doll and held it at arm's length.

Ursa lifted one shoulder. "You name her. She's yours."

"Um... Cyanide?"

"Be sensible."

"She looks like a Bonnie. You know, like Bonnie and Clyde." Luna stifled a smile.

Ursa tutted. "I expect to see her at your wedding. She's a good luck doll."

"We'll find the perfect spot for her." Olympus walked out of the back room with his coat on and smiled warmly at Ursa.

I hoped he considered the recycling heap at the end of the yard the perfect spot. That doll was going nowhere near our wedding or the house.

Ursa pulled her thick green cloak tighter around her shoulders and nodded. "Just don't let her near anything flammable."

"Will her clothing catch fire?" I asked.

"She's a fire bug. She can catch anything alight when she sets her mind to it. Have a good evening." Ursa swept out into the snow.

I set the doll on the bar and glared at her. "A good luck doll that's a pyromaniac. Most unfun, unwanted wedding gift ever."

"That was Ursa being nice," Olympus said.

I snorted a laugh. "I know. I've dealt with her when she's being mean. Let's get out of here." I yanked open the door, and a powerful swirl of icy wind and snow slammed into me and knocked me flat on my back.

Chapter 2

"Stay still. You hit your head when you went down." Olympus was crouched beside me, concern etched on his handsome face.

"Ugh. What happened?" My vision was blurry, my head pounded, and I was freezing.

"The weather's gotten weird." Odessa was on my other side, while Luna knelt by my head.

"That was not your average gust of wind. And the snow tasted metallic and bitter." I attempted to lift onto my elbows, but the room spun, so I sank back down.

"Stay there for a few more minutes," Olympus said. "Luna's using healing magic on you, so you'll feel fine soon."

I stayed on the cold floor, but my gaze moved to the window. A thick curtain of snow pelted down outside. "When did that start?"

"It was rolling in when we were walking here." Luna held her hands on either side of my head as she pulsed healing magic over me. "I thought I'd held it off with Storm. We were working with our magic for over two hours before we came here, but it felt as if something was fighting us the whole time."

"It makes sense that someone wants to dump a pile of snow on Witch Haven on Christmas Day," Odessa said. "Everyone loves a white Christmas."

"Sure, a white Christmas, but not a Snowmageddon Christmas." I succeeded in sitting up. Luna's healing magic was doing wonders, and my head no longer hurt.

"Go slowly." Olympus helped me to my feet.

"I'm good. Thanks for healing me."

"Anytime." Luna stood and rolled her shoulders.

"I'm not sure it's safe to go outside." Odessa peered through the window. "I might get my scarecrows to carry me home. They can withstand anything. They love going out in the worst storms and fighting them. I often see my boys running around the pumpkin fields, chasing lightning bolts."

"No news from Storm?" I asked Olympus as he settled me in a chair.

"They're still not back," Olympus said. "And you were out cold for fifteen minutes."

I arched an eyebrow. Definitely not natural weather if it had behaved that violently toward me. I touched the back of my head, where a small egg-shaped lump remained.

"They must have stayed inside because the weather turned bad so suddenly," Odessa said. "I'm sure they'll be here as soon as they can with Dobbie."

"I've sent Storm two messages, but she hasn't responded," Luna said.

"If someone conjured this amount of snow, the magic will interfere with communications." Olympus scowled at the snow. "When I find out who's behind this, they'll be spending Christmas behind bars. Especially if it ruins our wedding day."

"Nothing's been ruined." Odessa patted his cheek. "Limpy, don't get stressed. It makes you look constipated."

"Please, don't call me that. We need to know what's going on with Dobbie. This is our final chance to run through the ceremony."

Odessa glanced at Luna. "You two stay here. We'll visit the bed-and-breakfast and make sure everything is fine."

"We should go," I said. "We can run through the ceremony details while we're there and save Dobbie a battle through this freezing weather."

"Are you up to it?" Olympus asked. "You whacked your head hard."

"I want to get this over with, and then I can put my feet up. I need to relax before tomorrow or I'll break out in pimples."

"Stress pimples." Odessa nodded knowingly. "The last thing you need on your wedding day is a bright red pimple on the end of your nose that everyone stares at."

"Don't put that thought out there!" I said. "Let's go, Olympus."

He wasn't happy about me going anywhere and protested for a few minutes before I convinced him it was the right thing to do. This time, he went first, easing the door open and getting a face full of snow. Then we slid outside, keeping a firm grip on each other's hands, our heads bent, almost blinded by the driving snow as we shuffled toward the bed-and-breakfast.

There were slips and slides and plenty of curses as we became thoroughly frozen and soaked by the snow, so it was a welcome sight when we saw the bed-and-breakfast's glowing sign.

We dashed through the door, and I groaned inwardly in relief as the welcoming warmth seeped through my coat. There was no one at the small reception desk, but it looked occupied, suggesting the receptionist had only stepped away for a few moments.

"Dobbie's in room five," Olympus said. "I know where it is."

We walked along the corridor and found his room. Olympus knocked on the door. There was no answer. He tried the handle. It was unlocked. Olympus knocked again. "Dobbie, it's Olympus and Indigo. Did you forget our meeting?"

"Go in. Make sure nothing is wrong." The unsettling silence triggered an alert in me.

Olympus knocked again. "Dobbie's probably taken Monty and the others for a drink in the bar while they wait out the weather."

"Look in his room!" I tried to sound casual, but unease swirled through me. Where had everyone gone? If Storm had arrived and found Dobbie, she'd have dragged him back to the inn no matter how much he protested or how much alcohol he offered her.

Olympus inched open the door. He took two steps inside then stopped so abruptly that I bumped into him.

I peered over his shoulder, and my stomach dropped. Storm, Nugget, Russell, and Hilda were unconscious on the floor, and the room looked like it had been the setting for a wrestling match. And there was blood. A lot of blood.

I pushed past Olympus and hurried to Storm. She was on her back, her skin even paler than usual, and her eyes closed. "She's breathing." I tapped her cheek. "Storm! What happened?"

"Nugget's stirring." Olympus was checking my familiars. "Hilda and Russell are fine, too. Russell is moving a wing and blinking."

"Watch over Storm." We traded places, and I scooped Nugget into my arms and flooded restorative magic over him, ensuring our bond thrived. I was relieved to feel that reassuring tug between us. Nugget shuffled about, twitching his whiskers, and opened one eye. He growled.

"Hey, what happened? Who did this to you?" I asked.

Nugget opened his mouth, but nothing came out. He wrinkled his nose and tried again, but I got the same silence.

"Rest for a minute. I'll see to Hilda and Russell."

"Where's Monty?" Olympus asked. "I don't see him anywhere."

Nugget pointed a paw at the bed and growled again.

Olympus crawled over on his hands and knees and lifted the cover. "He's under here! He's unconscious, too." He shoved an arm under the bed then sighed. "He's breathing fine. Just can't get him to wake."

I spent a few minutes focused on my familiars, while Olympus watched over Storm and Monty, making sure they weren't injured and helping them regain consciousness.

"Can any of you tell me what happened?" I sat on the floor with my incredible familiars, a bundle of feathers, fur, and limbs, not wanting to let them go. We'd lost our bond years ago, but now I had them back, I always ensured our magical connection was strong and stable.

Hilda was wobbly on her limbs, but she hopped onto my knee and speed-weaved a beautiful shimmering web. When she was done, it showed an explosion.

"Magic did this to you?" I asked.

They all nodded. Russell squawked, startling himself as well as us. He flapped off my lap and settled on the floor, close to my feet.

"You'll all get your voices back soon," I said. "It must be a side effect of the spell used on you. Did you see who cast it?"

They shook their heads.

"And the blood?" I pointed at several worrying smears on the floor and wall. "Does it belong to Dobbie?"

There were several shrugs and a lot of shuffling. Russell mimicked being startled and then collapsing.

My concern turned to anger. I had to know who had done this. No one messed with my familiars or my wedding plans and got away with it.

"Monty is waking," Olympus said. "Help me to pull him out. He's so heavy, I can't move him on my own."

I settled Nugget and Hilda on the floor, shuffled to one side of the bed, and gently pushed Monty's dead weight toward Olympus. He had to slide under the bed so he could wrap his arms around Monty's enormous midsection before dragging him out.

Monty was whimpering and flapping his paws, but his eyes were blinking as he came back to consciousness.

Russell squawked again and flapped his wings, and Nugget was making grumbling sounds in the back of his throat, so whatever magic had hit them was definitely wearing off.

Olympus had Monty's giant head resting on his lap, one hand stroking his thick fur. "Who did this to you, old boy? You tell me, and we'll make them pay."

Monty stopped scrabbling his paws in the air and heaved out a sigh. "I feel weird."

"At least you've got your voice," I said. "Did you see who did this to you?"

He shook his head. "We came into the room with Storm and a huge bang went off. I fought against passing out for as long as I could, but I lost. I must have rolled under the bed. And I feel like I've eaten too much. Rub my belly."

"You didn't see who attacked Dobbie?" I asked. "Monty, this is important. I think Dobbie's been injured, and we need to find him."

"I didn't see anyone." Monty whined. "Pat my back. I'm so bloated."

"Stop focusing on your gassy stomach," Olympus said. "Is Dobbie alive?"

"The blood," Nugget said, clearing his throat. "Dobbie wasn't here when we arrived. The blood was on the floor, though. I spotted it before the explosion went off."

"Someone booby-trapped the room?" I looked around at the messy contents. "Were they hoping to conceal evidence of a fight?"

"They did a lousy job," Olympus said. "And who'd fight Dobbie? He's a laid-back guy."

I stood and inspected the room. There was a smashed lamp, an overturned chair, papers knocked off the small desk, and several glasses had been smashed against one wall. "Dobbie must have put up a fight when his attacker arrived."

Olympus glanced up, but he was too worried about Monty to focus on the crime scene.

I checked Storm was comfortable. She still hadn't woken, but her breathing was steady, then I walked over to the desk and discovered Dobbie's diary flipped open under a pile of paper.

Hilda crawled up my leg and settled on my hand, reading the diary as I flipped through it. "He's a busy guy."

I nodded at his crammed diary full of appointments. "There's no contact information in here other than what we already have for him."

"We need more help with this." Olympus shifted so he could pull out his mobile snow globe, using one hand to send a message. "I'll get backup from the Magic Council."

I instinctively winced. My past was murky with the Magic Council, and it still amazed me I was marrying a guy who'd spent so many years working for them.

Olympus got an almost instant reply and frowned. "They're sending people, but they're busy. They won't be here for a while."

"Did you say someone is missing? And that someone is badly injured?"

"They know all the information. It won't make them come any faster."

"Christmas Eve makes people misbehave," Nugget said. "They're busy dealing with fake Santas and drunk winter fairies."

Russell squawked his agreement.

"The holidays bring out the best in people." Hilda tapped a leg against my hand. "Acts of kindness. Gift giving. Sharing love and joy."

"Not always," Olympus said. "People overindulge. Food, booze, magic, fun. It goes to their heads, and things get messy. Christmas is a busy time for law enforcement."

Nugget hopped onto the desk and looked at the diary with Hilda. "What do those stars mean? Every week, Dobbie has a star meeting booked."

I studied the meticulously handwritten diary entries. "He looks after a range of celebrations. They could be magic ceremonies involving stars."

"Astral cults worship the stars, planets, and other heavenly bodies," Hilda said.

"Astral worship is rare, though," I murmured. "Dobbie has had star meetings all year. One a week."

"We'll ask him about them when we find him," Olympus said.

"If you find him." Nugget gestured at the blood. "I doubt he's doing so good."

"Yeah, that's not a good look for the carpet." I tilted my head as I flicked through more diary pages. "Why does Dobbie use star symbols when every other appointment has dates, names, and times? Look at ours." On the appropriate page and date, Dobbie had neatly written: *Marriage of Indigo Ash and Olympus Duke: three o'clock: Witch Haven.*

Monty groaned, and a foul stench filled the air. "I feel terrible."

Nugget hissed at him. "Control your bowels. I don't want to keep chewing on your rank stomach emissions."

"Olympus, give Monty some healing magic to settle his stomach," I said. "Those fear farts are making my eyes water."

"It's not fear gas." Monty staggered to his paws, shook out his fur, and gave the most enormous burp, making the air even riper. "I... I have a confession to make. I'm a terrible familiar."

"I'm always telling you that," Nugget said. "What have you done this time?"

Monty whimpered. "It's really bad. Unforgiveable."

Olympus knelt in front of him. "It's okay if you have an upset stomach. You've had a fright."

Monty dropped to his belly and hid his eyes under a giant paw. "No! I know what happened to Dobbie."

I turned to Monty. "You do? Who took him?"

"Me! I... I think I ate him."

Chapter 3

Olympus slumped onto the bed and dropped his head into his hands. "Please say I just heard you wrong."

Monty turned his head away from Olympus and refused to look at him.

Olympus groaned. "You didn't say you ate Dobbie, did you? Our missing wedding celebrant? The man who's marrying Indigo and me tomorrow."

Monty remained flat on the floor, hiding his eyes from all of us. "I feel awful. Like I've eaten too much. Way too much."

I stared at Monty. The overly bouncy leopard had a tangled history with Olympus and wasn't known for always being on his best behavior, but I'd never seen him interested in eating another magic user. "Monty, do you remember eating Dobbie?"

"No! But I was hungry when I got here. And do you remember the first time we met Dobbie, how delicious he smelled? Like roast beef. I had to be careful not to drool on his shoes. He exuded yumminess from his pores."

"I noticed that too," Nugget said. "The guy smelled good."

"Dobbie could have had a roast beef sandwich in his bag." Olympus stared at Monty with disbelief in his eyes. "It's his favorite food. He always requests that meal when he officiates a wedding."

"I must have smelled that and lost control." Monty whimpered again. "This is terrible. I munched him down, thinking he was a slab of roast beef. I'm a bad leopard."

I looked at my familiars, who sat silently on the desk. "Did any of you see Monty eat Dobbie?"

None of them spoke. They shuffled around as if the desk was suddenly uncomfortable to sit on.

"What aren't you telling me?" I walked over to them. "Did Monty eat Dobbie?"

"He didn't do it," Hilda said. "We all adore Monty, and we know he's not a killer."

"I'm a bad kitty." Monty whimper-burped.

"Nugget, what did you see when you arrived?" I leaned down until I was eye-level with my grumpy familiar.

He stared at the wall. "We didn't *see* anything."

An uneasy feeling swirled through me. "But you know something?"

Russell cawed and stamped his feet up and down, his talons clipping on the wooden desk.

"Help me! We have to find out what happened to Dobbie," I said. "If there was an accident, and for whatever reason, Monty ate him, we can figure this out."

"How?" Olympus stared at Monty. "How do we figure this out?"

"Nugget's telling the truth," Hilda said. "We didn't see Dobbie when we got here. But..."

"Go on. Something happened?" I asked.

"Monty disappeared for ten minutes," Hilda said. "Not to do anything he shouldn't, though. I'm certain of that."

I turned to Monty. "Did you pick up Dobbie's meaty scent and hunt him?"

"I... I don't remember. We got here, and everyone went inside, but something made me hesitate. It could have been the scent of roast beef, so I went to investigate." Monty smacked his lips together.

"You told me there was something you wanted to check outside," Hilda said. "Do you remember that?"

"I did?" Monty shook his head. "Are you sure?"
Hilda nodded.

"What's the last thing you remember?" Olympus said to Monty. "Did you find Dobbie?"

Monty shivered. "Maybe. I hit my head on the wall when I got caught up in the magic explosion, so everything is hazy."

"Wait! There were two explosions?" I asked.

Monty lifted his head an inch off the floor and nodded. "I arrived after the others, stepped into the room, and saw they were in trouble. The next thing I remember, I was flying through the air. I hit my head and then crawled under the bed."

I exchanged a worried look with Olympus, and he lifted one shoulder, seeming stuck as to what to do.

"Why do you think it's Dobbie in your gut?" Olympus asked, surprisingly calm, considering how astonishing Monty's confession was. "You could have found discarded food outside and gorged on it. The bed-and-breakfast must have industrial waste containers. And it wouldn't be the first time you've made yourself sick by eating something you shouldn't."

Monty whimpered and hid his face again.

"What aren't you telling us?" I asked.

"Dobbie's bloody shoe is under the bed," Monty whispered. "I must have brought it in with me after I gobbled him down."

Olympus got back on his hands and knees and peered under the bed. He sighed. "It's under there. I won't touch it in case it's evidence."

"Why bring Dobbie's shoe with you?" I asked Monty. "If you ate him, you'd want to hide the evidence, not carry a souvenir that would get you locked up once people figured out where it came from."

"I wish I could tell you. But I enjoy carrying Olympus's slippers when I'm at home. And look at my gut!" Monty rolled onto his back and exposed a hugely distended belly. "Prod it. I'm so full I'm ready to burst. There has to be a person in there!"

I stood over Monty, and Olympus joined me. "You do look like you've eaten a lot of food."

"It's Dobbie. I've ruined your wedding by eating him. I'm so sorry. Please don't banish me."

I massaged my forehead with my fingertips. "Let's look at this logically. You can't have eaten Dobbie."

Monty's left ear lifted. "Why not?"

"There's no blood on your fur. You'd have gotten messy if you attacked Dobbie."

Monty blinked slowly. "I could have cleaned myself off in the snow."

"Let me check your claws for any...bits." Olympus grimaced as he carefully pressed each paw pad and looked at Monty's claws. "Good. That's good. There's nothing gross stuck in any of them."

"I'm not saying you did it." Nugget leapt off the desk and landed on Monty's gut, causing him to groan and break wind at the same time. "But you don't like Dobbie, do you?"

Monty closed his eyes. "I don't remember if I do or don't."

"I say you don't. He kept telling you off for interrupting him."

"I... Maybe I don't love him." Monty grunted his displeasure as Nugget made biscuits on his belly.

"Monty, this is serious." Olympus crouched beside him. "If you've done this, I can't protect you."

Monty opened his eyes. "If I did it, and it feels like I did, I'll accept my punishment. But promise you'll visit when I'm behind bars."

I knelt beside Olympus and rested a hand on his shoulder. "Monty can misbehave, but he wouldn't do this. He's looking forward to the wedding day almost as much as we are."

Monty nodded his enormous head. "I'm so excited. Now, you won't let me go, will you?"

"Not if you ate our wedding celebrant!" Olympus stared at the wall. "Whatever you do, don't tell anyone you argued with Dobbie."

"I didn't know they argued," I said. "What was it about?"

Olympus gently rubbed Monty's bloated belly. "Monty doesn't always obey orders."

"I do the sensible ones," Monty said. "Any order that has to do with eating lots of food gets a paw up from me. Although not for a few hours. I need to give my stomach a break."

Nugget continued to knead Monty's belly. "There is a person-like squishiness to your gut. Dobbie could be in here."

"You're not helping," I muttered to him. "Olympus, what was their argument about?"

Olympus tipped back his head. "Monty's bad behavior. He wouldn't sit still when Dobbie talked me through the ceremony details. Dobbie got annoyed with him and told him to lie down. Monty got offended and tried to drag Dobbie out of the office by his collar."

I grimaced. "Monty! Why'd you do that?"

"Dobbie was bad-mannered, and he was behaving as if he owned me," Monty said. "I only obey orders from Olympus and you, Indigo. I like you."

"And me." Nugget settled on Monty's stomach and tucked his paws underneath himself, so he looked like a fluffy loaf cat. "Hilda and Russell too."

"Sure. You, too," Monty agreed.

"You saw an opportunity to get revenge by eating Dobbie?" I shook my head. That motive was too out there to be possible.

"Maybe Monty was hungry," Nugget said. "I've seen him eat all kinds of gross things when his belly is rumbling. And Dobbie did smell good. I'd have been tempted to take a nibble."

"And I keep telling everybody, I'm a growing leopard and need all the calories, but no one believes me," Monty said. "And Olympus is so stingy with the rations."

"I'm not stingy. You're greedy, especially this last week. But I didn't think you'd be greedy enough to do this." Olympus raked a hand through his hair. He looked at me. "What am I supposed to do with him?"

"Nothing. We find Dobbie alive and prove Monty's innocence," I said.

"You should put me in a cell in case I've turned evil," Monty said. "I don't want to eat a wedding guest and make things even more awkward."

Olympus gestured at the chaotic scene in the room. "There won't be a wedding if we can't find Dobbie!"

I touched Olympus's arm. "We need backup."

"I've already called the Magic Council."

"Not them. Something strange went down here, and until we locate Dobbie, or find his body, we won't know for certain he's dead." I sat beside Storm and checked her again. She was finally stirring.

Olympus nodded. "Okay. So, what do we do?"

"You keep looking for Dobbie. I'll get Storm on her feet, and then we'll round up the others. We'll get to work on finding a backup wedding celebrant."

"I'm happy to keep looking, but there's no chance of finding another celebrant at such short notice." Olympus stood. "Indigo, our wedding is tomorrow! And Dobbie only agreed to do the ceremony on Christmas Day because he owed me a favor. I tried half a dozen other celebrants before I twisted Dobbie's arm to get him involved. And as soon as the ceremony was over, he was leaving."

"With a roast beef sandwich in his pocket." Monty sighed. "I don't even have room for one small sandwich. Dobbie was super filling."

"We must try." I swirled magic over Storm as her eyelids fluttered. "Take Monty and look around. Check with the guests, ask at the reception desk, and then look outside. Dobbie's been injured, so you may find a blood trail. Monty, can you sniff that out?"

"I can! I can sniff for roast beef, too. Dobbie may have had another sandwich in his pocket. That's if it isn't inside me." Monty's ears lowered.

"Stop obsessing over the man's sandwiches," Olympus muttered.

"Roast beef, blood, sweaty socks, whatever gets your nose twitching," I said. "I'll go back to the inn and get everyone else to work."

Cautious optimism entered Olympus's eyes. "Do you think Monty is innocent?"

"Don't ever doubt your familiars," Nugget said. "Even when we're guilty, you always say we're innocent. Those are the Familiar Rules every good magic user must live by."

Confusion crossed Olympus's face. "But you've been making comments to suggest Monty could have eaten Dobbie."

"That's Nugget's way. He loves to find the worst option and then look at that option's dark side," I said. "If you're not used to it by now, you never will be. Storm, it's time to move. No more snoozing on the job."

She made a few weird noises in the back of her throat then jerked upright, magic flaring on her fingertips. "What the—"

"Easy! You got messed up in a magic explosion. How do you feel?" I kept a hand on her shoulder to let her know she was in no danger.

Storm took a few deep breaths, her narrowed gaze traveling around the room. "Angry."

"If you're up to it, we're moving. I'll get you up to speed on the way back to the inn." I lifted Nugget and settled him on my shoulder. Russell flapped over and sat on my other shoulder, while Hilda settled on my hand.

"I'm up to it. Whoever did this has just made me their enemy." She cracked her knuckles then hopped to her feet.

"Glad you're okay, Storm." Olympus kissed my cheek. "I don't know what I'd do without you."

I smiled at him. "You'd be a stressed mess, and your familiar would be about to go down for murder. I'll meet you back at the inn in an hour."

I was glad to leave the fart and blood-scented room, and I hurried out into the intense cold and dark, along with Storm and my familiars. Snow swirled around us in mini tornadoes, slamming into my cheeks and freezing my skin in seconds. This weather was seriously unnatural. A suspicious mind would think someone was trying to keep people inside and out of the way.

Despite the cold, the village was a breathtaking sight as we dashed along and I filled in Storm on what we'd found in Dobbie's room. Twinkling lights adorned the lampposts, casting an inviting glow upon the snow-covered ground. Wreaths adorned with shimmering ribbons and sparkling ornaments hung on every door, while garlands of fragrant pine branches stretched across the storefronts. It was beautiful, but I was certain I had an icicle hanging off the end of my nose by the time we got to the inn.

I pushed on the door, but it wouldn't budge. I knocked loudly. "It's Indigo and Storm. Let us in. I'm freezing out here."

"Same here," Storm grumbled. "And my head still hurts."

Hurried footsteps approached. "Come back in half an hour." It was Odessa.

"Unless you want me to have frostbite on my wedding day, open the door. What's going on?"

There was silence then the bolt slid across the door, and Odessa's face appeared. "There's been a small problem. A tiny one. Completely fixable. Don't get angry."

"I'm only angry because my toes are freezing." I shoved on the door, and after a second of resistance, she let me in. "What are you playing at?"

Odessa slammed the door shut and put the bolt back in place. "You need to be calm. Think zen thoughts and know all will be well."

"Odessa, what's going on? You're making me nervous. Did Dobbie show up? Is he okay?"

"It's got nothing to do with him. You didn't find him at the bed-and-breakfast?" She hurried after me as I headed to the bar.

"We found his room messed up and blood on the floor. Dobbie is missing. Storm and my familiars were also injured. Monty, too." I puffed out a breath. "And... Monty thinks he ate Dobbie."

Her eyes widened. "That would be unfortunate. Did he?"

"No!"

"We're ninety percent sure he didn't," Nugget said. "Maybe eighty. He ate something huge, though."

Odessa's forehead furrowed. "Like what?"

"That's what I've left Olympus to figure out. What's the bad news here?" I asked.

Her gaze went to the back of the inn to the door that led into the ceremony room where our wedding was to be held.

I turned to the door. "Let me see."

Odessa hurried to block my path and shook her head. "You don't want to look."

"I'm looking!"

She held up a hand. "Wait! Let me prepare you. There's been a break-in."

"In the ceremony room? Has anything been stolen?" I couldn't imagine what a thief would want with wedding flowers, candles, and twirls of white streamers.

Odessa chewed on her bottom lip. "Everything is still there. They must have snuck inside when we weren't looking. But... it's been wrecked. There's almost nothing left."

Chapter 4

I stood in silence with my familiars as we stared at the once beautiful ceremony room where my wedding was supposed to take place in less than twenty-four hours. The chairs had been overturned and broken, the flowers, what was left of them, were a sad, charred mess. The decorations had been torn down or burned, and graffiti was scrawled everywhere. There were long lines of black and red paint running across the ceiling, walls, and floor.

"I told you not to let her in." Luna marched over, her hands full of charred decor. "We can fix this. It won't take long."

"This can't be fixed." My throat was so tight, I could barely get the words out. I didn't realize until that moment how much I cared about this wedding. I'd told myself the venue, the decorations, and the flowers were extravagant fluff, and they meant nothing to me. But I wanted a beautiful, memorable wedding day just like everybody else. Now it had been destroyed. I couldn't see a single piece of decoration that hadn't been damaged.

"I've already made a few calls," Luna said. "Someone will help."

I checked the time. It was just past seven in the evening. "Everywhere will be closed. And the stores that open on Christmas Day won't have replacement wedding fluff."

"We can simplify things," Odessa said. "We'll find enough spare chairs and clean off the graffiti. You may have to make do without flowers or decorations, but we can make the space nice again. Add some magical twinkle with a little effort. Or we could go all out Christmas and cover the place in tinsel."

"I can weave pretty webbing," Hilda said from her perch on my arm.

Storm looked around, her expression not full of hope. "I got nothing. Unless you want rain clouds on your big day. My magic doesn't sparkle."

"Does Cornelia know about this?" I picked up a limp, frazzled flower and turned it over in my trembling fingers.

"We didn't want to worry her," Luna said. "She may cancel her holiday plans to come back to Witch Haven and see what's going on."

"Cornelia trusted me with this place. It wasn't easy to convince her to let me hire the inn while she went away." My heart thumped out its unhappiness in a slow and steady rhythm. "Is this... is this my fault?"

"I don't understand. Do you think you destroyed your own wedding venue?" Odessa asked.

I turned to my friends. They'd stood by me over the years, through my traumatic youth, the rejection I'd faced when I'd returned to Witch Haven to untangle the mess of my life, and through all of our adventures and trials. They'd always been there. But not everyone in the village had.

Luna grasped my hand. "This has nothing to do with you."

"People have long memories," I said. "They won't have forgotten how I helped my stepmother hurt all those people."

"Everyone knows why that happened," Odessa said. "The village was consumed by darkness, but you solved that problem. You saved Witch Haven!"

"With a little help from your friends." Luna smiled and nudged me with her hip. "People remember that, not what went before."

"Do they? I still get funny looks." I gestured at the ruined decorations. "Maybe there are still residents who don't want to see me happy."

"You're not to blame. And if anyone says otherwise, send them my way." Storm was perched on a charred chair, looking around.

"This wasn't done because of you," Odessa said. "If anything, it was someone Olympus arrested and put behind bars. Before you loosened him up, Limpy was the most uptight member of the Magic Council I knew. He's made a lot of enemies."

"This is his fault?" I arched an eyebrow.

"It's not the wackiest idea Odessa's ever had," Luna said. "Someone on parole got revenge when they learned Olympus was marrying you. Why should he get to be happy when he ruined their life?"

I inwardly groaned. "If that's true, the list of enemies is too long to tackle tonight."

"We'll worry about who did this after you're married," Odessa said. "The most important thing is we find a solution. We can move anything that's salvageable to a safe place and find you a new venue."

"Where will we find a suitable venue in less than a day?" As hard as I tried to be optimistic, this wedding was slipping through my fingers. "Dobbie is missing, and now the venue is trashed. Is this fate telling me something?"

Odessa tapped a finger against my forehead. "Less thinking, more action. We can pull this off. This time tomorrow, you'll be happily married and have a stomach full of delicious wedding cake."

I drew in a deep breath and let it out slowly. "You're right. My wedding isn't cursed. But before we deal with the destruction, we need a backup wedding celebrant in case we can't find Dobbie."

"Or in case he's been digested by Monty," Nugget muttered.

"What's this?" Luna asked.

"I'll fill you in," Odessa said. "I'll get a list of every wedding celebrant, and we'll contact each one. Someone will have room for you. And we've got an amazing sob story to soften the hardest heart. You'd planned a beautiful Christmas Day wedding, but evil tyrants destroyed your venue and stole your faithful celebrant. You were about to marry the love of your life, and you won't let anything stand in your way." She sighed. "It'll be a happily ever after of epic proportions."

"Let's leave out the trashed bed-and-breakfast room," I said. "We don't want to scare anyone away."

"I really have missed out on all the gossip," Luna said. "Is Dobbie injured?"

"I already told you, Monty ate him," Nugget said.

"Hush now." Hilda jumped on Nugget's back. "There's a vague possibility that Monty ate Dobbie, but we're almost positive he didn't."

"Monty ate something big," Nugget said. "That wasn't made up. That cat has issues."

"He's not the only one." I settled Nugget on a seat. "Let's get calling and messaging. Once we have a celebrant, we can figure out where to move the ceremony to."

Ten minutes later, I was sending messages and calling people from the wonderfully long list of celebrants Odessa had pulled together at lightning speed. I wasn't surprised when most of the numbers went to voicemail, and I swiftly became familiar with the messages I heard, which said they were closed over the holidays, wishing me a Happy Christmas and New Year, and they'd return my call in a week's time.

So, I was surprised when someone answered. "Celebrant Central. The place to call when you want the event of your dreams. How may I help?" The woman's voice was cool, professional, and held a hint of boredom.

"Hi! I'm glad you're there. I have a wedding emergency."

"Sounds serious. What kind of emergency?"

"I'm getting married tomorrow. My name is Indigo Ash, and—"

"Tomorrow? And you forgot to organize your wedding celebrant until now?"

"No! He's been booked for ages. But... he's unavailable due to an unexpected illness. I'm calling to see if anyone can step in."

There was a gentle sigh. "On Christmas Day? Do you know how many weddings take place on that day?"

"Not many? It'll be a short ceremony. We've kept everything simple and uncomplicated."

"It can be as simple and short as you desire, but celebrants get booked up years in advance. I'm sorry, but we're unable to help. And if you find any wedding celebrant who is free tomorrow, then they're most likely bad at their job."

"They can be drunk, give the service in Japanese, and arrive naked on the back of a unicorn," I said. "I just need them to legally marry me and my husband-to-be."

There was silence. "I wish you luck with your search. Goodbye."

I tipped back my head and scowled at the ceiling.

Luna looked over. "Any joy?"

I shook my head. "You?"

"I've left a dozen messages. Keep going. Someone will take pity on you and come spend Christmas in Witch Haven. With all the snow, it'll be beautiful in the morning."

"Unless we freeze to death because it doesn't stop snowing, and then there won't be anyone to worry about this wedding." Nugget had curled up by the open fire in the bar.

I made a few more calls but then took a five-minute break to grab coffee for everyone and some of Odessa's delicious pumpkin-spiced chocolate cookies she'd brought with her. After handing around the coffees and treats, I walked back into the ceremony room and stared at the graffiti scrawled across one wall.

I tilted my head from side to side then stepped closer and squinted. Underneath the messy red and black lines, the images weren't random scribbles. They were stars. Dozens of stars.

I stood with Luna, Odessa, and Storm. I'd sent Nugget, Hilda, and Russell to fetch Dobbie's diary and bring it to the inn.

"You're right." Storm stood with her legs apart and her arms folded across her chest. "They're easy to miss if you're not paying attention, but there are stars all over this place. And it's a pattern. Twenty stars on each wall."

"And another twenty on the floor." Luna looked up. "A hundred stars in total. Why?"

The door opened, and my familiars returned. Between them, they carried Dobbie's diary.

We walked to a clear spot on the floor, and they put it down.

"Find the pages where the star meetings are shown," I said.

Nugget flipped through the pages of the diary, and we all peered at the symbols.

"They match!" I said. "The shape of the star in Dobbie's diary is the same as the stars left here."

"What's the connection?" Luna asked.

No one spoke as we studied the images.

"Do you think the attacks on your wedding have to do with Dobbie?" Odessa asked.

Storm growled low in the back of her throat. "If this is Dobbie's fault, I'll kill him if he's not already being digested by Monty."

I gave her elbow a brief squeeze. Whenever Storm threatened to kill someone on your behalf, you knew it was because she loved you.

"We need to find out what the star meetings mean," Odessa said. "Maybe Dobbie was meeting with another client to look after their wedding, but it clashed with your plans."

Luna nodded. "Dobbie chose to officiate for you and Olympus, which put the other person's nose out of joint? It's possible."

"Olympus had to twist Dobbie's arm to get him to do this," I said. "Apparently, he owed him a favor. But if there was a clash of dates, Dobbie would have arranged something else. He's a nice guy. He wouldn't have strung anyone along."

"Bridezillas get insanely intense," Storm said. "I once had to stop a mermaid from drowning a siren when they wanted the same venue on the same day. If your wedding rival figured out Dobbie chose you over them, this could be their way of getting revenge."

"Revenge on me and Olympus for something Dobbie did?" I wrinkled my nose. "Would they be that petty?"

Storm shrugged. "Bridezillas. There's something about lace and fruitcake that tips people over the edge into insanity."

"You'll be just as bad when you marry," Odessa said.

Storm smirked. "Never gonna happen. I'm happy living in sin with my guy."

"We need to research these star symbols." I turned to Odessa. "You know about astral cults and star worship, don't you?"

"A little. I know nothing about these star configurations, though. The best place to find that kind of information is the library." She checked the time. "Although it'll be closed now until after the holidays."

I grimaced. The librarian, Nazan Grizig, was grumpier than Nugget. He was a dragon hybrid and fiercely protective of his books. Actually, all books. And if anyone broke into his precious refuge of paper and ink, he was happy to roast them alive as a reminder not to do it again.

"We need that information. I'll deal with Nazan," I said.

The door opened, and Olympus walked in with Monty. They were covered in a thick layer of snow, and Olympus's face was bright pink from the cold. "Any sign of Dobbie?"

I shook my head. "He still hasn't shown up. I'm guessing you didn't find him, either?"

Olympus wiped snow off his coat. "No one at the inn has seen him recently. I asked the receptionist, and she said Dobbie didn't have any guests today, so whoever planted that magic in his room and attacked him must have snuck in when her back was turned."

"Unless it was me." Monty belched quietly.

"No one thinks you ate Dobbie!" Odessa walked over and tickled the top of his head. "You're too much of a good boy to do that."

"I wouldn't be so sure," Olympus muttered. "We couldn't find any tracks outside, but the snow is coming down hard, so it's concealing everything in minutes. If there was a blood trail, it's been obscured. We have no idea where Dobbie was taken."

"Or if he was taken," Storm said. "Maybe he got injured and staggered away because he didn't feel safe. He could be in the snow, freezing to death."

"I tried a location spell, but it didn't find him." I frowned at the thought of Dobbie hurt and helpless. "Any more news from the Magic Council?"

Olympus pursed his lips. "I spoke to someone again, and they said this case wasn't a priority."

"Dobbie is missing! The blood in his room shows something bad happened."

"The officious nincompoop I spoke to said the blood could have been from an accidental cut. They won't file an official missing person's report until forty-eight hours have passed. Until then, I'm the only person investigating." Olympus shook his head.

I caught hold of his hand. "We're in this together. We'll figure out what happened to Dobbie and make sure our wedding goes ahead as planned."

His wonky smile made my heart flutter. "Have you found us a new celebrant?"

I tensed. "Almost. We've been in touch with all the names we could find."

"I almost got someone to say yes by crying," Odessa said. "Then they pretended the connection was bad and hung up. I was so close to guilting them into doing it."

Olympus cupped my face in his hands. "If we have to postpone, and I'll be disappointed if we do, we can rearrange. Maybe a spring wedding would be better. At least our guests won't be at risk of getting stuck in a snowdrift."

I gritted my teeth. I didn't want a spring wedding. I wanted my winter wedding as planned. My mobile snow globe buzzed. I didn't recognize the number, but I answered it.

"Is this Indigo Ash?" a weedy male voice asked.

"Yes, who's this?"

"I'm Zephir Monkton. I got your message about your wedding issue. I love a Christmas Day celebration. It's such a magical date to hold your ceremony."

"We agree!" Hope fluttered through me, and I smiled at Olympus. "We had everything planned, but now our wedding celebrant is unable to attend. Are you free?"

"As luck would have it, I am. I had a last-minute cancelation when my bride-to-be discovered her almost husband on top of his mother-in-law-to-be. Can you believe it?" Zephir's chuckle was tinged with embarrassment.

"Oh! That's bad."

"Bad for them, but fortunate for you. May I ask who was planning to conduct your ceremony?"

"Dobbie Doubleday," I said. "Do you know him?"

There was a sharp intake of breath.

"Is something wrong?" I asked.

"No, it's just that..." His voice trailed away.

"You haven't changed your mind, have you?" I tightly squeezed Olympus's hand. "We can triple your rate. Whatever you need to get here, we'll make it happen. Please, we need someone to marry us."

"My regular rate is fine. I always think it's a delight to hold the service on such a special day, so I'll be glad to assist you. But there's something you need to know about Dobbie," Zephir said, a note of caution in his voice.

"What about him?" I lifted my eyebrows as my gaze locked with Olympus's.

"It's better I explain everything when we meet," Zephir said. "I'll pack my things and be there within the hour."

I joyfully gave Zephir the details of our wedding and the address before ending the call. I let out a breath of relief. Everything was working out.

Olympus hugged me. "At least there's nothing stopping us from getting married."

Odessa cleared her throat. "Um... your venue—"

"No! We can find somewhere else." I looked at her and shook my head. Charred flowers I could deal with.

"What about the venue?" Olympus looked at the closed door leading to the ceremony room. "Is there a problem?"

I smiled up at him. "Nothing we can't fix. Now we just need to figure out what happened to Dobbie."

"There is one suspect we haven't considered yet. A small, evil suspect who could be behind all of this." Luna pointed at the creepy doll gift I'd tucked into one corner of the inn. "Didn't Ursa say she was a firebug?"

I scowled at the doll. "Maybe Ursa's wedding gift isn't such a good luck charm after all. Let's find out, shall we?"

Chapter 5

"What do you mean, my delightful gift is causing trouble?" Despite the freezing conditions outside, Ursa hadn't invited us into her eerie manor house when I knocked on her door with my familiars.

"Exactly what I say! Since I got her, there have been mishaps," I said. "Big mishaps."

Ursa stood straight, her glare almost as icy as the weather. "Such as?"

"Invite us inside, and we'll tell you," Nugget said.

Ursa remained by the door, blocking our way in. "That doll will bring you good luck. I told you that. Unless..."

"Unless what?" I asked. "What have you cursed her with?"

"Nothing! But if you've been mistreating her, she has every right to defend herself."

"Of course I haven't been mistreating her! But I need to ask you some questions about her. She can't keep jinxing things."

Ursa sighed dramatically. "Shouldn't you be worried about your wedding, rather than my gift?"

"I'm worried it won't take place if this doll gets her way." I took a deep breath to check my anger. "Please, Ursa. I need your help."

Her scowl deepened then she sighed again. "Ask away."

I staggered as a gust of frigid wind slammed into me. "Can we do this inside? I lost feeling in my toes a couple of minutes ago."

"That's not convenient." Ursa glanced over her shoulder. "I'm having a Christmas tea party."

I arched an eyebrow. Was she trying to get rid of us? Guilty conscience, maybe? "You have guests? I don't see many lights on."

She tutted as if I'd said something dumb. "With my dolls. They can see in the dark."

"Of course they can." I shuddered.

"We'll join them." Nugget slid past Ursa, and Russell flapped over her head, leaving me shivering outside with Hilda perched on my shoulder.

"Your familiars have no manners." Ursa scowled at Nugget as his butt disappeared along the gloomy hallway. "I don't trust him anywhere near my dolls, not after the last time. My precious darlings experience daily trauma after his vicious attack."

"Nugget has a few flashbacks, too," I said. "And you've got to admit, your dolls weren't on their best behavior when we met them. We had to defend ourselves."

Ursa opened her mouth to protest but settled for a nod. "Fine, but make this quick. We were about to eat cake."

"I figured your dolls only ate flesh."

"Keep talking like that and I'll have them lock you in the coal cellar over Christmas."

"Sorry," I muttered as I stepped inside.

The hallway was decorated in traditional festive reds and greens, and an open fire crackled close by. Ursa led us into a surprisingly warm room, lit with a few twinkling fairy lights. Still, my blood ran cold when I saw twenty-five dolls dressed in their best Christmas outfits settled around a table with a spread in front of them.

"Ladies, we have uninvited and unwanted guests," Ursa announced. "I hate to trouble any of you, but would someone mind giving up a seat for Indigo? You all remember her, I'm sure."

There were muttered grumbles from the dolls. Fortunately, none of them moved.

"I'm fine standing." I didn't want any of these dolls to do me a favor, in case they wanted it repaid in blood.

There was a faint giggle at the far end of the room, and a chair scraped back, making me tense.

"There! Valerie is happy for you to take her place," Ursa said. "And it's at the head of the table, so you can sit by me and ask your questions. Hurry up, now. I'd just poured the tea when you so rudely dropped by."

"We can stay for a cup of tea," Hilda whispered to me. "We don't want to appear impolite."

"Too late for that," Nugget said from somewhere under the table. Russell cawed softly, suggesting he was hiding under there, too.

"Sure. Tea would be great." I didn't want to be at the mercy of these dolls when their mood soured, but I could keep things civil if it got me the answers I needed.

"Ellen was about to play for us on the piano." Ursa sat in an empty seat. "She's been practicing all month so she can entertain us with Christmas carols."

I couldn't see which creepy doll was sitting by the piano, but a second later, off-key plinking and plonking began. It might have been The First Noel, but she'd added a darker undertone of malice to the beat.

I shuffled to the seat offered to me. Nugget jumped up beside me.

"Off the table!" Ursa shooed him away with a wave of her festive napkin. "He should be in the yard where the beasts belong."

"Nugget's not a beast. He's my familiar. You know that." I glanced at Russell, who'd subtly crept out from under the table and was on a candle sconce, giving the dolls his beady-eyed attention.

Ursa muttered to herself several times. "He can stay, but no jumping, and no attacking my darlings."

"If they don't attack me, I won't go after them." Nugget growled, his hackles lifting as he glared at the dolls. But other than a few soft giggles, they seemed to be on their best behavior.

"This looks nice." I eyed the spread. There was a tower of cranberry scones, miniature eclairs glistening with a glossy chocolate sheen, chunks of iced fruit cake, and pots of tea. "The dolls eat real food?"

"I always indulge my girls during the holidays." Pride resonated through Ursa's words. "Other than that unfortunate hiccup you witnessed when my girls became unruly, we're the best of friends."

"Unruly!" Nugget said. "These bug-eyed nightmares almost killed us."

"I'm glad everyone's having fun." I rested a hand on Nugget's head to calm his grumblings. "Your home feels more welcoming than the last time I was here."

"Yes, well, I suppose you had a small part to play in that." Ursa reached over and set cakes on plates. "It's why I got you the good luck doll."

"Is she really good luck?"

"Of course."

"Where did you get her from?" I discreetly fed Nugget a small piece of cake.

Ursa poured me a stewed cup of tea in a patterned china cup. "At a doll collectors' event. I'd almost given up hope of finding the perfect doll for you and Olympus, but I was at the event just the other day, and she spoke to me."

"Literally or figuratively?" Nugget asked.

"She talked! What else would she do?"

"Of course she did." I looked down at Nugget and winked. "And she said she'd make the perfect wedding gift for us?"

Ursa sighed gently. "I know everyone mocks my doll obsession, but we understand each other. They're my only friends. Ever since I was a child, the dolls have understood me. They came to me during a dark time and helped me through. You're fortunate. You have Olympus and your familiars. I have my dolls. They're a great source of comfort."

Movement at the table caught my eye, but when I turned to look, the dolls were still. I was certain the second my attention returned to Ursa, they'd continue enjoying their feast while conspiring to destroy me.

"It's good you have them to support you," I said. "But I'm concerned about my doll. How do you know she's not a mischief-maker?"

"I asked the seller, and I saw her papers. They're difficult to forge."

"But not impossible?" Nugget asked.

"Well, no. Unfortunately, fraud is prevalent among the doll-collecting community. There are unscrupulous people out there, and they know that people who desire to expand our collections can be exploited. But that wasn't the case with this doll. The paperwork has the authentic stamp, and I even had her magic recharged. There was no mention of anything untoward."

"Have you heard my wedding celebrant, Dobbie, is missing?" I sipped the tea. Although stewed, it was flavorful. I was tempted by a scone, but a sharp look from a doll sitting opposite me made me resist for fear of getting a butter knife thrust into the back of my hand.

"I don't keep up with the village gossip," Ursa said. "Are you sure he's missing? Perhaps he got a better offer."

"Something bad happened to him," I said. "Could my doll have had anything to do with it?"

Ursa bit into a chunk of fruit cake. "Why would she want to do something to your wedding celebrant?"

"Ursa, let's be real." Nugget stamped his paws on the table. "The last time we tangled with your crazed dolls, we barely got out alive. Now, you gift a creepy-eyed creation to Indigo and Olympus, and suddenly, they're dealing with a missing wedding celebrant, insane snowy weather, and a ruined wedding venue. What's next? Are you kidnapping the bridesmaids?"

Ursa sat up in her seat, the cake she'd been planning to cram into her mouth suspended in the air. "I know nothing about any of this. Why would I wish harm to your special day?"

"Because you haven't forgiven me for what happened the last time I entered your house," I said. "You lost most of your doll collection, and I know how much they mean to you."

Ursa grimaced. "I haven't forgotten, but I have forgiven. I love my dolls, and I want to protect them, but they behaved badly toward you."

"They turned into killer monsters who wanted to gouge our eyes out and skin us alive," Nugget said.

"That's a little dramatic," I muttered, but he wasn't far from the truth. We'd barely escaped the last time we'd tangled with Ursa's hexed dolls.

"My darlings are well-behaved now," Ursa said. "And that attack was my fault. I allowed my collection to grow too big and wasn't paying attention to who was in charge. That's been remedied. This is my entire collection. Well, apart from the few I have in the cellar, but they're chained up."

I gulped down panic. "You have more misbehaving dolls living here?"

"They're under control. And I assure you, I wish you well for your special day, the same for Olympus. Although he's inefficient and a touch pompous, he has his moments of effectiveness. You've both been helpful to me."

"Have you got the doll's paperwork?" I asked. "I'd like to check it, just to be certain you missed nothing."

"I've learned my lesson when purchasing unsafe dolls. Her paperwork is authentic." Ursa pushed back her seat, stomped to a desk, and pulled out a folder full of papers. She flipped through them and returned to the table, shoving something into my hand.

I took a moment to read the document. It was written in an old style of English with lots of *thees* and *thous*. As far as I knew about authentic paperwork for potentially murderous dolls, it seemed authentic, and it clearly stated the doll was imbued with positivity and good fortune for anyone who cared for her.

"Perhaps the doll wants to stay with you," I said. "She could be doing this to make a point."

"She knew the arrangement when I purchased her. And she wasn't cheap, so I hope you're grateful," Ursa said.

I stifled a sigh. I'd hoped to give the doll back. "You shouldn't have spent so much."

Ursa simply shrugged. "She was excited to meet her new family. Ask the doll. She'll confirm everything. And if you still have doubts, you can contact the auction house. They know me on a first-name basis since I spend so much money there. And I'd have spent more if it wasn't for Peony interfering."

"Peony Cashmere?" I asked. "I didn't know she was into doll collecting."

"She outbid me on some exquisite antique doll cards. I confronted her after the auction ended, and she said she was considering opening a new store. I offered to pay her for them, but she said no." Ursa arched an eyebrow. "That's who you should go after if you think your wedding is jinxed. There's something about Peony that sets my teeth on edge. She was rude to me, and I know she had a thing with Olympus."

"It was more than a thing," I said. "They have a daughter together and were once engaged."

"There you go. If you're looking for someone who wants to spoil your wedding day, go bother Peony." A hint of evilness slid across Ursa's face. "And if she needs bail money when you arrest her, she can always sell me those collector cards."

A flicker of worry lit inside me. I'd briefly wondered if Peony was behind this but surely not. We were friends. She'd given us her blessing, not that we needed it, but I didn't want her to feel like she was being left out.

"As I said, I wish nothing but the best for you and Olympus. One day, I hope to have my happily ever after, just like you," Ursa said.

Nugget sounded like he was coughing up a furball, but I ignored him. "I'm sure the right one will come along one day."

"I'm not lonely. Well, not too lonely. My dolls keep me entertained." Ursa pointed at the food.

"Now, how about a slice of something special? Fruitcake?"

I shrugged. "Sounds good."

Ursa clapped her hands together. "Excellent. My girls made it from a secret recipe."

Oh, crud.

Chapter 6

"It's not Ursa behind this." I stood in front of the pile of mildly soiled wedding paraphernalia we'd saved from the vandalized venue and brought back to my house.

"The auction house confirmed the doll is legit." Odessa put an arm around my shoulders and squeezed me tight.

"I had to get Olympus to use his official voice and mildly threaten them before they revealed all, but Ursa bought the doll from a registered buyer," I said.

"She could have cursed the doll herself," Storm said. "I hate those things."

"One tiny doll could do all that?" Luna shook her head. "It wouldn't have had enough time. We left the ceremony room empty for an hour at the most. Maybe less."

"Stuffed with enough evil desires, maybe it could." I gestured at the mess.

"How about we make a bonfire?" Storm suggested. "You should go for the minimalist look for your wedding. No flowers. No décor."

"No wedding celebrant," Nugget said from the corner of the room, where he'd curled up on a piece of paper.

"We'll make this work." I was putting on a brave face, but panic swirled in my stomach like I'd swallowed a rancid potion and it was fighting to make its way back out.

"What about using this place as the wedding venue?" Luna stood in the middle of my festively decorated living room. "Hilda's done a great job with the decorations."

Hilda had spent one morning weaving beautiful, sparkling webbing around the ceiling. With Russell's help, she'd added a touch of shimmering magic, so the room sparkled and gleamed when the light caught the webbing. We'd also added a small tree in one corner, which Nugget was determined to knock over before Christmas Day.

"It's a nice thought." Olympus came in with one final box of salvaged items. "But for the marriage to be legal, we'd need a venue license."

"Limpy! Can't you pull a few strings?" Odessa asked.

"Whose strings am I supposed to pull? Everyone has clocked off for the holidays."

"Even better. They'll be full of the joys of the festive season, so more likely to help a friend in need." Odessa beamed at him.

He glanced at me and lifted one shoulder. "I'll send a few messages, make some calls, see if anyone will sign off on a last-minute license."

I walked over and kissed his cheek. "I knew there was a reason I loved you."

"For the power and influence I have over the Magic Council?" Olympus quirked an eyebrow. "It's a long shot."

"That's all we've got, so I'll take it," I said. "When is Zephir arriving?"

"He said within the hour, but I imagine it'll be at least another hour, given how intense the snowstorm is."

I looked outside and winced as a blast of snow slammed against the window. "That gives me time to go to the library. I want to investigate what those star symbols mean."

"I'll come with you," Olympus said.

"Stay here with the others. Sort through everything we've brought back and see if there's anything we desperately need to make tomorrow perfect. I won't be long."

"The only way to get into the library this late at night is to break in," Olympus said. "And if Nazan catches you, you don't want to be on your own."

"I won't be alone." I winked at Nugget. "Get up, lazybones."

Nugget grumbled but stretched and shook out his fur.

Olympus still didn't look happy, but he nodded. "If Zephir arrives before you get back, I'll fill him in on everything that's going on."

"Perfect. Everything is coming together." I sounded as hopeful as I could. I was marrying this man, and nothing would stop me.

I rounded up Nugget, Hilda, and Russell, but rather than face the snow again and getting unwanted cold therapy exposure, I translocated us to the library.

It was an imposing gothic building with tall spires and small, dark lead-lined windows. It reminded me of something out of a Victorian novel. The bricks were a dark red, looking almost black in the gloom. As expected, the lights were out and the front doors locked.

An icy wind blasted past me, almost knocking me off my feet. My heel hit a patch of hidden ice, and I lost my balance. Russell squawked and leapt off my shoulder, while Hilda clung on. Nugget wasn't so fortunate. He yowled as he landed headfirst into a snowdrift, only his butt and tail visible.

I plucked him out, wiping the worst of the snow off his black fur. "I should have gotten you sweaters as a Christmas gift if you've taken to snow bombing."

Nugget hissed his irritation. "I do not wear clothing." He scrambled back onto my shoulder, digging in his claws to show his displeasure. "Let's find a way inside before my whiskers freeze and snap off."

It was too risky to go through the front door. Nazan had alarms that would trigger him into action the second I touched it. Instead, we slid around the side until we found a window that looked into the cellar.

"Allow me." Hilda twirled off my shoulder. She spun shimmering webbing around the bars on the window. There was a fizz followed by a pop, and the bars melted away.

I had to use several unlocking spells before the window would budge, but after a few minutes of muttering and blasting spells, I was shimmying my way through and dropping onto the cold concrete floor. I lifted Nugget in and then Hilda. Russell was happy to fly in and swooped over my head.

I waited a moment, getting acclimated to the gloom, then headed up a set of steps. I inched open the door at the top of the steps and peered into the dark corridor. There was no sign of Nazan, although I wouldn't put it past him to patrol on Christmas Eve. He loved books more than life.

We stopped by the information sign and scanned the different sections.

"Let's try *Religion and Alternative Beliefs*," Hilda whispered.

We dashed to the third floor and hurried along the corridor and into the main library. The air held a hint of old paper and cinnamon. The towering shelves, adorned with garlands of holly, reached up toward a vaulted ceiling, and the intricately carved wooden furniture was draped in rich red and green fabrics, inviting visitors to settle in and immerse themselves in the mystical atmosphere.

It took several minutes of searching along the stacks, but we found what we were looking for. I pulled down several books about astral cults, settled on the floor, and flipped through the pages. My familiars did the same, scanning for images that looked like the star symbols that we'd found at my wedding venue.

"These have too many points. These are inverted. These have to be a certain color to work," I muttered.

"All the stars in the wedding venue were black, right?" Nugget asked.

I nodded. "Only red and black paint was used to wreck the joint. The stars were all black."

Russell squawked and jumped up and down. I peered over to inspect the page he'd been reading, and my gut filled with an icy dread.

Russell flapped his wings and jabbed his beak at the page until we'd all turned our attention to his discovery.

"Those are the symbols," Nugget said. "Shadow Weaver marks. I've never heard of them. What do they believe in?"

I gulped and licked my suddenly dry lips. "It can't be them."

Hilda balanced on the back of my hand. "What do you know about Shadow Weavers?"

"Everything I know about them is bad." My head turned as a door creaked.

"It could be a library ghost," Hilda whispered. "I'll take a look." She scuttled into the darkness.

I rested a hand on the page and traced the star symbol. It was an exact match for the symbols left at the wedding venue. But why were Shadow Weavers interested in my wedding?

There was a squeak from Hilda, a fierce, grumbling growl, and then a blast of flames lit the darkness.

My heart raced as I scooped up Nugget and Russell and clambered to my feet. Nazan had found us!

"Who dares to violate my library?" His deep, rage-filled voice boomed through the darkness.

"We need to find Hilda," I whispered.

Russell struggled in my grip, so I let him go. He flapped to the top of the bookshelves. It was impossible to see his gorgeous inky wings in the gloom, but they were the perfect concealment so he could snoop on Nazan without attracting his attention. And although I couldn't see Russell, I followed the tiny tap of his claws against the wood.

"I know you're in here. Things will only get worse if you continue to hide. I have the power to destroy anyone who steps foot inside this library without my permission."

Nazan wasn't joking. He'd kill to protect his books.

Russell reappeared, swooping down and settling on my shoulder.

"Is Hilda okay?" I asked.

He nodded and tapped his beak against my cheek.

I took a deep breath. "Then it's time to confront our angry dragon and hope he's feeling in a festive mood."

"His mood sounds murderous," Nugget said. "We're going to die."

I hurried along the book stack, gathering up the books we'd used to investigate the star symbols. By the time I got to the end of the row, Nazan was waiting for us, fire smoldering in his amber eyes, the red scales on his face barely visible in the low light.

His expression showed a flash of surprise when he saw me before the rage reappeared. "Indigo Ash! You're not a lover of my library, so your reason for breaking in had better be sublime if you want to see tomorrow."

I kept my voice level and low, catching Hilda as she dropped from the ceiling. "I'm on a mission to save my wedding. I'm marrying Olympus Duke tomorrow."

"I'm aware. I received your invitation to the evening reception."

"I don't remember if you RSVP'd." I narrowed my eyes. "You're coming?"

"I'll stop by for five minutes."

"You may not have that option. Someone is sabotaging our wedding. Our celebrant has been taken, and the venue was trashed and covered in strange graffiti. I needed access to your books to learn what it meant and if it's anything to worry about."

Nazan was silent for such a long time that I grew uneasy. I glanced toward the exit, but I was too far away. If I ran, Nazan would incinerate us.

"I was once married," he finally said.

My eyebrows rose. "I didn't know that."

"She left me. She said I loved books more than her."

"Um... Sorry to hear that."

"She was right to leave. My books bring me more comfort than the arms of a woman ever could, no matter how luscious her curves. But I remember what it was like to have a companion. When you find the right person, a union makes sense."

Hope flickered inside me. "I agree! Which is why I'm determined to marry Olympus. But someone doesn't want that to happen."

His gaze went to the books I clutched. "Have you located your enemy? Can you obliterate them with the knowledge in those pages?"

"I wasn't thinking so much about destroying them, although if they keep messing with us, it'll be on the agenda. But yes, your books helped. I'm not happy with the answer, but I know what we're dealing with."

"Destruction is the best course of action," Nazan said. "They'll never bother you again if you grind them into the dirt."

"If she does that, Indigo will end up behind bars again," Nugget murmured.

A flicker of amusement crossed Nazan's face. "Of course. I sometimes forget your colorful past."

"You're one of the few who do around here," I said.

"I also remember your recent past and how you saved us. Witch Haven owes you a debt of gratitude." He stepped to one side. "You may leave. But give me the books."

I'd planned on taking them to do more research, but since I'd identified the symbols, there was little more they could reveal, so I handed them over willingly. "Thanks, Nazan. And when the wedding happens, you're welcome to come to all of it. The main ceremony is at three, then we're eating at six."

Surprise crossed his face. "I always spend Christmas alone. I have bookbinding to attend to and a ham hock to devour. I've been marinating it in cider for a week."

"The books will understand if you'd like to spend a day with your friends," I said. "Why not look after your books in the morning and join us in the afternoon? We'd be happy to have you with us."

A rare smile crossed Nazan's face. He bowed. "If your nemesis doesn't destroy you, it would be an honor to attend the wedding. I shall bring a suitable gift."

I choked back a laugh. "I hope they don't destroy me. If we can pull it off, we're holding the ceremony at my house. If not, meet us there anyway, and we'll lead the wedding party to wherever we can find that'll marry us at such short notice."

He bowed again.

"Let's get out of here before he changes his mind," Nugget muttered.

I gestured for Russell to follow us on the wing then hurried out of the library, shocked Nazan had a softer side. I was intrigued he'd been married, but it was something to ponder another time.

Once we were outside, I cast a spell to get us home. Two men were speaking as I entered the house, and I discovered a man with a round belly, equally round red cheeks, and a white bushy beard settled in my most comfortable armchair. He had a plate of cranberry and orange cookies beside him and a mug of hot chocolate in one hand.

"Indigo! How did you get on?" Olympus hurried over to me.

"I got what I needed." I looked at the stranger. "You must be Zephir."

He stood and shook my hand. "I am indeed. It's a great pleasure to meet you, Indigo."

Luna, Odessa, and Storm came out of the kitchen and joined us. We settled in seats, all eager to hear what Zephir knew about Dobbie.

Zephir took a moment to get settled before stroking his fingers through his bushy, white beard. "I'll get to the point. Dobbie is a vicious, untrustworthy person. His disappearance should be seen as a blessing in disguise."

Chapter 7

"Why is he such a terrible person?" I looked at Olympus, and he seemed equally surprised by Zephir's stark statement about Dobbie.

"Do you know him well?" Zephir helped himself to a cookie.

"I've worked with Dobbie at the Magic Council for years," Olympus said.

"Interesting. You've had no complaints about him?"

"We work in different departments, but our paths cross at conferences and social events," Olympus said. "I've never heard anyone say a bad word about him."

"You would if you spent time with other celebrants." Zephir finished his cookie and sipped his hot chocolate, leaving a ring of cream on his beard. "Dobbie steals jobs and undercuts prices. I've even heard a rumor he pretended to be a different celebrant to take a job he wanted."

"I didn't realize being a celebrant paid so well." Storm leaned back in her seat.

"The pay is average, but Dobbie doesn't do this for the money," Zephir said.

"For the accolade?" I asked. "Does he target celebrity weddings?"

"Nothing so crass. Dobbie is obsessed with weddings. Do you know how many times he's been married?" His question was directed at Olympus.

"No clue. He never talked about a wife. I didn't even notice a wedding band on his finger."

"Probably because he doesn't want to say the wrong wife's name." Zephir tutted and shook his head. "Dobbie has been married eight times. And again, if you believe the rumors, some of those marriages overlapped. It wasn't because he fell in love with an amazing woman and found his soulmate. He did it because he loves being at weddings. He loves being the center of attention on special days. It's an unnatural obsession."

"That should have gotten him into a heap of trouble," Luna said.

"I agree. Yet he's still free to work and faced no criminal charges." Zephir cocked his head. "I wonder why that would be?"

"Magic Council immunity." Storm smirked. "Won't be the first time they've pulled strings for an employee."

Olympus's forehead furrowed, but he didn't disagree with the bold comment.

"There must have been complaints made about him," Odessa said.

"Did you run any background checks on Dobbie before hiring him?" Zephir asked.

"Well, no. But I know the guy. I trust him. At least, I did." Olympus looked at me, his eyes wide with concern.

"It's an unhealthy behavior. But the man loves a ceremony, and he sees no harm in fueling his desire. And he cares nothing about stepping on other celebrants' toes or lying about who he is to secure the wedding of his choice."

"His diary was crammed with bookings," I said.

"I've heard he's worked for free because he was so desperate to attend a particular event," Zephir said.

"The guy needs a new hobby," Storm said. "Weddings are so dull."

Luna nodded. "That behavior could get him in trouble. Or hurt."

"It absolutely has! Dobbie's been jumped on, threatened, and I believe he's been reported to the Magic Council for misconduct." Zephir arched an eyebrow. "Yet, somehow, he's still getting away with it."

"He wouldn't if I'd known about this," Olympus said. "And if he'd been reported, he'd have been investigated. This wouldn't have been swept under the rug."

"You sure about that?" Storm stretched out her legs.

"There must be records of his sneaky behavior on file," I said to Olympus.

"Most likely. But I never thought to run a check on Dobbie. Like I said, I've known him for ages. There was no hint he was obsessed with weddings or marrying multiple times to feed his addiction."

"There are worse addictions," Odessa said brightly. "At least no one's getting hurt."

"The women he abandons after the shine fades would say otherwise," Zephir said. "And then there are the wedding celebrants whose noses are put out of joint because they've lost work. Dobbie has no scruples in stealing from others." His gaze settled on me. "You said Dobbie was unable to attend your wedding. What happened to him?"

I shifted in my seat. "I didn't want to scare you off by telling you the whole truth, but hearing this, I doubt you'll be surprised."

"I've seen plenty of terrifying things at wedding ceremonies. I once attended an event where there were over a hundred inflatable unicorns, and the guests had to sit on them. When they did, the unicorns started fighting. And another where the couple was naked! So were the guests. It was a liberating experience. I even joined in but found it a touch drafty around the nether regions."

"It must have been." I glanced at Olympus, and he nodded at me to continue. "Dobbie can't conduct our ceremony tomorrow because he's missing."

"Missing! He'd never abandon such an important event. Are you sure he hasn't disappeared to find a unique finishing touch for the special day? He does that. He likes to be remembered by his couples."

"We're taking his disappearance seriously," Olympus said. "Dobbie was late for the final run-through of the ceremony, and no one's seen him since."

"He prides himself on his punctuality." Zephir set down his mug. "Is there anything else that's concerning you about his disappearance?"

"There's evidence to suggest he fought with someone," I said.

Zephir let out a soft sigh and leaned back. "This is bad news. I don't like the man and will never forgive him for stealing the wedding of Lady Isabella Tinkletoes from me, but I wouldn't want to see him hurt."

"Maybe just roughed up a bit?" Storm smirked.

His round cheeks flushed. "I make no apologies for having issues with Dobbie. Do you think someone took him?"

"We're looking into it," I said.

Zephir caught hold of my hand. "My dearest bride-to-be, focus on tomorrow, not worrying about what mischief Dobbie has gotten himself into."

"Maybe it was another wedding celebrant," Luna said. "It sounds like none of you like him."

Zephir's eyebrows rose slowly. "I'd be surprised if it was. They'll all be busy. Christmas Day weddings are popular with magic users. It's the purity of the magic, you see. It makes the day extra special and the spells and potions stronger. It's always been my favorite day to conduct a wedding. I was so disappointed when my groom ran off with the bridesmaid, canceling my scheduled wedding."

"The groom ran off with a bridesmaid?" I asked. "I thought it was the groom and the mother-in-law enjoying each other's company that caused the friction?"

"Oh! Of course. My mistake. Weddings get canceled for all kinds of scandalous reasons. I sometimes get muddled. You're right. It was the mother-in-law misbehaving."

I sat back in my seat as Zephir entertained us with the story of an amorous groom and a granny, a frown on my face. Had he just lied to me?

An hour later, I stood shivering beside Olympus outside the main entrance of the Magic Council headquarters. It wasn't my favorite place, since I'd been hauled here as a criminal many years ago. And what we were about to do felt criminal.

The building reached high into the sky, commanding attention with its intricate architectural details. The entrance was adorned with shimmering magical symbols.

"Stop looking so nervous." Olympus accessed the building with a wave of his hand and a waft of magic, revealing a vast main hall and corridors, leading off to different departments. "We're doing nothing illegal. Don't forget, I work here."

"Sneaking in somewhere that's closed on Christmas Eve feels wrong." I kept my voice low and remained close to Olympus as we dashed inside.

"You had no problem breaking into the library."

"That was different."

"True. We don't have book-obsessed fire breathers as guards. Did you find anything useful?"

I hesitated. Discovering the star symbols were linked to Shadow Weavers had shocked me.

Olympus arched an eyebrow then smiled. "Don't be nervous. I know why you don't want to be here. Stick with me, and we won't get into trouble. And this is the easiest way to find out if Dobbie's been hiding things. This way." He strode along the corridor, confident in where he was going.

"I'm not nervous. It's just... have you ever heard of the Shadow Weavers?"

"Sure. Old school dark magic. Time benders? Or was it dimensional magic? They're long defunct. Why do you ask?"

"Those star symbols. They looked like the work of Shadow Weavers."

"Can't be. They don't operate anymore. That magic was outlawed because it was too unstable."

"Yeah, maybe. But the symbols looked the same to me." I rubbed my arms.

"It can't be them. Besides, what do they want with our wedding?"

"That's what I can't figure out."

"This has to do with rival celebrants. I'm certain of it." Olympus stopped me and pressed a finger to his lips then gestured to keep going.

"Maybe we should have questioned Zephir for longer," I said. "If he's involved in Dobbie's disappearance, he could have let something slip."

"He was only interested in telling scandalous stories about the weddings that never happened. Your friends will keep him entertained. If Zephir lets slip anything useful, they'll pass it on. Hurry! We don't want to be here long. Even though it's Christmas Eve, there are still patrols."

"You said it was okay for us to be here." I sped up as Olympus led us through a series of corridors and into a silent office.

"It is. We should keep the lights off, though. Questions will be asked why I'm here," Olympus said. "There's no point in raising the alarm about Dobbie unless we have to."

"We should run a check on Zephir, too," I said. "I'm not so sure it was an accident he got the facts about his latest wedding scandal wrong."

Olympus was busy keying in passwords on the system. "I'll check his background, too. Give me a minute. The system is warming up."

While Olympus went to work, I kept a lookout, scanning the room. The walls were adorned with tapestries woven with shimmering threads, depicting the history of the Magic Council. The desks looked expensive, crafted from rich, dark wood, and crystal orbs emitted soft, pulsating lights.

Olympus gestured me over. "It looks like there's been a feud raging between Dobbie and Zephir for years."

I looked at the information he'd pulled up. "Dobbie filed six complaints about Zephir stealing jobs!"

Olympus nodded. "Zephir lied. It's Dobbie who has a problem with Zephir stealing his jobs, not the other way round."

"Maybe Zephir's the celebrant who has eight wives, too. He's wedding-obsessed. Did Zephir deceive us so he could get to our wedding? He learned Dobbie was our celebrant and got envious?"

"He could have snuck into Witch Haven, attacked Dobbie, and dragged him off somewhere because he knew we'd be desperate for a celebrant and would jump at the chance to have him."

I shook my head. "Why? We're not special."

Olympus quirked an eyebrow at me. "Indigo! You always underestimate yourself. We're a magical power couple."

I snort laughed. "You're sure of yourself."

"Take this seriously. With your Ash witch magic and my position in the Magic Council, we could be a target."

"A target for what?"

"Um... I'm unsure. But what if Zephir has bigger plans than conducting our marriage?"

"You're thinking he wants to take over our wedding so he can abduct us and demand we unleash terror on the unsuspecting residents of Witch Haven?" I wiggled my fingers in the air.

"I don't know his plans! But he could have already been in the village when we contacted him to find a replacement. He set this up to get Dobbie out of the way and have access to us."

I still wasn't convinced we were in the middle of a wedding-obsessed celebrant's devious plans. "Is there anything else useful in the file?"

"Nothing. Other than accusations of him stealing work, he's clean."

"Check Dobbie's background."

Olympus took a few minutes to bring up the information. "Huh! There's a note on his file. None of his records are publicly accessible, but there are paper copies of a closed dossier in storage."

"Where do we find this dossier?"

"It'll be in the cellar. Let me make a note of the reference number so we can grab it."

We left the room and headed back along the corridor to a set of steps, with Olympus leading the way. The atmosphere grew colder and darker as we descended.

"How far underground are we going?" I asked.

"Only another twenty steps or so. Watch out for the ghosts," Olympus replied.

"You have ghosts guarding your old records?" There was a hint of disbelief in my voice.

"No, they live here. They're mainly harmless."

"Mainly!"

Olympus chuckled in the gloom. "Just be polite, and they won't cause you harm."

Finally, we reached the bottom of the seemingly never-ending staircase. Olympus flicked on a light, revealing row upon row of storage units.

"The Magic Council loves to keep records of everything." I stifled a sneeze as dust zoomed up my nose.

He shrugged. "We need paper trails in case someone makes a complaint. This way."

A whisper in my ear made me jump, but when I turned around, there was no one there. "No fun and games tonight, ghosts," I declared to no one in particular. "We're on a mission to save our wedding." I took a few more steps and found my way blocked by a pale ghost in a tattered wedding dress.

She stared at me. I stared back.

"Is there something I can do for you?" I asked.

"Indigo! Keep up. Don't get lost in this place," Olympus called out as he headed off. "It stretches back for miles."

"I'll be with you in a second."

The ghost opened her mouth, revealing a gaping black hole where her teeth should have been, and pointed behind me.

"Sorry, I'm going this way, and we're on a deadline." I maneuvered past her and caught up with Olympus, who was scanning the shelves.

"It's not here! There's a space where the dossier is supposed to be." He checked the number he'd written down and shook his head.

The ghost in the wedding dress appeared once again, silently screaming, and pointing frantically over my shoulder.

I grinned. "I know where it is. Our new friend will lead the way."

The ghost smiled and whisked along briskly, occasionally looking over her shoulder to ensure we were keeping up. Finally, she stopped by a shelf and hovered in place.

Olympus inspected the box she pointed out. "Who filed it here? I'd never have found it."

"But we did, thanks to some help from our ghostly friend." I waved at our spectral assistant, who waved back before disappearing.

Olympus opened the box and pulled out a pile of papers.

"Good news or bad news?" I asked.

"Complaints. Lots of them about Dobbie's poor conduct."

"Complaints about his work at the Magic Council?"

"No, just as Zephir said, Dobbie was sneaking around and stealing wedding jobs that didn't belong to him. There are dozens of complaints. They're as bad as each other."

"Let me guess, it was brushed under the rug because of his position here?" There was a touch of bitterness in my tone.

Olympus started to defend the place he worked but then sighed. "I'm not confirming or denying that, but it wouldn't be the first time something like this has happened."

I pressed my lips together. My opinion of the Magic Council had never been favorable, and it had just lost a few more points with this unsettling revelation.

"Let's take this with us." Olympus tucked the information into an inside coat pocket. "If and when we find Dobbie, I'll confront him and see who he's getting to conceal his bad behavior."

I was relieved to leave the chilly cellar as we ascended the stairs. As soon as we reached the surface, my mobile snow globe pinged, signaling a message from Luna. My heart skipped a beat as I read it.

We found out who trashed your wedding. Get back here ASAP.

I showed the message to Olympus, and he sighed in relief. "Ask Luna who it is."

I tapped out a message and got an almost immediate reply. When I read it, I felt dizzy. "Um... Olympus."

He nodded. "Who'd they catch?"
"Your former fiancée, Peony."

Chapter 8

Even though I'd used a translocation spell to get us back to Witch Haven as quickly as possible, I felt breathless. Peony, my husband-to-be's former fiancée, was ruining the wedding. Why would she do that? She'd not always been friendly toward me, but she was civil to Olympus whenever they met to discuss Bloom, and I'd sensed no lingering romantic feelings on her part toward him. Had I gotten it wrong?

I grabbed Olympus's hand before we stepped through the doorway of my house. "Whatever happens, we'll make this right."

He shook his head. "It makes no sense. Why would Peony want to stop us from getting married? And what has she done to Dobbie? She's no killer."

A dozen possibilities flew through my head, but I kept them to myself. I pushed open the front door, and we strode into the living room. Peony sat in a straight-backed chair, her hands and feet shackled, and a panicked expression on her face. Her cheeks were red and sweaty and her clothes rumpled, suggesting she'd put up a fight.

Luna and Odessa occupied separate chairs, both looking concerned, while Storm lurked close to Peony, a thunderous look on her face, and her fingers flexing.

"This is a mistake," Peony pleaded, her gaze locking onto Olympus. "I didn't mess with your wedding venue, I promise."

I trusted my friends with my life, and they wouldn't have shackled Peony without good reason. I looked at Storm. "What happened?"

"I went back to check on the ceremony room, and I found her snooping." Storm jerked a thumb toward Peony.

"No! I wasn't snooping," Peony said.

"But you were there?" I asked.

Peony chewed on her bottom lip for a second. "Yes, but not for the reason you're thinking."

I slowly crossed my arms and stared at her. "How do you know what I'm thinking?"

Peony's gaze shifted to Olympus. "You know me! Would I do something like this?"

His brow furrowed. "You don't want me to marry Indigo?"

"She's jealous," Storm said. "She's still desperately in love with you, although I can't think why. Or she's insane. The reason doesn't matter. We caught her before she could do any more damage. Time to teach her a lesson."

"Hold on," I said. "I have to know why Peony did this."

"She's not ruining your wedding," Storm said.

"Keeping me tied up solves nothing." Peony's gaze was full of fear as lightning crackled across

Storm's palm. "Whoever wants to stop you from getting married is still out there. You'll soon see when they make their next move."

Storm kicked one of the chair legs. "You're working with someone else? Do you really hate Indigo that much?"

"No! I don't hate Indigo! I... I like her. She can be scary at times, but Bloom adores her."

"You didn't welcome her into the family when you found out she was involved with Olympus," Luna said.

"I don't care about Olympus." Peony looked up at him. "Sorry, but we both know our relationship has been dead and buried for a long time. Neither of us has a desire to reignite that old flame."

"Agreed. But you weren't always kind to Indigo," he said. "Maybe you don't want her to be happy."

"I wasn't unkind, but I was cautious." Peony's tongue traced her bottom lip. "Indigo was in my daughter's life, and I couldn't risk putting Bloom in harm's way."

I nodded slowly as realization dawned. "When you learned about my past, you figured there was still a big bad witch hiding inside me. A witch who might hurt your daughter if you took your eye off me."

"Even though Indigo helped with Bloom's rehabilitation after she got free from dark magic scum, you still didn't trust her?" Luna asked.

"I'm sorry! I should have, but I was worried. I couldn't always be around when Indigo was with Bloom. So yes, I was overprotective when I visited and said some things I shouldn't. I regret that," Peony said.

"Not enough to quit your plans to ruin their happy day," Odessa said.

"I don't want to ruin anyone's happy day." Peony fell silent for a moment, her gaze fixed on the floor. "I'll admit, I was jealous when I heard you were getting married."

"You just said you had no interest in Olympus." I scowled at Peony.

"I don't! Not him as such. But... I never got a happily ever after. I haven't found anyone I want to spend my life with."

"So, you thought you'd get back into Olympus's life and give it another go? Never gonna happen." Storm kicked the chair again.

"Easy now," I murmured to Storm. "Let's give Peony a chance to speak."

Storm grunted her compliance and took a step back as she glared at Peony.

"Hand on heart and on my daughter's life, I don't want Olympus back," Peony said.

"Why do you want to ruin Indigo's special day, then?" Odessa asked.

"I don't!" Peony's gaze lowered. "My conflicted feelings have nothing to do with Indigo or Olympus. But... I'm lonely. I'm not unhappy, but I miss having someone special. I have a wonderful daughter and friends, but ever since I left Witch Haven, I haven't felt like I fit in anywhere. I've moved house three times, thinking it was the wrong place for me, but wherever I am, it doesn't change how I feel."

"Your problem isn't your physical location." Odessa's tone was gentle. "You need to spring clean your internal issues before you find your forever home and happiness."

"Here she goes," Storm muttered. "The woo-woo is getting started. Think only happy thoughts, and the world will be a happy place."

"Don't disrespect the woo-woo," Odessa said. "I'm right about this. Peony, if you have unfinished business or unhappiness lurking inside you, if you don't address it, you'll always feel like this. You could move to a tropical island where there are bare-chested hunks offering you exotic drinks and sensual massages all day, and you'd still be miserable."

"I'm beginning to realize that," Peony said after a few seconds of silence. "I shut myself away after Bloom disappeared. I didn't want to deal with the pitying looks and the veiled discussions that I was at fault."

"It wasn't your fault. That was on me," Olympus said.

"Neither of you were at fault," I said. "No one knew about the dark powers infiltrating our village. We were all tricked."

"I still wonder if I could have done more," Peony said. "Been around more. Worked less."

I crouched in front of Peony. "Come back to Witch Haven. You liked living here, didn't you?"

She blinked several times, surprise in her eyes. "I love it here. I loved having my store. And I have great friends close by."

"Then come back. You can reconnect with the people you left behind and find somewhere to set up your business again if that's what you want. Bloom would love having you so close. It would make life easier for everyone."

"I'd wondered about opening a new store. I've even been to some auctions and picked up a few things I could turn a profit on."

"You wouldn't mind?" Olympus asked me.

I shook my head. "It makes sense. Once we marry, we'll become a blended family. I consider you a part of that family, Peony."

Her eyes filled with tears. "I'd like that. Whenever I come here, I feel like I'm returning home. Everywhere else feels temporary."

"We still have a big problem to deal with," Storm said. "Before you make plans to live together in a commune and smoke strange-flavored herbs from a giant bong, we still don't know why Peony was snooping around the wedding venue or what she's done to Dobbie."

All eyes shifted to Peony.

She tensed in her seat then sighed. "I heard some locals gossiping about there being a problem with your venue, so I took a look. I wanted to see if I could help."

"More like check you'd done enough damage so the inn couldn't be used for the wedding," Storm said.

I glanced at my suspicious friend. Storm was being super protective because she cared. "Did you see inside?" I asked Peony.

"Only through the windows," Peony said. "Well, to begin with. The door wasn't properly locked, so I opened it to get a better look."

"She was standing close to one wall and staring at it," Storm said.

"You were interested in the graffiti?" I asked.

Peony paled. "Did you see the star symbols underneath the lines of paint?"

"Sure. Not at first, but we picked them out. What do you know about them?"

"I know they're trouble."

"You're covering your butt," Storm said. "You put those symbols there. You've brought trouble to Witch Haven. You're probably behind this lousy weather as well."

"I promise, I had nothing to do with those symbols. I know they're bad news, though." Peony's fear-filled gaze darted around. "Have you ever heard of the Shadow Weavers?"

Chapter 9

My pulse picked up. "Funny you should ask. I've been refreshing my memory about them."

"Which means you know what the symbols represent?" Peony asked.

"In a way." I nodded at Storm. "Remove Peony's shackles."

"We can't trust her!"

"If you need my alibi, speak to Mystica Shade. I'm renting a spare room from her. Other than when I dropped by the inn to give you your gift and let you know I was coming to the wedding, I've been there this whole time. We even had dinner together the night I arrived."

I made a mental note to double-check, but the more Peony talked, the less I considered her a suspect. "Storm, she's not a threat. Let her go."

Storm grumbled as she removed the restraints.

"Tell me what you know about the Shadow Weavers?" I asked Peony.

She rubbed her wrists and flexed her fingers. "Wherever they go, trouble follows."

"Are you one of them?" Storm asked.

"No! But they only mean harm. And if they've targeted your wedding, you need to hide. You can't risk going through with the ceremony. You'll be too vulnerable."

"Vulnerable to what?" Olympus asked.

"I'm not buying this," Storm said. "You're misdirecting us so you can escape."

"I don't think she is," I said. "And my visit to the library proved useful. We found books with pictures of the symbols left at the inn. They're Shadow Weaver marks."

Olympus shook his head. "Their practices have been outlawed and the groups disbanded. No one practices that kind of magic anymore. And if we catch anyone doing it, they go to prison."

"Are you sure about that?" Storm asked. "These shadow jerks don't practice whatever twisted magic they're into because you tell them so? Is the Magic Council really so scarily effective?"

A flush crept up Olympus's neck. "Maybe there are a few still active. It's hard to keep track. They weave their power into the shadows, so they're almost impossible to detect until their actions turn chaotic."

"I... um... haven't told you this before," I said, "but I met a Shadow Weaver while I served my sentence. She bragged about an underground network of Shadow Weavers. She even tried to recruit me to the ranks, but I wasn't interested. I just wanted to serve my time and get on with my life."

"That was years ago," Olympus said. "And she could have been lying. Few magic users have the skills to control shadow magic."

"I don't know how she did it, but she showed me her power. It made me queasy to be in the same room as she spun a spell through the dark corners, and everything turned gray. The little energy I had vanished, and I passed out."

"The star symbols left at your wedding venue show you've been marked," Peony whispered.

"Marked by Shadow Weavers?" Luna asked.

Peony nodded. "They either want to recruit you or destroy you for something you've done that's offended them."

"Olympus, have you had recent dealings with Shadow Weavers?" Storm asked. "Put some sleazy dark shadow-weaving scumbag on ice, and now he's coming for you?"

"No Shadow Weaver cases have come across my desk in years. They don't want me."

"They want you." Luna looked straight at me. "Recruit an Ash witch into their ranks, and their power would triple."

I drew in a slow breath as I considered this option. Ash witch magic was ancient and tapped into the earth's primal power, and I had to use it regularly, or the excess would spark out of my fingers and give people electric shocks.

"It has to be you they want," Odessa said. "No offense, Limpy, but you're half as powerful as Indigo."

"None taken. I know how incredible she is," he said.

"But Olympus isn't useless," I said.

He arched an eyebrow. "Thanks for that endorsement."

"You said it yourself. Your position in the Magic Council holds sway. You can pull strings and get things done quickly."

"I wouldn't say quickly," Storm said. "But Olympus can be effective."

"Please, I'm not sure my ego can take any more inflating," he said.

"What's their endgame?" Luna asked.

I shrugged. "I can't tell you."

"They don't give out unicorns, rainbows, and sparkles to people," Peony said. "If they're on a mission, it's to destroy something or someone. They take pleasure in sucking the joy out of the world."

"They won't do that with us around," Storm said.

I sank into a chair. "Dobbie had star symbols in his diary. Does that make him a Shadow Weaver?"

"The only people who use that specific symbol are users of shadow magic or associated with them," Peony said.

"How do you know all of this?" Olympus asked. "You were never interested in powerful magic when we were together."

Peony ducked her head. "When Bloom went missing, I lost my way. I saw no point in goodness since what I loved had been taken. I dabbled in some dark stuff, but it did nothing to help. It just made me feel worse."

Storm loomed over Peony. "You know about the Shadow Weavers. Shadow Weaver symbols appear on the walls of Indigo and Olympus's wedding venue, and now you tell us you practiced the same magic. Someone give me five minutes alone with this witch to get her to confess."

"I know! It looks bad, but please check my alibi. It wasn't me." Peony cowered from Storm.

"We'll check your alibi, but I don't think you're involved," I said to Peony. "And I know all about sinking into darkness. It seems like the easy route, doesn't it? You've got nothing positive left, so why not try something different? Anything so you feel something."

"Exactly! I felt like I'd lost a vital part of me when Bloom was taken. I couldn't see a way back. Nothing I did made a difference."

"So you tried increasingly more deviant things," I said. "Darker spells, twisted potions, anything to dig out that horrible feeling in your gut."

Peony stared at me, blinking, then nodded. "I wouldn't ruin your special day with Olympus. And Bloom adores you. She's so excited we're joining as a family. We think you're good for Olympus. He's so much less uptight these days."

I smiled as Olympus grumbled under his breath. "I'm glad we're becoming a family, too. And I'll take the best care of Bloom."

"I know you will. Sorry I ever doubted you. If I can help to figure out what's going on with your wedding, I will. My Shadow Weaver knowledge is rusty, but whatever I know, I'll share."

Nugget strode in from outside, with Russell and Hilda beside him. They were all covered in snow. "We've figured out what Monty did in those missing ten minutes when we looked around Dobbie's trashed room. Where is he?"

Monty slunk in from the kitchen, his ears lowered. "Did I eat Dobbie?"

"From the clues we've uncovered, it would have been simpler if you had." Nugget glowered at the giant leopard.

"Monty didn't eat Dobbie, though, right?" I asked.

Nugget shook snow off his fur. "It's so much worse than that."

"You can't get worse than Monty eating our wedding celebrant the night before our big day," Olympus said. "Not that I think you did, buddy."

Nugget drew in a breath and made sure he had everyone's attention. "Monty ate your entire wedding buffet."

My heart sank as my gaze drifted over what was left of the gourmet buffet. The food had been partially consumed or knocked over. And large paw prints covered the floor. They were Monty-sized prints.

My familiars were with me, along with Olympus. Monty was there, too, but he was hiding. Luna and her uncle Albert stood beside me in his bakery kitchen, his face ashen, and his hands clasped in front of him. "I didn't know anything was wrong until your familiars arrived and asked to check the food. I was busy making the finishing touches to your wedding cake when they showed up. I told them there was nothing to worry about, and it was safely stored, but Nugget was insistent."

"I had a bad feeling in my gut," Nugget said. "Monty's enormous stomach came from somewhere, and since we were almost convinced that he hadn't eaten Dobbie, I looked elsewhere and found this."

"Eat Dobbie?" Albert looked at me. "I'm lost."

"It's a long story." I swallowed against the tightness in my throat. I couldn't ask Albert to make the food from scratch. He baked his magic and his love into everything he made, often exhausting himself in his desire for perfection. It would have been the best meal I'd ever tasted.

Olympus had his eyes closed. "Pinch me. This is a nightmare."

"You need to feed Monty more," I muttered to him.

"I need to teach him basic manners. I can't believe he did this."

"I checked everything with your familiars to see what we could salvage," Albert said, "but it's all been tasted or licked or trodden on. Most of the meat is gone. There was a whole ham and a side of roast beef. They've vanished."

"That's what made Monty look so chunky," Nugget said. "He swallowed the ham and the beef down in one bite. He never chews his food. It would have made him feel terrible and look like he'd eaten Dobbie. Or at least his head."

"I know Monty is a giant cat, but he couldn't have eaten it all. He'd have been violently unwell," Albert said.

"Monty can pack away a lot when he sets his mind to it," Olympus said, "but I agree. Even this is beyond him. Monty! Get in here and explain yourself."

Monty slunk in, his belly scraping the floor, and his ears lowered so they were flat.

Olympus turned on him, anger coloring his cheeks. "Why conceal this from us? You must have realized we'd figure out what happened."

"I've been stress eating because of the wedding preparations. And you've been distracted and not paying me enough attention. You keep forgetting to feed me."

"I do not! You'd never let me get away with your dinner being even five minutes late. This is inexcusable, Monty." Olympus had his arms crossed, a severe frown on his face.

While Olympus chastised Monty, I walked around the destroyed buffet, being careful not to slip in anything sticky. Monty had stepped in the food, and his paw prints were all over the place. I looked at him. "Did you have friends eating with you?"

"No! Just me. I'm the guilty one. All me. Only me. I'm a bad kitty."

I didn't believe him. There were different-sized paw prints mixed in with Monty's. "Nugget, you had nothing to do with this, did you?"

Nugget hissed at me. "I'm insulted you even ask. You've been bleating about how important this wedding is for months, so I wouldn't even risk sniffing a salmon souffle in case I get yelled at." He swished his tail. "If I need extra food, I'm capable of hunting."

"Or visiting the neighbor. She leaves you treats on her porch," Hilda said.

"That too. It's important to have backup plans."

"You're not coming to the wedding," Olympus said to Monty. "You don't deserve to be a part of our special day."

"I'm sure Monty is sorry," I said. "And you'll miss him not being there."

"No! He's done enough damage. I'm putting him in a cell as punishment. He can sit in there while we get married and think about what he's done."

Monty whimpered but didn't protest over his punishment. "At least I'm not a killer."

"Was the story about you eating Dobbie a cover for this?" Olympus's voice lifted an octave.

"No! I woke with his bloody shoe near me and panicked. I... I remember sneaking here to get food, but when I got hit with the magic blast in the bed-and-breakfast, I genuinely got confused memories. With the shoe, blood, and Dobbie missing, plus my gut being so sensitive, it made me wonder." Monty hid his eyes under a large fluffy paw.

I touched Olympus's arm and leaned in close, keeping my voice low. "We can figure something out with the food. And we have bigger things to worry about."

"Monty's humiliated me! He's supposed to support me and make my life easier, but he only makes it worse. I'm done with that leopard."

Monty shuffled to the door, his belly dragging on the floor. "Don't lock me up for long, though."

"I should lock you up and throw away the key," Olympus grumbled. "You're a menace."

"We'll bring you snacks if you're worried about getting hungry," Hilda said.

"It's not me I'm worried about." Monty looked up at Olympus and whimpered. "I don't like being inside a cell."

"Get used to it. I'm so disappointed in you, Monty."

"We'll clean up," Luna said. "And we can pull something together for your wedding buffet, right, Uncle?"

Albert's eyes widened, and his face paled, but he nodded. "We'll make sure your wedding day food is perfect."

I looked at the destroyed buffet while my angry fiancé stalked away with his disgraced familiar. The way things kept going wrong, I'd be lucky if we ever got a wedding.

Chapter 10

I opened my eyes and took a breath. It was Christmas Day, and I was getting married. Maybe. I hadn't slept much, partly because we'd stayed up late putting a plan together on how to deal with the Shadow Weavers. If they risked showing up and following through with their less-than-subtle threats, we needed to be ready for them.

There was a tap on the bedroom door.

"I'm awake."

Odessa walked in with a huge tray of breakfast treats. She was followed by Luna and Storm. "You can't be one of those brides who faints at the altar because she's been starving herself for weeks to fit into her dress." Luna thumped down the enormous tray of tasty goodies.

"There's enough for all of us." I inspected the mound of muffins and pancake stack.

"Of course. We're eating, too. Fainting bridesmaids are also unacceptable." Odessa lifted an iced cranberry muffin and took a bite. "How did you sleep?"

"It was patchy. But I'm confident our plan will work."

"You bet your sweet cheeks it will." Storm sipped on a black coffee. "When the Shadow Weavers attack, we attack back until there's nothing left but a smoldering pile of ash."

I checked the time. "I should get up. We have so much to do."

"Relax. It's your special day, and you don't need to get involved with casting spells or putting up the protective barriers." Luna patted my hand. "Your fabulous bridesmaids can look incredible *and* kick butt."

I cocked my head. "How long have you all been up?"

They grinned at each other.

"We left you a few things to finish," Storm said. "We didn't want you feeling left out on your special day." She air-quoted the last two words.

"But you must focus on the most important thing," Luna said, "finally marrying Olympus."

I smiled. "How's the weather looking?"

"The snow stopped a couple of hours ago, and it's beautiful out there. It's the perfect setting for an outdoor wedding." Odessa grinned at me. "You'll be a stunning winter bride."

I slid out of bed and pulled back the curtains. A blanket of crisp snow stretched as far as I could see, and a smile crossed my face.

There was another knock on the door. "I know it's bad luck to see you before the wedding, but I got us a license," Olympus said. "It's all systems go!"

"You can come in. We've had enough bad luck thrown at us that a little more won't hurt."

Olympus poked his head around the door. "I could only get an outdoor license, though. We're getting married in the snow."

I let out a sigh of relief. "So long as it's legal, I don't care if we marry in an enchanted dragon dung pile. But we need to talk to Zephir about what we learned."

"Get dressed. He arrives in an hour." Olympus nodded at us then disappeared.

Zephir had lied to us, and I didn't trust him. I had to know if he was involved in Dobbie's disappearance.

After Odessa had shoved a hearty breakfast down my throat, I showered, dressed, and headed down the stairs. Olympus met me in the hallway.

"Zephir's just arrived," he said.

"Let me talk to him alone."

"I figured you'd want to shake the truth out of him without me watching."

"If I need to rough him up, it's best you don't see." I kissed his cheek.

"I'm happy to look the other way. I just need nothing else to mess with today."

I squeezed his arm then headed into the living room.

Zephir smiled when he saw me. "I hear we're having an outdoor wedding. How delightful. I'm glad I brought my thermal robe."

"It won't be cold," I said. "We'll use spells to keep everyone toasty warm."

"I enjoy an outdoor wedding. It brings a flush to everyone's cheeks. I'm surprised you wanted me here so early, though. I hope there's nothing wrong."

"There's nothing wrong with me or Olympus," I said. "But we have concerns about you."

"Me? I assure you I've conducted hundreds of weddings and other celebratory events. I could read the vows with my eyes closed. In several languages."

"It's not that I'm concerned about," I said. "We ran background checks on everyone who's involved with our wedding. You're the troublemaker who steals other celebrants' couples."

Zephir spluttered for several seconds before sinking into a chair. "Oh, dear."

"You're not denying it?"

"I... I can't deny my addiction. It's a sickness I can't control. My counselor tells me it's wrong, and if I don't face the truth, the problem will only grow." He hung his head. "I'm too weak. I see a wedding I want, and an urge comes over me."

I loomed over him. "Did you do something to Dobbie? Is that the reason you were available to look after our wedding?"

"No! I was heartbroken when I got the news that I wouldn't perform a wedding ceremony on Christmas Day. Then I got your call. Fate had shone her benevolent light upon me, and I was to have my perfect Christmas Day celebration. I was overjoyed. Of course, the circumstances were difficult with Dobbie disappearing, but it worked out for all of us."

"Not for Dobbie. He's still missing," I said. "And I'll be honest, I'm uncomfortable with you being involved in the wedding."

"I couldn't have hurt Dobbie. I was at another wedding when he vanished. Check with the bride and groom. It was why I didn't pick up your call."

I narrowed my eyes at him, still unsure I trusted him. "Give me their details."

Zephir pulled a small book from his pocket and flicked through it. "Here! They're on their honeymoon, but I'm sure you can get hold of them."

"Olympus!"

He appeared in the doorway. "All good?"

"Almost. Find out if Zephir looked after this wedding."

He took the details and nodded. "I'll make a few calls."

Zephir slid from his seat and fell to his knees. "Please, don't send me away. I'll waive my fee! It'll be an honor to host the service for you and Olympus. I've done wrong in the past, but I'm getting help. I'm having weekly therapy sessions. And I haven't asked a woman to marry me for at least a month."

I repressed a snort. "That's progress?"

He sighed. "It's a daily struggle, but I'm doing my best."

Some people's version of best verged on the terrible, but who was I to judge when my past was so murky?

Olympus strode back in. "Zephir was at the wedding. He couldn't have been in Witch Haven when Dobbie was attacked."

Zephir remained on his knees. "I'm so embarrassed, Olympus. I'm trying to convince your charming fiancée to let me stay. I'll be on my best behavior. No matter how pretty the single ladies are at your wedding, I won't even ask them to dance."

I wrinkled my nose. I still didn't like him being involved.

"We need someone to marry us," Olympus said to me.

I nodded. "No messing around. And stay away from everyone."

Zephir clapped his hands together. "That's wonderful news. And, of course, I'll behave. Is there anything I can do to help while I'm here?"

"We're looking good," Olympus said. "Nugget and Russell are decorating the wedding arch. And I've sent messages to everyone coming to the ceremony to notify them of the venue change."

"I'll go to the inn and put up a notice." Storm appeared in the doorway. "Anyone who doesn't get the message will know to come here."

Zephir stood. "I'll be back promptly at two-thirty for the three o'clock service." He smiled at everyone then hurried out.

"Any sign of the Shadow Weavers?" I asked Storm.

"It's quiet. I swept the village with Luna and Odessa, and nothing strange stirred."

"They could have changed their mind," Olympus said. "Decided it was too dangerous to tackle us."

"I'll believe that when I see it," Storm said. "We'll keep patrolling."

"I'll help. I have hours before I need to get ready." I turned to Olympus. "You should let Monty out. He's been in a cell all night."

He frowned. "I was planning on keeping him there until the wedding was over, but..."

"You're feeling bad?"

Olympus nodded. "An overnight stay in a cell should have calmed him down."

I kissed his cheek. "He'll be fine at the wedding. We won't hear a peep out of him for the whole day."

"If we're lucky." Olympus grabbed his coat. "I'll go get him."

"Ready to look for trouble?" Storm asked me.

I smiled and rubbed my hands together. "Let's go trouble hunting."

Hours of walking around Witch Haven, looking for the Shadow Weavers, had done little to calm my nerves, and a riot of tiny knife-wielding gnomes stabbed my insides as I stared at myself in the full-length mirror. My dress was cream with purple accents and simple lines, the hem brushing the floor.

Although we'd found no evidence the wedding was under attack, I had one final, giant challenge to face, which ensured these nerves were staying. Marriage.

When I glanced up, Odessa, Luna, and Storm stood behind me, all smiling at my reflection.

"You scrub up nicely," Storm said. "I can't remember the last time I saw you in a dress."

"You should talk," I murmured. I'd chosen classic dresses for my bridesmaids, nothing floofy. Luna was in a beautiful burnt orange dress, Storm in black, and Odessa wore a stunning red number.

My gaze went to the window. "Oh, boy. This is really happening! No Shadow Weavers have messed with us, and Olympus is waiting for me at the altar."

"It's too quiet," Storm said. "I don't like it."

"We scared them off," Odessa said. "They must have snuck in to take a look and found all the protection magic and barriers, so they gave up."

Although I nodded, I shared Storm's sentiment. Why would they give up when they'd gotten so close to ruining everything?

"We need to hurry," Luna said. "The guests are all here."

I took one final look at myself in the mirror, smoothed my hands down the front of my dress, and then took the bouquet Odessa handed me. "Let's go get married."

As I descended the stairs with my best friends, my nerves finally faded. Nugget, Hilda, and Russell waited at the bottom. Russell's feathers gleamed, and he had an adorable black bowtie around his neck. Hilda had spun herself a delicate sparkling cape, which she wore over her back. Nugget also wore a smart bowtie and had clearly spent time grooming his fur.

Bloom was also there as my flower girl. She wore a cute pink dress with a full underskirt and had a cascade of winter daisies woven through her hair. She jigged on her toes when I arrived. "You look pretty."

I hugged her. "So do you."

She blushed, and then a worried look crossed her face. "I heard what's been going on. Is everything okay?"

"Everything is perfect." I peeked out of the door. "Are you ready to lead the way?"

Bloom's grin was a touch self-conscious, but she nodded as she lifted her basket of flower petals.

After getting a hug from my friends, my familiars led the way out of the house. An arch of glittering webbing and glistening feathers had been built to protect me from the cold and lead me to a short aisle, where a handful of friends and family sat. Zephir and Olympus stood by a twinkling altar. Monty stood beside Olympus, looking proud.

Bloom had littered the path with petals, and she stood beside Peony at the front, close to the altar.

Russell and Hilda settled on my shoulders, and I lifted Nugget into my arms. A lump formed in my throat from the happy tears that gathered in my eyes. I'd come such a long way since those dark days when I thought I'd never be accepted back into Witch Haven. I'd been certain I didn't deserve love, friendship, or even familiars. I'd chosen a path of loneliness. But returning to Witch Haven had changed that. I'd rekindled friendships, bonded with amazing familiars, and been surrounded by love. It was a happily ever after I'd barely been able to dream of, but here it was.

"You did a great job on the decorations," I whispered to Hilda.

"I have no webbing left, but it was worth it," she replied. "And you're always worth the effort."

I slowed as the hairs on the back of my neck stood up. I glanced around.

"Everything okay?" Nugget asked. "You can still back out. Olympus has his uptight moments, so everyone would understand if you've changed your mind."

"I'm good. Just nerves," I assured him.

"Once you're standing opposite Olympus, they'll vanish," Hilda said. "He's always had a calming influence on you."

I drew back my shoulders, and Olympus caught my eye. His smile calmed my jitters as I began the walk along the aisle. Twenty steps separated me from my future with this wonderful man.

A movement out of the corner of my eye had me turning my head. "There's someone out there."

"Even if there is, nothing can get through the barrier magic," Hilda said. "We checked it a few moments ago. It's strong."

I squinted and turned in a slow circle.

Nugget growled, and his hackles lifted. "What's wrong? Your heart's racing."

"That." My breath escaped me as a black star encased in a circle appeared in the snow.

Chapter 11

I ran up the aisle to Olympus, clutching Nugget to my chest. "Do you see it?"

His smile had vanished, concern filling his eyes. "See what?"

"They're here! The Shadow Weavers have gotten past the magic."

Storm, Luna, and Odessa were by my side in an instant.

"That's not possible," Storm said. "We checked everything."

"I don't know how they've done it, but they've gotten past our defenses," I said. "Look!"

They looked around as a low mumble of concern came from the waiting guests.

"I'm not seeing anything," Luna said. "Anyone else?"

Odessa shook her head. So did Storm.

"Our wedding party is encased inside a giant Shadow Weaver's symbol. It's in the snow!" I jabbed a finger at the dark mark.

"Is there a problem?" Zephir asked cautiously.

"This wedding is under attack," I said.

"I'm also not seeing anything," Olympus said. "But I trust you. What do you want to do?"

"Get the guests inside. Zephir, too. Make sure everyone is safe. Go! And Monty, guard them. Keep everyone inside." I remained with Olympus, staring at the symbol as my friends and Monty hurried our guests into the house. Despite protests, everyone sensed my alarm and were soon safely inside.

My friends rejoined me, and their calm determination reassured me. "Nugget, Russell, Hilda, look around. But be careful. The Shadow Weavers are out there, and I don't want you getting hurt."

Russell took to the wing, while Nugget leapt out of my arms. I set Hilda on the snow then pressed my hand to her back, and she grew into an enormously magnificent, hair-covered spider with giant fangs. She scuttled off after the others.

Russell made it thirty feet in the air before letting out a pained screech. Magic sparks flew around him, and then he was falling. I hitched my dress and ran with one arm out, catching him before he hit the snow. His feathers smoldered.

He cawed softly as I stroked him.

"They put up their own wards?" I whispered.

He nodded.

"I'll heal him." Luna gently lifted Russell into her arms. "Hey, sweet boy. Let's get those wings flapping again." She was incredible with animals, as her thriving sanctuary revealed. It took a few minutes, but Russell was soon back on his feet and snapping his beak.

"We don't see anything." Hilda scuttled back to the group. "How's Russell? I saw him fall."

He cawed joyfully and flipped snow in the air with his wings.

"No one lurking close by?" I asked Hilda.

"If they're here, they're hiding from us."

My frustration grew. How was I able to see the star symbol when no one else could?

I stumbled back as swirls of dark mist whirled up and enveloped everyone. I reached for Olympus, but the mist burned my skin, and I could only watch his struggle as it curled around him and down his throat. Magic sparked on my fingertips as I looked for a patch of shadow that wasn't twisted around someone, so I could slam a spell into it.

Before I found my mark, dark forms appeared through the mist, floating toward me.

I squinted at them, rage heating my insides and flaring my magic. "Let them go."

"Happily, if you come with me." The murky stranger's eyes gleamed with a twisted fervor, and the air crackled with power that made my skin crawl.

My fingers twitched, instinctively forming a protective shield of shimmering light around me, my friends, and my familiars. The stranger laughed, chilling and taunting, as he hurled shards of obsidian magic in my direction. They collided with my shield, creating a shower of sparks that cascaded like shattered stars.

A whispered incantation escaped my lips, and the snow responded to my call, swirling into a cyclone that sent the shards hurtling back, but he deflected them with ease, each shard evaporating into tendrils of shadow before they touched him.

Our gazes locked. I extended my hand, summoning the earth's energy to respond to my command. A wall of snow erupted from the frozen ground, reaching toward the stranger. Before it could cover him, he exhaled dark fumes, and the snow melted.

He thrust out his hand and sent me flying, slamming into the barriers and jarring my bones. I hit the snow and wheezed out a breath. "What do you want?"

"You. This has always been about you."

I checked on the others. They still struggled in the dark mist. "Release my friends and familiars. If you don't want them, let them go."

"Join me, and they will live."

I growled at him as I drew upon my power and threw out more magic, but the misty attacker sliced through it with ease. "You cannot escape me, Indigo. The shadows know your every move."

Determination blazed within me, and another incantation spilled from my lips as I blasted out ethereal fire. It surged toward the misty form, the magic clashing with the enveloping shadows that swirled around him. His form wavered, his hold on the darkness faltering.

With a guttural roar, he summoned a vortex of shadows. The sky darkened, the sun's feeble attempt to break through the inky veil falling short. "I will destroy them. Then you'll have nothing. I keep my magic under control to save their lives, but my patience is limited. Join me, and they survive.

Keep fighting, and I destroy them, and it'll be your fault. Or do you want even more blood on your hands?"

My magic surged within me as I called upon my ancestors. I wouldn't lose anyone I loved. I'd lost so many people I cared about, and it was never happening again.

An aura of luminescence enveloped me as the spectral form of my stepmother, Magda, materialized. Her gaze went from me to the wedding arch then my dress, and her eyes widened.

"I know! I'm getting married. We can talk about that another time. Right now, we have a big problem. That misty jerk wants to stop my wedding and kill my friends." I staggered to my feet and grabbed for her outstretched hand. The second our powers fused, flames shot toward my attacker, and the collision created an explosion of energy so dazzling I could barely see.

Magda surged forward, taking me with her, her eyes blazing as we channeled our energy toward our enemy. The air sparked as light and dark smashed together.

His form wavered as we pressed closer, his grip on the shadows faltering. He snarled, and his dark powers lashed out again and again. But Magda and I stood strong, a barrier of ancestral energy and love shielding us from his malevolence.

With a surge of magic, Magda extended her hand, her guiding, supportive touch a beacon of unyielding strength. A brilliant light enveloped the mist man, his twisted powers unraveling as her pure energy stripped away the darkness that consumed him. He thrashed and roared, but his resistance was futile against our combined magic.

Magda looked at me and winked as the vortex of shadows dissipated, releasing everyone. Our mysterious attacker was splayed in the snow, not moving.

I inched toward him, Magda's hand still in mine. The air shimmered around us, and six people appeared. Dobbie Doubleday was among them.

"Magda, hold him!" I pointed at the unconscious attacker, and she surged around him and flared out a light barrier. I turned to confront Dobbie. "You're behind this?"

Dobbie looked battered, with dried blood in his hair and bruising on his face. His gaze flicked to the man in the snow, and he winced. "Come with us, Indigo. No one else needs to get hurt as long as you obey."

"Obey! What do you plan to do with me? I figure it has something to do with whatever this misty loser was tossing out."

"We... we need your blood." Dobbie glanced at one of the younger men in the group.

As I looked at the younger guy, I realized how similar he was to Dobbie. "You two are related?"

The guy strode over to Dobbie. "Dad! We need to finish this. She's almost killed Carlos. Time is running out. It'll be dark soon, and then it'll be too late. You said the witch would come with us. You said you had everything under control."

"This attack on our wedding is a family affair?" I glowered at Dobbie.

There was a hint of regret in his eyes, but he kept his chin up. "Please, I don't want bloodshed."

"Except mine!"

The younger guy tugged on Dobbie's arm. "Finish this! Prove to me you meant what you said about wanting to help."

"We still have a few minutes, Isaac. And if we're taking Indigo, she deserves an explanation," Dobbie said to the fierce-faced young man.

I glanced at my friends and familiars. They looked stunned but were recovering from the attack. "You're taking me nowhere. You ruined my wedding!"

"This is your fault," Isaac spat at me. "You had to pick today to get married, so it was an opportunity too good to miss."

"Why is Christmas Day so important to the Shadow Weavers?"

Dobbie inhaled sharply. "You know who we are?"

I nodded. "We recognized the symbols when you trashed the wedding venue. Thanks for that, by the way."

"We were stating our intent," Isaac said proudly. "We're scared of no one. We don't care if you know we're coming for you because we're unstoppable."

"Did you teach him to be so arrogant?" I asked Dobbie.

"He's young. Please excuse his behavior. He's testing his power. So is Carlos. My sons are willful."

"No can do, since Isaac wants my blood, and Carlos basically just tried to kill me and my friends," I said. "Who are the other guys? Murderous nephews?"

Dobbie's cheeks flushed. "Something like that. We're all family."

"I'm done messing around. Get her! And make sure Carlos isn't dead." Isaac gestured to one of his companions who'd been lurking behind him, his face smeared with dark marks that looked like wonky Shadow Weaver symbols smeared on when he'd had too much to drink.

Several spells flew over my head, but before I could retaliate, Luna and Odessa had my attacker face down in the snow.

"You're good," Odessa said over her shoulder to me. "And I've got my scarecrows on alert if we need reinforcements."

"There'll be no reinforcements coming to save your skin." Isaac stood beside Dobbie, crouched in a defensive position. "The only people who can get past our star mark is us. You're trapped. And when your guests realize the only way they're getting free is to give you to us, they'll hand you over. We know about your murky past. You're perfect for us."

I stared at Isaac in wide-eyed surprise. "You want me to join the Shadow Weavers?"

"No, but we need you to open a door for us. It doesn't have to hurt."

"That's enough, Isaac," Dobbie said. "Indigo, I am sorry. I didn't think it would get this far."

Isaac scowled at him. "I knew your heart wasn't in this. I said we shouldn't let you join, but the others wouldn't listen."

"You joined the Shadow Weavers to protect your sons?" I asked Dobbie.

"When you have children, you'll understand that you'll do anything to keep them safe," Dobbie said. "I had to protect them."

"You may have gotten us a way to Indigo, but we don't need you anymore," Isaac said. "Step aside, unless you want to get hurt again, old man."

"Hey! Don't speak to your father like that." Odessa still had a Shadow Weaver pinned as she wagged a finger at Isaac.

He sneered at her.

"You injured your own father?" I said to Isaac. "You took him from his room?"

"He lied to us, so he deserved it," Isaac said. "He doesn't want the Shadow Weaver power. He was just keeping tabs on me and Carlos to stop us from getting what we need."

"And what exactly do you need?"

"To release your blood's energy, so we can open the portal."

A chill slid through my veins. I'd heard about the dimension portals Shadow Weavers' mythology was founded on. They believed, with the right combination of spells and blood, they could open a portal to a different magical realm. A realm they could rule over.

I planted my feet in the snow. I glanced at my friends, familiars, and Olympus, and they all nodded. They knew what had to happen.

I drew in a breath and primed my magic. "If you want my blood, you'll have to come and get it."

Chapter 12

The air crackled with tension as we stared each other down. My heart raced, adrenaline pumping through my veins. I stood alongside Nugget, Hilda, and Russell, while the others watched. The sky darkened, the clouds pulsing with yellow light.

Isaac's top lip curled, his eyes filled with malicious intent. He raised his hands, conjuring misty shadows. The magic lashed out, hitting Luna and Storm, sending them sprawling and freeing Isaac's friend from the snow.

"Odessa, shield Luna and Storm until they're back on their feet!" I yelled.

Odessa nodded, creating a barrier of shimmering energy around our friends. With their safety ensured, I focused on Isaac, Dobbie, and his companions.

Dobbie lifted a quivering hand. "We can stop this! Find a solution."

"It's too late for that, Dad." Isaac tossed out a bolt of jagged black lightning.

Russell took to the wing, swooping and pecking at Isaac. Hilda scuttled forward, her eight hairy legs carrying her with incredible speed. She spat globs of gooey web binder at him, trapping Isaac for a second, but he burst free in a roar of defiance.

Nugget prowled at my feet, his feline instincts honed for combat. As Isaac and his companions unleashed dark spells, I called upon my magic, a surge of power emanating from within. I weaved protective barriers and launched a counterattack, bolts of energy surging from my fingertips with ease as Isaac thrust out blast after blast of dark, unstable magic.

Olympus appeared by my side. His magic gleamed, slicing through their defenses. Together, we formed an unbreakable bond, our magic entwined and our love only making us stronger. Magda weaved through the air as fast as Russell, her spectral energy flooding across the Shadow Weavers and knocking them down.

Spells collided in mid-air, releasing bursts of energy that crackled and illuminated the snow. I fought with every ounce of strength and determination, refusing to yield to their dark desires.

It was clear that Isaac was in charge. The others looked to him for orders every time the fighting slowed.

"You can't stop us!" His voice was laced with arrogance. "You didn't even realize we were here until it was too late."

I gritted my teeth. With a surge of magic, I unleashed a torrent of fire from my fingertips, engulfing the Shadow Weavers in a blaze of heat and destruction, melting the snow.

Olympus swung an arc of magic at them, his strike calculated and fierce. But the Shadow Weavers weren't easily defeated. They retaliated with a barrage of spells, each one striking with painful precision.

I winced as Isaac's spell hit me and searing pain lanced through my body.

Luna and Storm, now recovered, rejoined the fight. Luna summoned a tornado, buffeting the Shadow Weavers and disrupting their spells. Storm unleashed bolts of lightning crackling with raw power, striking around them, and leaving them momentarily stunned.

I locked eyes with Dobbie, his face contorted with anger and desperation.

"You can't win, Indigo! Please, let Isaac have this victory. It's the only thing that'll make him stop."

I met his gaze with unwavering resolve. "No one screws with my wedding day and gets away with it. Whatever I have to do, I'm marrying Olympus, even if that means taking out your entire family so you leave us the hell alone."

"You say the sweetest things." Olympus grunted as a spell winged him.

My gaze flashed around the group. Luna, Storm, and Odessa held off several Shadow Weavers with Magda's help. My familiars circled Isaac and the fallen Carlos, and I focused on Dobbie, who kept pleading with Isaac and me in turn to stop.

I gathered the energy within me, channeling it into one final, devastating spell. Light enveloped me, casting a brilliant glow across the snow. I raised my hands high, unleashing a burst of magic.

The Shadow Weavers screamed. Two of them fled, smashing through the barriers.

"Hilda! Fetch," I yelled.

She dashed after them, and from their continuing screams, she hadn't let them escape.

Isaac, bruised and bloodied, staggered beside his father, his eyes burning with an unsettling mix of anger and desperation. He locked his gaze with mine, a twisted smile playing on his lips.

"You think this is over?"

"It can be if you give up. But I won't stop fighting until I get the chance to put a ring on Olympus's finger."

"And... um, stop the Shadow Weavers from opening a dimension portal and messing with all of us?" Odessa brushed her damp hair off her face.

I jabbed a finger at Isaac. "That, too."

"Look around, witch. Your wedding day is over. The only thing you have left is to give yourself to me and let me drain you. The light is fading. And I need your blood." Isaac held out a hand as if he expected me to take it.

"What you need is to grow up and stop playing with magic you don't understand."

Isaac's eyes flashed with anger as he clenched his fists, dark energy swirling around him. He raised his hand, prepared to unleash more magic. But I stood my ground, my own power simmering within me. I refused to back down. I summoned every ounce of magic, and my love for my friends, my familiars, and Olympus fueled my determination. I'd protect them at any cost.

"Uh-uh. You're not doing this alone. How many times do I have to remind you of that?" Odessa grabbed my hand, and my friends, familiars, and family linked hands, arms, legs, and paws.

The air crackled with the intensity of our confrontation. Isaac's dark powers surged, but we held our ground, our magic intertwining. We unleashed a flood of light, a beacon of hope against the encroaching darkness and chaos. The magic collided with Isaac's malevolence, creating a powerful surge that sent shockwaves through the snow and knocked over my beautiful wedding arch.

The ground shook, yet we stood firm. With a final surge of power, one hand holding tight to Magda, I unleashed a magical blast aimed at Isaac. The impact sent him sprawling, his dark energy dissipating and smoke swirling around us and concealing Isaac, Dobbie, and the remaining Shadow Weavers.

I stood amidst the aftermath, my body trembling with exhaustion.

"Is Isaac dead?" Luna waved a hand in front of her face. "I can't see anything."

"He'd better be," Olympus muttered. He squeezed my hand. "Nice job."

"I told you nothing would get in the way of us getting married."

A raspy roar filled my ears, and Isaac was suddenly in my face, his fingers curled around my throat. He lifted me off my feet and turned, tossing me toward Dobbie.

Dobbie backed away, shaking his head. "Son, we've lost. Let it go."

"We must try! I'll kill her if I have to." Isaac shot a twist of dark magic at me.

Dobbie lunged and blocked the spell, the magic slamming into his chest.

Isaac screamed and dropped to his knees, catching his father before he hit the snow.

We stood back for a few seconds, all of us stunned, including the remaining Shadow Weavers, their fight gone now one of their own had fallen. Dobbie had sacrificed himself to save me. He'd seen Isaac had lost himself to darkness and couldn't let him become a killer.

Olympus stepped forward and bound Isaac's hands in magic. He made no move to protest as he sobbed over Dobbie's body. A second later, Hilda, Russell, and Nugget restrained the remaining Shadow Weavers.

Odessa cleared her throat. "Isaac, you've been a very naughty boy, but if you want me to, I can help your father."

"Help him how?" Isaac wiped his nose on his sleeve. "That witch killed him!"

"You killed him," I said.

"That spell was meant for you. He shouldn't have gotten in the way."

"Isaac! Let me help him." Odessa crouched beside him.

"He's gone."

"Not quite. His essence is still here. One of my many talents is to use the energy of the newly deceased in my scarecrows."

"Are you sure that's a good idea?" Storm asked. "You've got a lousy track record when shoving undead energy into your scary straw creations."

Odessa grinned. "I'm much more stable these days. Besides, I've always thought having a scarecrow to officiate at weddings would be fun! Think how popular he'll be at Halloween." She focused on Isaac, tipping his chin up with a finger until he looked into her kind eyes. "If I hurry, we can give Dobbie a second chance. What do you say, Isaac? Shall we turn your dad into something truly magical?"

Chapter 13

"The fact Isaac said yes to turning his dad into a monster scarecrow proves he has more than a few screws loose." Storm lounged on the bed in my room.

Odessa whacked her leg. "Stop being rude about my scarecrow. And get up! You'll wrinkle." She forced Storm to stand. "Look at your hair. It's frizzy again now you've rolled around on it."

Storm shrugged. "I don't mind frizzy. Luna is frizzy."

Luna sat on the floor, rubbing at a stain on her dress. "I have bigger things to worry about than my messy hair."

"You should mind frizzy!" Odessa said. "Everything needs to be perfect for Indigo and Olympus. And my scarecrow celebrant will be perfection, too, once he's been properly trained."

"Wild, uncontrollable, killer perfection." Storm dodged a slap and laughed. "Just don't let him near this wedding."

"Scarecrow Dobbie is shackled in a barn until I can focus on him. My boys are watching over things back home. He'll be no bother."

"And the Shadow Weavers won't bother us anymore," I said. "Olympus has already gotten them in a cell, and they're being charged as we speak. Isaac was heartbroken he hurt his dad, and he's already confessed to everything."

"So he should. He was disrespectful to his father and all because he wanted to play around with power far outside of his control." Odessa shook her head. "Shame on him."

"But you helped him keep Dobbie alive! You're too soft-hearted," Storm said.

"There's nothing soft-hearted about saving a soul."

Luna tossed a pillow at them. "Quit it, you two!"

I tuned out my friends' good-natured bickering and inspected my dress. It was torn, stained, and my makeup had gone from gorgeous to Gothic. This wedding was toast. Beyond saving. I had no choice but to postpone things.

There was a quiet cough from under the bed.

Storm lifted the cover and jumped back, a spell flashing on her fingers. "Ugh. Creepy doll face has been spying on us! Ursa's gift needs to be destroyed."

The doll coughed again, and she turned her head to me. She held out a hand.

I inched closer. She didn't look evil, more curious about what was going on.

"Don't touch that thing!" Storm said.

The doll hissed at her then beckoned to me.

"Ursa said she was good luck. And I checked the paperwork. Maybe she wants to help," I said.

"Besides, there's nothing else that can be done that hasn't already happened."

"She wants to light a match under what's left of this wedding." Storm bared her teeth at the doll.

I touched the doll's small, cold hand, and warm magic flooded the room. It swirled around me, lifting my stained gown and hair. A soft, feather-like stroke kissed my cheeks and eyes.

"Oh, my goddess! We're even more gorgeous than usual." Odessa twirled in front of me. Her stained, damp bridesmaid's dress was fixed, her hair restyled, and her makeup perfect.

I looked down at my dress, and it looked like new, a fusion of witchy elegance and gothic style. The bodice was now a rich shade of deep purple, adorned with intricate silver embroidery that resembled delicate spiderwebs glistening with frost. The skirt flowed gracefully, fashioned from layers of iridescent lavender and midnight blue tulle. Completing my outfit was a cape made of blue velvet, embroidered with silver stars and moon motifs.

I stared at the doll. "You really are a good luck gift."

She giggled then slid back under the bed.

As much as I appreciated her help, I'd find her an alternative spot to chill out, but she had a home here for as long as she wanted.

"The doll hasn't just helped us!" Luna stood at the window, her dark hair gleaming.

I joined her with the others. The wedding arch was restored, and all signs of the battle were wiped away. Olympus stood by the arch, his gaze darting around and confusion on his face as he took in the restored décor and seating. I laughed. I was about to marry that wonderful man.

"It's almost dark," Odessa said. "We'll light the way if you're ready."

I blew out a breath. "I'm ready."

They each kissed me then left the room. Before the door closed, Hilda and Russell zoomed in. Hilda scuttled up my dress and settled on my left shoulder, while Russell took the other shoulder.

"Everything is ready," Hilda said. "And you look beautiful."

"You can thank my new doll for that." I glanced at the space under the bed.

Russell cawed and flapped his wings.

"You look splendid, too. Both of you. But where's Nugget?"

Hilda tapped her leg on my shoulder. "You'll see."

"He's not walking with us?"

"He'll be there. Hurry!"

I grabbed my restored flowers and headed down the stairs. The front door was slightly open, and as I stepped outside, Bloom was waiting for me, ready to do another round as a flower girl.

A picturesque, snow-covered image greeted me. Twinkling fairy lights entwined the wedding arch, casting a soft, ethereal ambiance. The winter air nipped at my cheeks, but the warming embrace spell cast over the yard meant the icy conditions barely touched me.

I hugged Bloom again. "Let's see if we can get it right this time."

She nodded, her eyes wide. "I can't believe those jerks tried to grab you. I'm glad I'll have you as a step-parent. I mean, I will, won't I? I know I already have two parents, but I'll never be scared with you and your familiars at my back."

I hugged her fiercely this time. "I'll always be there for you. You and Peony. We're family."

Bloom grinned at me. "Then go marry my dad!" She bounced away, scattering flowers with abandon.

I approached the arch, nodding at the guests. Ursa was there, accompanied by three dolls, all dressed like tiny brides. I smiled warmly at her. Nazan stood beside her, dressed in a striking red velvet suit. Magda drifted at the back, winking at me when our eyes met. My stepmother had been there when I needed her the most, and I'd never forget that gift.

Russell and Hilda climbed off me and settled on a perch close to the altar, so they had a perfect view of the ceremony.

As I reached the altar, Nugget hopped onto a small podium. I stopped walking and stared at him. He wore a collar made of deep purple velvet, encrusted with tiny moonstone gems. He also had on a miniature top hat crafted from dark purple silk, embellished with a silver crescent moon and stars.

"You look..." I was lost for words.

"Ridiculous. But I figured I'd make the effort since I'm your new celebrant."

My eyes widened. "How'd that happen?"

"While you were repairing the damage following the fight, I took an online course. Took me less than ten minutes."

"For which organization?"

"Does it matter? I can wed you legally. I think." Nugget adjusted his top hat.

I turned to Olympus. "What happened to Zephir?"

"Gone. He made a move on Storm, and she almost broke his arm. I suggested he leave, and he was happy to run before Storm came for him again." Olympus shrugged. "I checked Nugget's credentials, and they look legit."

I grinned. Who needed a sleazy wedding celebrant when I had my wonderful sassy familiar to look after us?

Nugget cleared his throat, his gaze fixed on me. "If you're ready, let's dive into the realm of matrimonial madness."

I cast a sideways glance at Olympus. His polished exterior did little to mask the excitement and anticipation in his eyes.

Nugget swiveled his attention toward Olympus, his whiskers twitching. "Olympus Duke, are you willingly subjecting yourself to the grand adventure of being tied to Indigo Ash for eternity?"

Olympus let out a hearty laugh, undeterred by Nugget's sassy commentary. "You bet your nine lives on it. After all, who needs a conventional happily-ever-after when you can have a captivating let's-see-where-this-crazy-journey-takes-us?"

Subdued laughter rippled through the gathering. As Olympus took my hands in his, his expression transformed into one of sincerity.

"We've faced our share of dangers, even danced with a few vicious, drunken gnomes along the way, but I always knew you were the one for me. Indigo, you're not just my partner in crime; you're the essence of my uncharted adventure. From that first encounter, I sensed something extraordinary in you—a strength that defies the odds and a loyalty that knows no bounds."

Swallowing the lump that formed in my throat, I blinked back the threat of tears.

Olympus continued, "You've turned the darkest moments into opportunities for growth. Your belief in our love is unwavering even in the face of life's fiercest storms. And with your laughter, your tender touch, and your enduring faith in the enchantment woven into our lives, you've illuminated my world in ways I never thought possible." The sentiment in his voice carried an undeniable weight, a promise etched into each word.

I gripped Olympus's hands. "We've faced trials and tribulations that would have shattered others, yet we're stronger than ever. You're my rock, my guiding light, and my source of strength."

Nugget sighed. "Very good. I'm getting hungry. Shall we—"

I held up a hand to stop his grumbles. "I'm not done. In the darkest of times, you stood beside me, and you amaze me by bringing light into my life."

Nugget drew in a breath, but a glare from me kept him silent.

"You've taught me to believe in the impossible, to embrace the unknown, and to cherish every moment we have together. Our love will continue to defy the odds."

"And we're done?" Nugget licked a paw.

"You just need to do your official bit," I said.

Nugget took his sweet time inspecting both front paws. "Do you, Indigo Ash, take Olympus Duke to be your lawful husband?"

I focused on Olympus, trying hard not to cry happy tears. "I absolutely do."

Nugget turned his gaze toward Olympus. "And do you, Olympus Duke, take Indigo Ash to be your lawfully wedded ball-and-chain?"

"Enough of the sass," I hissed.

Nugget flicked an ear.

Olympus grinned, undeterred by Nugget's snark. "Sure do. I definitely do."

A few stifled chuckles escaped from our guests.

"Olympus, you may now smooch the bride," Nugget said. "Congratulations."

Applause erupted from our guests as we did indeed smooch, and moon and star-shaped confetti floated around us.

As we walked along the short aisle, I looked at our assembled guests and frowned. "Where's Monty?"

Olympus furrowed his forehead. "Probably sulking. He hasn't forgiven me for locking him up overnight. Don't worry, he'll show up soon. Most likely when we're about to eat."

I looked around, smiling and thanking people as they congratulated us. "He was here earlier.

The last time I saw him was when he was getting everyone safely inside."

"He won't be far away. My mother's gesturing at me. Be back in a minute." Olympus kissed the back of my hand and hurried away.

A second later, I spotted Monty's long, fluffy tail disappearing into the nearby trees, so I lifted my dress and trudged through the snow. I didn't want there to be bad blood between Monty and Olympus on our wedding day.

Reaching the tree line, I peered into the gloom. There was a soft growl, followed by several squeaks. I shuddered, hoping Monty wasn't gathering rat gifts to replace the buffet he'd destroyed. I had no appetite for rodent cuisine.

Taking a cautious step closer, I froze as a pair of small amber eyes appeared, followed by more, until there were five sets of blinking eyes looking at me from the shadows under the trees. Monty leaped in front of them, growling, but the sound cut off as soon as he recognized me.

"Indigo! What are you doing here? Have you had a fight with Olympus? He can get grumpy when stressed but feed him and he'll be fine. You should go back to the wedding."

"We're good. We've literally just tied the knot," I assured him. "I wanted to know what you were doing. You missed the ceremony." I looked over his head to see what he was hiding, but he blocked my view.

"I'll come back now. Give me five minutes." Monty's voice was tinged with guilt. "Don't wait for me. It's cold."

"Monty, what are you keeping in the woods that you don't want me to see?"

"Nothing! No one. You didn't see me. Please, just go."

"I see you." I arched an eyebrow. "What's going on?"

"No! I'm not... please, Indigo. Olympus will be so mad at me." Monty sounded worried.

"Why? What have you done?"

"I've been a bad kitty. I didn't mean for this to happen, but..."

A tiny hissing ball of fluff and fury rolled into sight, followed by another identical ball of fluff. They hissed and spat, their little paws a blur as they engaged in a miniature battle.

I gasped. They were tiny versions of Monty.

He whimpered as he pulled the sparring cubs apart. "They were an accident. A happy accident, and I love them, but Olympus will be cross. He's always telling me to be careful and think ahead, but I got lost in the joy of the moment."

I struggled to hide a smile. "I'd say you definitely got lost in the joy of the moment if these were the result. Where's their mother?"

"Gone. She was only here for the weekend. We had a great time, and I wanted her to stay, but she had other plans. Then, a few nights ago, she showed up with the cubs. She said they were mine, and I had to look after them. And then she left!"

Realization hit me like a witch's cauldron knocked off its tripod. "Oh! This is why you destroyed the wedding buffet. I knew all those paw prints weren't yours."

"I didn't eat it all. I brought most of it back for the cubs after we'd all had a nibble. They've been feeding from it ever since. They're excellent feeders, just like their father. And always hungry." Monty's eyes gleamed with pride.

I crouched and held out a hand as more cubs appeared. There were five fluffy, clumsy, adorable babies with enormous eyes. After a moment of hissing and cautiousness, they approached me and sniffed my hands.

"Monty, they're adorable." I was unable to contain my delight.

"I think so too. But Olympus always tells me I'm too much for him. Imagine me in a smaller version times five. He'll throw us out. We'll be homeless at Christmas."

"He won't, but if he tries, I'll have words with him. And I'm sure he'll have a serious conversation with you about responsible behavior when enjoying yourself with a lady. But we're past that now. And you've got these gorgeous babies as a result."

Monty's ears lifted. "You don't think he'll be too angry?"

"Angry about what?" Olympus appeared behind me, his voice filled with curiosity.

I grinned and scooped up two of the cubs. "How's this for a wedding gift?"

Olympus stared at the cubs then at Monty. "I... I don't understand."

I chuckled. "We've got new additions to the family. We'll need to clear a space for them. The old barn may do. It's warm and well-insulated. We could use spells to keep the temperature constant."

"Wait, a minute. Monty, do these belong to you?" Olympus stared at his cowering familiar in wide-eyed disbelief.

Monty glanced at me and nodded. "I didn't want to bring them home because I thought you'd be angry."

The cubs I held squirmed with displeasure, eager to rejoin their siblings and play in the snow.

Laughter burst from Olympus. "This is why you've been acting so strangely?"

"I didn't want you to tell me off for being irresponsible," Monty said. "I'm doing the right thing. I'm giving them love, attention, and plenty of food. And I found them a cozy den in the woods. But I think they might like the barn better."

"It's why Monty ate our wedding buffet." I squeezed Olympus's elbow. "Given the circumstances, we can forgive him for that, can't we?"

Olympus walked over and took hold of Monty's huge head in his hands. "You ridiculous creature. Your cubs are welcome. I'm sure they'll exhaust me, annoy me, and frustrate me as much as you do, but they'll also bring me endless amounts of joy. Just like you."

"You want them to stay?" Monty swished his tail, sending the cubs into a riot of boisterous play as they chased it.

"As much as I want you to be my familiar for the rest of time."

Monty launched himself at Olympus, and they crashed to the ground. After a second of stunned silence, the cubs joined in, barely leaving Olympus visible under the mound of fur and licking tongues.

Olympus grunted as he pulled himself out from under the leopards. He brushed down his damp, fur-covered suit then sighed. "Let's take them back with us. We can introduce them to the wedding party and get them settled in the barn. What do you say, Monty?"

"I say yes! And I haven't named them yet, so you can help me. I was thinking about warrior names."

"This one looks like a Fluffy to me." I held up one squirming cub.

"No Fluffies," Olympus grumbled.

"How about Thor? Or Legend? I like Ranger, too. Or maybe Zeus. And Diana is good for the girl. Four boys and one girl. So many decisions to make." Monty grabbed one cub and tossed it onto his back.

Between us, I carried two of the cubs, and Olympus took two more. The fifth cub rode on Monty. As expected, the wedding party welcomed them, and the cubs even got to take part in the photos. I couldn't wait to see how hilarious they turned out as the cubs pounced, snarled, and caused delightful chaos every time we posed.

Half an hour later, everyone was inside, getting warm and mingling.

"There's one problem we've yet to fix," Olympus whispered in my ear as we stood back while our guests enjoyed champagne and conversation. "Albert hasn't shown up with a replacement for the buffet."

Luna waltzed over, looking a little shame-faced. "I know what you're whispering about. And I'm sorry to say there was a tiny snafu when I helped Uncle Albert get the food together. A few things got burned. There may also have been a tiny explosion. No eyebrows were lost, though. Well, Uncle Albert got singed, but he's fine."

"It was a cremation of epic proportions." Storm sauntered over and joined us. "The bakery was full of smoke for hours."

"Luna! You said you'd be hands-off with the food," I said.

"I couldn't resist. And Uncle Albert was tired. But I left the wedding cake alone, and it's perfect."

"So, it's champagne and cake for our guests?" Olympus asked. "I can think of worse."

"It's the best cake you'll ever taste. Uncle Albert pulled out all the stops." Luna stepped back to reveal Albert wheeling in a ten-tier wedding cake.

"That will feed a hundred people." Olympus gaped at the cake. "It belongs in a gallery."

"It's something else." I breathed out as I studied the bottom layer. A cosmic dance unfolded in a symphony of colors and swirls, and edible stars adorned the surface.

"Is that fourth layer an underwater world?" Olympus took my hand as we studied the cake.

I nodded. Sugar seashells and coral formations reflected the iridescence of the ocean's depths. "And that's us on the top!" Albert had made tiny replicas of me, Olympus, and our familiars.

The crowd oohed and aahed as we stood around the cake, admiring its beauty.

"And each layer is a different flavor," Albert said. "Something for everyone." He looked at me and Olympus. "I hope it'll do."

"It's perfect," I said. "It looks so beautiful that I'm scared to eat it."

"Grab the knife and get cutting," Odessa said. "I've been looking forward to cake all day."

"It's the best bit of any wedding," Storm said.

Odessa elbowed her. "Cynic. Wait until you get a ring on your finger."

Storm smirked. "My guy knows better than to propose. I'll have a slice of chocolate."

We stood by the cake, cutting into the first slice as the guests watched, guessing what each layer would be.

Olympus held my hand in his as the knife slid easily through the bottom layer, his grip warm and firm. "We did it," he said. "Despite the obstacles, we got married."

I looked at him and smiled. "I never doubted us for a second."

He chuckled. "You did, but I always knew you were the right one for me. And now, nothing will stop us."

I kissed his cheek. There'd be plenty of things that would stand in our way, whether that was Shadow Weavers, Magic Council rules, or dark magic testing our limits, but with Olympus by my side, my familiars at my back, and my awesome group of friends surrounding me with the ride-or-die love that was rare but so special, together, we'd take on anything and win.

You are cordially invited to the wedding of...
Luna Brimstone and Cole Kellam

Chapter 1

How much stress could we handle before our perfect wedding day became a magical battleground?

"We could always elope." I leaned against Cole Kellam's broad chest, his chin resting on top of my head as he wrapped his solid arms around me. My farmhouse living room was a whirlwind of wedding paraphernalia. Piles of gifts. A stack of cards. Details of seating plans that had been altered ten times. My mother had even set up a whiteboard against one wall with a huge list of tasks to tick off. Just looking at it made my stomach churn.

"Whatever you want, it's yours. Although I've heard the flowers are non-refundable. Three times." Amusement swirled through Cole's words as we stayed out of the way of the latest flurry of wedding decisions that overwhelmed me daily.

"They'd forgive us for sneaking off, wouldn't they?" I asked. "All this pressure isn't fun."

"Our mothers thrive on pressure." Cole kissed the top of my head. "We'll get through this and out the other side. Then we can do exactly what we want."

I rested a hand on his and squeezed. "I knew it would be like this. What with my mother, and..."

He chuckled. "You can say it. Mine is way worse than yours. She's an alpha from the tip of her nose to the end of her tail."

"Mine is the same, minus the tail," I said. "I didn't realize a werewolf-witch wedding would cause such a stir, though." I backed up as one of the many assistants who'd been hired to ensure wedding perfection almost stood on my foot.

"You underestimate the influence our families have," Cole murmured.

I was only too aware of the influence the Brimstone Dynasty had. We were ranked number two in the magically competitive field of baking magic, and my parents constantly vied for the number one spot. And my marriage to Cole may get them what they desire. The Kellams were top of the werewolf hierarchy. Along with Cole, his three brothers, and his parents, they couldn't be bested. That meant there were healthy egos lurking around all my wedding decisions.

It sent an unpleasant chill through me. "If we elope, we can keep it simple. Just us and a few close friends. Could you convince Reuben to join us? You'll want your best man with you. And I know my friends would be okay with sneaking away. Storm has been threatening to hex anyone who asks her to go for another dress fitting."

"Reuben would be fine with whatever we decide," Cole said. "So, where shall we go?"

I grinned as he indulged in my impossible escape fantasy. I turned and looked up at my tall, muscled fiancé, his patient dark eyes settling on mine and calming the chaos within me. I reached up and pushed his shoulder-length dark hair off his face. "You'd really do it?"

"For you, anything."

"Even face the wrath of our families if we sneak away?"

"Luna, the only thing I care about is having you as my forever mate. Whether that takes place at a lavish ceremony our parents have spent a fortune on or in a quiet forest glen surrounded by a few friends. So long as it happens, that's all my heart wants." His gentle kiss softened the anxious edges around the spiky ball of panic that had been lodged in my stomach for months.

After our whirlwind introduction, which had involved chasing a debt collector who'd been stalking me, several near-death experiences, and a surprise marriage proposal from me, we'd settled on a lengthy engagement. We'd had breathing space, but our parents had kept nudging for a wedding.

And the more they nudged, the more I realized what I'd gotten myself into. When the Brimstones and the Kellams had first met, sparks flew, and soon, wedding plans were being formulated like a military battle. Not that our families always agreed on the tactics to win this wedding war.

Cole gently pressed a finger against my forehead. "The cogs are spinning. I can hear them. I thought we agreed to lean into this and accept whatever they did. If you've changed your mind, I'll go speak to my parents. If it's not what you want, we'll change it."

"Is it what you want, though? The elemental blessings. The shapeshifting ritual. Our spellbinding feast. Your midnight howl. And then we have the three-hour ancestral worship."

"I want you. So long as you make this official with me, that's all that matters."

"That's all I want too, but I don't want to disappoint my parents. They've been so generous." I'd seen a few of the bills, and they'd made my eyes water.

"They're as pushy as my parents. If we elope, it may take them a few decades to forgive us, but they'll understand why we snuck off to do this our way." Cole brushed a kiss across my lips.

I nudged a wrapped gift on the table. "How about we open a few of these to take our minds off the stress?"

"Before the wedding?"

"We start now, or we'll be unwrapping gifts during our honeymoon. We've already received so many." Every day, more and more gifts were delivered from well-wishers across the country.

He nuzzled my neck. "There's only one gift I plan on unwrapping on the honeymoon."

I giggled and gently pushed him away. "This one's from Zodiac Black. He's a pack alpha, isn't he?"

Cole crinkled his nose. "And not a great one. What's he gotten us?"

I opened the package and discovered a set of carving knives.

Cole rolled his eyes. "Original. His company makes knives. He probably didn't even pay for them."

"They were on the register. And the amount of steak you go through, we always need sharp knives."

He flashed his teeth and chuckled. "Forget the gifts. Name a place, and I'll swoop you away so no one will find us. We can get hitched on the beach and be drinking from coconuts before midnight."

"You're planning an escape?" Odessa Grimsbane stood in the open doorway of my farmhouse with my two other friends, Storm Winter and Indigo Ash, beside her.

"No! Well, maybe. Look at all of this." I gestured at the wedding chaos surrounding us. "My mother showed up at six this morning with a list of fifty things I needed to approve. I don't know why she bothers. She's already decided for me."

Storm cocked a hip and rested a hand on it. "Getting out of here is the perfect idea. My head would have exploded from the stress. Keep it simple. Local registrar's office then straight to the inn to drink the place dry before grabbing a takeout bucket of chicken and collapsing into bed together."

"Sounds like a fun evening." Reuben Whitehaven strolled in from the kitchen, a cheeky smile on his handsome face. "I could be persuaded to go on that date if you're up for it."

Storm smirked. "My chicken-eating partner and I already have plans. Thanks for the offer, though."

Reuben sighed as he inspected the knife set I'd opened. "All the best girls are taken. Isn't that right, Luna?" He winked at me.

Reuben had shown up a week ago, renting a room at a local hotel, after Cole put in a plea to have an impartial negotiator by his side. They'd known each other for decades, and the second I'd met Reuben, I'd warmed to him. He was flirty, cheeky, and fiercely loyal to his best friend. His shaved head and glowing red tattoos that covered his scalp marked him as a master illusion mage.

"You've already snagged your perfect woman," I said. "Where are Serenity and the girls? I thought they'd be here by now."

"Soon. Serenity had trouble getting time off work. Last-minute crisis. They'd love this, though." He looked around at the wedding chaos and chuckled.

"I'm glad someone will," I said.

"You're really thinking about sneaking off?" Odessa strolled into the living room with the others and inspected a pile of linen napkins in various shades of pink.

Indigo threw an arm around my shoulders. "Never! And miss all this?"

I gently shoved her away. "I want a wedding like yours. Outside, just a few people, beautiful, simple."

"And almost didn't happen because a group of crazed Shadow Weavers tried to drain my blood." Indigo shook her head. "No trouble will find you while you're surrounded by hordes of pacing, uptight werewolves who have vowed to protect you."

"Hey! We're not all uptight." Cole huffed out a breath, his eyes gleaming amber.

"You have your moments." I kissed his cheek. "Although the way my parents keep ordering the werewolves around, they barely have time to check in with us, let alone protect us."

"You need to get the wolves on the prowl. There are more paparazzi snooping around." Storm wrinkled her nose. "I chased off a couple of van loads earlier. They were wandering around the village and asking questions about you and Cole, trying to get the inside scoop so they could print scandal about you."

I groaned. "That's the last thing we need." There'd been interest from the paparazzi ever since the wedding announcement went out. It was something I was used to, given my family's lineage, but I wouldn't say I was comfortable with it.

"We've already agreed on the running order." Morrigan Kellam announced her arrival by slamming open the front door and striding in. She was a magnificent alpha werewolf, tall and imposing, wearing black heeled boots, tight black jeans, and a form-fitting shirt.

Beside her was my mother, who was also no slouch. Impeccably dressed, her familiar scent of freshly baked chocolate chip cookies filled the room. But one look into her dark eyes made me flinch. The mothers were fighting again.

"I should break them up before the verbal sparring gets physical again," I whispered to Cole.

"They can handle themselves," he said. "I'm almost certain my mother won't injure yours too badly before the big day. It would be impolite."

I thumped his arm. "Don't even joke about it. The last time my mother complained about yours, she was talking about making her a 'special' meal.

You do not want one of my mother's special meals. You'd be in bed for a week with a stomach ache and hallucinations." Although my parents were bakers par excellence, they weren't above using underhanded tactics to maintain their position near the top.

"Sounds like the side effects I had after eating one of your stodgy breakfast muffins." Storm poked out her tongue.

I shot her a scowl as I hurried toward the bickering mothers. I'd left my disastrous baking days behind and was content to live at my farmhouse and run my animal sanctuary. Alongside the teaching I did at the gremlin rehabilitation school, life was perfect, especially now it didn't involve inedible muffins, stale scones, or slices of cake I baked that tasted like boiled socks.

"Is there a problem?" I threw as much authority into my tone as I could muster. Meekness around these women wasn't tolerated.

"Your mother-in-law-to-be is being unreasonable again." My mother, Clovis Brimstone, stood with her hands on her narrow hips and glared at Morrigan. "She's changed the running order again. It was perfect just how I'd set it."

The alpha female werewolf glared back just as fiercely. "This allows for more mingling. Werewolves are sociable, and some of my guests haven't seen each other for years."

"Your guests? Isn't this our wedding?" I asked.

Both women slid their gazes my way. Neither of them flinched.

"Of course it is, darling," Clovis said. "We want everything to be perfect for you."

"And it will be perfect if it's done my way." Morrigan pulled a sheet of paper from the back pocket of her jeans.

I didn't take it as she thrust it at me. "You can't keep doing this. I don't even feel as if this is my wedding day anymore."

"Things must be organized properly," Clovis said. "Otherwise, your special day will be a shambles. The families will become a laughingstock."

"Speak for yourself," Morrigan said. "It'll work if we do things my way."

I held in a sigh. They were flashing their alpha cards because they wanted the best wedding for me and Cole, but if only they didn't have different versions of what best was.

We settled on silence and glaring. It went on for several minutes, and Morrigan only blinked twice. She finally sighed. "I'm doing my best to ensure all werewolf traditions fit into your witch customs. That doesn't make things simple."

"It could be simple," I said. "We could do away with all of this and focus on what's most important."

"Your father is ensuring the media has all the details," Clovis said. "Everything will be reported properly. Nothing can be left out, or people will gossip."

"I care nothing for mean-spirited gossips! The most important thing to me is Cole. We want to marry without caring if the flowers clash or if the table napkins are perfect."

"Which is why you have me, darling." My mother tried to hug me, but I stepped back and shook my head.

"Both of you take a time out. Think about why we're doing this. Morrigan, is this wedding happening because you want to show off your family's spectacular status among the werewolves? If so, you've got it wrong. And Mother, before you interrupt me, I'm not doing this to yank our family into the top echelons of the baking dynasty." I sucked in a breath. "I'm doing it because I've found the love of my life, and I want to spend the rest of my days with him. I want to join our families so they share in our joy. But you're both making it impossible with your demands and bickering. Don't think I won't ban you from the wedding day if you keep being so bull-headed."

Morrigan growled softly, and her eyes flashed amber. "I'd never do such a thing to my son. I'm doing this because Cole deserves the best."

I lifted my chin and met her gaze squarely. "He has the best. I make him happy. And I intend to make him happy forever, but you're making it so hard for us. Things need to change."

It was only then that I noticed the conversation and chaos in the room had died down as everyone watched us fight. But I wouldn't break my resolve. These two alphas needed to be taken down a peg or two, and if that meant upsetting my mother and making an enemy of my future mother-in-law, then so be it.

"Does my son agree with this opinion?" Morrigan finally asked.

"I do." Cole's voice was a deep rumble behind me, and I felt his body heat. "We appreciate your investment in our wedding, but we don't want to remember the day because it was full of bickering and family feuding."

Clovis sighed. "Perhaps I've been a touch overbearing. But it's because I love you. Both of you. I want the absolute best for your magical day."

"I know," I said. "And we appreciate that."

Morrigan shoved the paper back into her pocket. "When I face another alpha, my hackles lift. Apologies, Clovis. We can come to an agreement. If necessary, my son can mediate. He's the best we've got."

"There'll be no need for that," Clovis said. "Let's stop for coffee. I've made some of my chocolate and cherry cake."

Morrigan grinned. "With the frosted icing and triple layers?"

"I saw how much you enjoyed the last one. You ate the entire thing."

"Why didn't you say you had cake? Lead the way."

The women headed off together, arm in arm.

"If only every problem could be solved with one of my mother's cakes." I turned to Cole. "I need a break. How about we get out of here and take a walk?"

Chapter 2

"Your mother is smart," Cole said, holding my hand as we strolled off the porch and into the wooded area that surrounded my farmhouse. "Food is an ideal way to a werewolf's heart."

"She didn't get to where she is without having a decent amount of brain cells," I said. "But my mother can be manipulative, and when she doesn't get her own way, she turns mean. And she sometimes forgets what's important."

"Mine is the same. She legitimately wants the best for the pack and her family, but being at the top means she's always dealing with sneaky offers or requests for favors. She gets jaded. My dad is often away overseeing the silver mines, so she does a lot on her own. Not that you'll ever hear her complain. But it's good to have a partner by your side when making important decisions." Cole squeezed my hand.

"Like how to deal with the fencing at the bottom of the hill that's always collapsing?" I grinned up at him.

He returned my grin with a warm smile that made my heart flip. "I was happy to figure out how to stop it from rotting."

I'd hidden my farmhouse on the outskirts of Witch Haven for years, using it—and I wasn't proud to admit this—as a place to trap other magic users so I could exploit their powers. I'd done it out of necessity, as I'd struggled to figure out why my baking magic had been so unstable. But now I knew the origins of my power didn't come from baking, but in the elements, thanks to my mother's affair with a powerful weather warlock. I hadn't known that for over three decades, and it had left me confused as to why I was different from everyone else in my family.

Once the truth was revealed, I no longer needed to exploit others and had turned my farmhouse into a huge animal sanctuary. I'd found my purpose.

"Are those clouds yours?" Cole pointed to the horizon, where a stack of gray, angry-looking clouds piled on top of each other.

I bit my lip. "Most likely."

"Relax. I know it's not easy, but we've only got a few more days to go, and then this will be over."

"I don't want to think about our wedding like that," I said. "I want to feel excited and nervous and giddy."

"Don't you feel any of that? After all, you get to spend the rest of your life with me," Cole teased.

I nudged him in the ribs with an elbow. "Of course! But the crazy preparations are overshadowing things."

"Our mothers will see sense. They'll back off. And if they don't, we'll keep telling them. They'll get the hint eventually," Cole said.

I raised a hand as I spotted Ridley Vandyke stride out of a barn, pushing a wheelbarrow of used straw. Ridley had been one of my captives, and I'd given him shelter when he'd killed a demon whose friends vowed revenge in return for some of his magic. He was a cheerful, slightly naive guy, who'd been happy to remain at the farmhouse after I'd released him and work at the animal sanctuary.

As we grew nearer, I saw Faye Calhoun in her usual seat, a mug of coffee beside her, as she focused intently on her knitting.

"There they are! Our almost happily married couple." Gloria Barkridge appeared next, a huge smile on her face. "You must be so excited."

"We were just talking about that," I said. "How's the injured deer doing?"

"He had a good night." Ridley set down his wheelbarrow. "He took a while to get into feeding, but he's healing. In a few days, he'll be ready to be set free."

Cole had found the deer while hunting and had brought it to the sanctuary. For a werewolf, he had the softest heart.

"This is the last piece of your wedding gift." Faye held up a beautifully knitted square.

"I can't wait to see the finished product," I said. "You've been working on it for months."

"Over six months," Gloria chimed in. "She rarely does any work around here."

"I want to make this gift perfect for Luna and Cole," Faye said. "Perfection takes time. And I do my bit. I always make sure you're both well-fed. And look, I'm keeping the kittens warm." She pulled down the top of her dress to reveal two tiny kittens nestled between her ample bosoms.

Ridley roared with laughter. "That's an incubator I wouldn't mind being in."

She waved away his comment, her cheeks flushed. "Behave yourself, young man. What would your lady think of you making comments like that?"

I raised my eyebrows. "I didn't realize you were seeing someone."

Ridley grinned. "Early days. We've got our first date next week."

Gloria's attention shifted behind us. "You have a visitor. Who's that? I don't recognize her from the village."

Cole inhaled deeply. His body stiffened, and his expression blanked.

I turned and saw a stunning blonde strutting toward us in a style I'd come to recognize as werewolf. She held a wrapped box in her hand, and when she caught my eye, she flashed me a smile.

"Do you know her?" I asked Cole.

Cole nodded woodenly. "Jade Silvermoon, a former girlfriend." He rarely talked about previous girlfriends, but I'd heard from others that Jade made things difficult for Cole when they'd been together. She'd lied about his behavior and even faked a pregnancy to make him stay with her.

"There you are!" Jade kissed Cole on the mouth, a full-on lips number that made me scowl. "I had to come see you as soon as I arrived in Witch Haven. Let me look at you." She stepped back, and her gaze roved over Cole. "You're as heartbreakingly handsome as ever. Why did I ever let you go?"

"You didn't. I let you go. What are you doing here?" Cole's tone was curt.

"I've come for your wedding, silly. Well, some self-care time, too. My therapist told me I needed a break, and your wedding has been the talk of the werewolf community, so I couldn't resist. I assumed my invitation got lost in the mail?" Jade's smile was sly.

I stepped forward and held out my hand. "Luna Brimstone, Cole's fiancée. We'd have been happy to invite you, but we didn't know which pack you were affiliated with."

Jade's bright smile faltered. She looked at my hand then engulfed me in a honeysuckle-scented hug. "You adorable little thing. I'm a footloose and fancy-free werewolf these days. No pack can claim me."

"Because no pack will have you," Cole said. "Jade, you shouldn't be here."

She hugged me for an uncomfortable length of time, her arms tight as she squeezed. "You're just as lovely as everyone said. But color me surprised when I heard Cole had fallen for a witch."

"I don't care what magic Luna possesses. I knew she was my perfect mate the second we met. Let her go." There was a growl laced in Cole's words.

"Ignore him. He can be so grumpy. Does he get grumpy with you? He probably needs a snack." Jade's grip was now painful.

I squirmed my hands around until they were flat on her back and sparked her with a warning zap of lightning.

She squeaked and let go. "Hey! There's no need to be bitchy, little witchy. Us girls must stick together. We should meet for drinks later, and we can share war stories about Cole. I have tales to tell that will turn that pretty hair white."

"Why are you here?" Cole wrapped an arm around my shoulders and tugged me away from Jade, no doubt to stop her from crushing me to death in another hug.

"To give you this! Your wedding present." Jade thrust the box out. "Don't worry, it doesn't contain my shattered heart after I learned you're marrying this witch instead of me, but I had to mark your special day with a unique gift."

I could imagine she'd rather mark it by raking her claws down my face. "We appreciate the gift, but you didn't have to come all this way. You could have mailed it."

Jade lifted one shoulder. "I wanted to be here. After hearing about you and learning about your cute rural lifestyle, I couldn't stay away. And, like I said, my therapist recommended a break."

"She sounds crazy," Riley muttered.

Jade flashed her teeth at him. "Careful there, pretty boy. Werewolves have excellent hearing, and we never forget the scent of something we'd like to devour. I could eat you right up, and there'd be nothing left."

"Don't threaten my family." I stepped into her personal space. "Everyone here is under my protection. If you have a problem with them, you come through me."

"And mine," Cole grumbled.

"Goodness, aren't we serious?" Jade let out a fake laugh and tossed the gift to Cole.

He caught it and stared at it.

Jade pouted, and her radiance dimmed. "I... I didn't mean harm by coming here. I know I behaved badly when we were together, but I'm getting help. I want to make amends. I even spoke to your parents. They said I could visit."

I bristled at that comment. Although Cole rarely mentioned Jade, Morrigan talked about her, and I had a feeling she'd have preferred Jade as a daughter-in-law. I couldn't imagine why. Sure, Jade was so stunning I needed to wear sunglasses, but her aura was unstable.

"If Luna doesn't mind, you can stay for a short visit," Cole said.

I shrugged. "I have no problem with that."

Relief flooded across Jade's face. "You'll love my gift. I put a lot of thought into it. It's handmade. Well, I should go. I didn't mean to intrude. Sorry for making things awkward. I'll say hi to a few people then get out of your fur." She turned to leave.

"Wait," I said. "You're here now, and we can fit one more person in at the ceremony."

"Luna," Cole grumbled. "Are you sure about that?"

Jade clapped her hands together then engulfed me in another bone-crushing hug. "I love weddings! Thank you. And I promise, no dramatics. I'm sure Cole has talked about me incessantly and told you

I'm a handful, but I won't misbehave. I'll zip my mouth and smile. I'll watch the ceremony, and I won't think that it should be me standing beside Cole. I mean, no. Wait a minute." She stepped back and did some weird rapid tapping around her head and shoulders. "That's better. My therapist gave me techniques to use for stress relief. Tappity-tap-tap and I'm all better. Well, not as bad as I used to be."

As she talked, I was doubting my decision to invite her to the ceremony by the second.

"Anyway, enjoy your gift, have a wonderful wedding day, and I'll be there, smiling sweetly and enjoying myself. Good luck." Jade turned and strutted away.

"You should not open that gift," Ridley said. "It'll explode in your face."

"Or give you a thousand years of hexes," Faye said. "Burn it."

Cole sniffed the box. "It smells wooden. It's safe." He yanked off the paper.

"Isn't it bad luck to open your gifts before you're married?" Gloria asked.

It was too late to worry about that. Cole had torn open the cardboard box to reveal two carved wooden figures. One was a magnificent werewolf and the other a hunchbacked witch carrying a broomstick and wearing a pointed hat.

I bit my lip to stop from smiling. "Whoever made these has talent. Look! I even have a wart on the end of my nose."

Cole tossed the figures back into the box. "I'll have words with my mother about why she thinks it's appropriate to invite Jade to our wedding."

"I'll get my friends to keep an eye on her to make sure she doesn't misbehave." I peered into the box. There was a card in the bottom, which I fished out.

"I'll do the same with Reuben. He knows what a nightmare Jade is," Cole said.

I turned over the card and frowned. It wasn't a card. It was a graphic, naked picture of Jade splayed on a bed. I showed it to Cole, who rolled his eyes and tore it in half.

"I feel sorry for her," Gloria said. "Once you get past the craziness, there's an air of terrible sadness about that young lady. Loneliness, too. Her aura gives off the feel of a bucket with a hole in the bottom, and no matter what she does, she can't keep anything in it. Poor creature. What a sad, tortured life she must lead. No wonder she needs all that therapy. I hope it helps."

"All she needs is the right person to rub her belly," Ridley said. "If she wasn't so unstable, I'd do it. What a stunner."

"Stay away from that stunner," Cole said. "She'll eat you alive, literally, if the moon is full and her emotions are on the fritz."

"Noted. Now, I need to get this straw dumped and top up the hungry residents with fresh stuff." Ridley grabbed his wheelbarrow and strode away.

"Before I forget, there was a man here who was asking for you," Faye said to me. "He was nosy and wanting to know all about you and the farmhouse."

"What man?" Cole snapped.

I giggled. "I love it when you go all alpha on me."

Faye chuckled. "He didn't give a name. An older man. Refined and powerful. He didn't use any magic, but it was oozing from him. It was intoxicating. Attractive, too. I checked and there was no ring on his finger."

"What did you tell him about me?" I asked.

"Nothing!" Gloria said. "He was handsome, but it was none of his business."

"More paparazzi," Cole said. "If he hassles you again, give him my mother's contact details. She'll deal with him."

We said goodbye to the gang and headed into the trees. Cole pushed ahead, and when I slowed to tie my shoelaces, a flash of movement caught my eye. A man stood some distance away, partially concealed behind a tree. I took a step toward him, but in a flash of magic, he vanished.

"Something wrong?" Cole appeared beside me as if sensing trouble.

"More media types lurking about in the trees. I wish they'd leave us alone."

"When we get back, I'll get some friends to do a walk around and discourage anyone from lurking." He took my hand. "But you have to remember, the Brimstones and the Kellams' uniting is big news."

"It's big news I could do without."

"Hey. No regrets?" Cole kissed the back of my hand.

I looked into his deep, honest gaze and smiled. "With you by my side, I regret nothing."

Chapter 3

For months, my dreams had been full of wedding day variations, mainly involving Cole's mother standing up and objecting before sending an army of werewolves after me. But this dream was full of noise and pain. My nose hurt, and it sounded as if someone was letting off mini explosions every few seconds. *Bam, boom, thud.* Over and over again.

"Wake up!" Earl's panicked voice hissed in my ear.

I opened one eye just as he whacked my nose with his paw. He must have been doing it for a while because my nose was almost numb. "What are you doing?"

"There's somebody outside. They've been knocking for ages."

I removed the earplugs I'd taken to wearing recently. I found that blocking my senses helped me sleep and prevented my mind from spiraling into a wedding whirlwind of ifs and buts. A second later, I heard the knocking at the front door.

I scooped Earl, my chunky, fluffy cat familiar, into my arms, slid out of bed, and hurried to the window. I pulled back the curtain but couldn't see who was out there. The moon was waning, but dawn had yet to arrive, so the front yard was gloomy and full of shadows.

There was more frantic knocking, so I stumbled down the stairs with Earl.

"Who is it?" I called out.

"It's Reuben! Open up. I must talk to you."

I didn't hesitate in flicking the locks and opening the door. His anxious tone had sped up my heartbeat. Reuben never got anxious. "What's wrong?"

He stumbled inside, his usually impeccable clothing disheveled. "Cole's been arrested for murder."

I stared at him and then burst into laughter. "Did Cole put you up to this? He's always trying to get me up early so we can go on dawn hikes. Where is he?" I peered past Reuben into the gloom.

"Sorry, Luna. This is no joke. I've been trying to get more information about what happened, but then I came here. I figured you wouldn't know what was going on." Reuben ran a hand across his shaved head, his red tattoos glowing in the low light.

My stomach flipped and then sank. I walked into the kitchen, grabbed the back of a chair, and let Earl go so he could sit on the table. "Murder? You're sure?"

Reuben followed me. "I'd planned an early morning run with Cole. I went to his place, but there was no sign of him. Then I spoke to a neighbor, and she said the Magic Council had taken him in. Apparently, he didn't go without a fight. It got messy."

I gulped down panic, but it surged back up, threatening to choke me. "Why do you think it was murder they want him for?"

"That's what the neighbor said they'd charged him with."

"Take about a hundred steps back. Cole's already been charged?" Dizziness swept through me, and a second later, Reuben was helping me into a chair.

"Breathe deep. It almost knocked me flat on my back when I figured out what was going on," he said as he crouched in front of me.

Earl jumped into my lap and leaned his head against my stomach. "Maybe this is Olympus's version of a stag night. He pretends to arrest Cole, but they're secretly at a lap dancing club, stuffing notes into sparkly thongs and drinking beer from hooker shoes."

"Olympus and Cole aren't into that kind of thing." I looked up at Reuben, a flicker of hope jabbing at me. "Could it be that?"

"If it is, why aren't I there? We've been debating what to do for his stag night for a while. It's the only thing we can't agree on."

The air in the kitchen heated, and a second later, Indigo, Odessa, and Storm appeared. I held in a groan as their worried faces confirmed my worst fears. They rushed at me, and even Storm hugged me. No one spoke for several seconds. I was grateful to be surrounded by my friends' love, but I needed answers. I gently pushed them away and focused on Indigo.

"What do you know?" I asked. "Was Olympus involved in the arrest?"

She kneeled in front of me and clasped my hands. "He's getting the information as we speak."

I gulped. "So, it's true? The Magic Council has really arrested Cole for murder?"

Indigo nodded. "Olympus doesn't have all the details, but they got an anonymous tip-off from someone who claims they saw Cole commit murder. Apparently, there's evidence at the scene, too."

I shook my head, failing to dislodge the horrifying news. "This is a mistake. Do we know anything about who died?"

They all shook their heads.

The front door smashed open, and Morrigan stomped in, her teeth bared, and her eyes a brilliant, dazzling amber. "This is your fault. You made him do it."

I shot to my feet and stared at the furious werewolf. "You know what happened to Cole?"

"The second one of my own is involved in any crime, it comes to my attention. And he'd do anything to protect you."

"Not murder a stranger!" I said. "I know nothing about this."

Morrigan snarled and lunged at me. My friends blocked her, magic sparking on their fingers.

"Back off." Storm growled in Morrigan's face.

Earl hissed, and his hackles rose. I rested a hand on his head to stop him from attacking.

Claws extended from the tips of Morrigan's fingers. "Cole is my son!"

"And Luna is Cole's fiancée," Odessa said calmly. "She'd do nothing that would risk his freedom. She loves him."

"There's no other reason for this insanity." Morrigan snarled, her teeth sharp and her bones cracking as her werewolf fought to get free and destroy. "He's obsessed with this witch. It's the only explanation for why he'd be so careless."

I touched Storm's shoulder, gently moving her to one side before facing off with Morrigan. This was my incensed almost-mother-in-law, so I had to handle her. "I've only just found out what's going on from Reuben. I didn't order Cole to murder anybody. I never would."

Morrigan's angry glare flashed around the room. "How convenient that you are tucked up in your shabby farmhouse while my son's life is ruined."

"If Cole's life is ruined, then so is mine." I pressed a hand against my stomach.

Reuben stepped forward, effectively using his body as a barrier between Morrigan and me. "We'll figure this out. There's no way this was Cole."

"I know you're behind this!" Morrigan jabbed a clawed finger at me. "You can only hide behind your friends for so long before I get the truth from you. If I have to tear it from your lying throat, I will." She turned and swept out of the kitchen and through the front door.

Earl hissed again before settling back on the table and shutting his eyes.

"The nerve of that wolf," Storm said. "Why would she think you had anything to do with this? You want me to go after her and teach her some respect?"

"No! She's upset and taking it out on me because she doesn't know what else to do." I looked at Reuben. "Is there anything more you can tell me?"

"You know as much as I do," Reuben said. "I got what I could from the neighbor then came straight here."

I looked at Indigo.

She shook her head. "As soon as I heard from Olympus what was happening, I got the gang together and we arrived. It's only just happened, so there's not much information available."

I drew in a breath, my nerves jangling and my throat tight. "I want to see Cole."

"That's not possible while they're processing him, but Olympus will be in touch the second he knows anything," Indigo assured me. "He'll get you in to see him."

"I need to do something! I'm not waiting here while a bunch of strangers debate Cole's innocence."

Odessa tightly hugged me. "Whatever you need, we're here for you."

I stepped back and looked at my friends. A fiery determination radiated from them. I picked up Earl and hugged him. "Then help me figure out who framed my fiancé for murder."

I was on my fourth mug of strong black coffee, and it was only nine o'clock in the morning. My nerves buzzed with a mixture of caffeine and anxiety as I paced my kitchen. Reuben had left an hour ago to see if Morrigan had gotten any updates about Cole. There was no point in me contacting her and asking since she'd made her hatred for me clear.

I stopped by the window and stared out. A snowstorm raged, despite the forecast being cold and bright. This was my snow, and it represented the maelstrom of emotions rampaging inside me.

Odessa caught me by the shoulders, turned me, and sent me back to the table, urging me to sit. "We're making progress. We already have a list of people who might want to frame Cole."

I stared at the scribbled list on a piece of paper in the center of the kitchen table. At the top of the list was Morrigan Kellam. I grabbed a pen, holding it over her name. My almost-mother-in-law loved her son. She couldn't be behind this, could she?

"Don't even think about it." Storm yanked away the pen. "The monster-in-law stays on the suspect list. She has a temper. She's fiercely proud of the family reputation, and she hates you."

"Hate is a strong word," Odessa said. "Fierce, almost uncontrollable dislike would be preferable."

"However we describe it, she's staying on that list," Indigo said. "She's never hidden her dislike of Luna, despite how happy she makes Cole. Some people think witch and werewolf unions are weird."

"It's all about the beautiful bouncing cubs that won't make an appearance, full of pure Kellam blood to carry on their oh-so-important lineage. Wolves and their dumb hierarchies," Storm said.

"We may not even have beautiful bouncing cubs of any variety," I said. "Cole loathes the violence that comes with a werewolf lifestyle. We've even talked about adopting. We'd like a family, but more werewolves, he's not so sure. Maybe we'll adopt witch babies."

"And that's another reason Morrigan despises you," Storm said. "She thinks Cole's reluctance to be involved in the bloodlust most werewolves enjoy is because of your influence. It won't be acceptable if her grandbabies are raised as peace-loving fluffballs."

I looked at the next name on the list. It was an obvious choice. Jade Silvermoon. "Having met Cole's ex, I won't be surprised if she's behind this."

"I'll go interrogate her." Storm turned to the door.

"No! I need to do this. I have to look whoever framed Cole in the eye and make sure they live to regret their stupid decision." My finger rested on the third name. Reuben Whitehaven. "I'm still unsure whether to include him, but he had planned to meet with Cole for a run first thing."

"It could be a coincidence," Odessa said. "He's a nice guy."

"Or Reuben set it up so Cole would be in the area where the murder took place to make him look guilty." I felt bad about having his name on the list, but until I'd determined his alibi, he remained a suspect.

There was a knock at the front door, and I jumped to my feet. A few seconds later, Indigo brought

Olympus into the kitchen. Tiredness sat beneath his eyes in lumpy purple bags. His black cloak was crumpled, and he was missing the hat he wore when working.

I rushed over to him. "Tell me everything."

He drew in a breath, his shoulders slumped. "Could I have a coffee while I talk? I've had barely any sleep."

"Sit. Odessa, get coffee and food." Indigo took charge, leading Olympus to the kitchen table. "You too, Luna. Sit down, take a breath, and stop crowding Olympus."

I gritted my teeth, my fingers flexing, but I did as she ordered. Time stretched painfully as I waited for Olympus to tell me what he knew.

After he'd had a long sip of coffee, he rolled his shoulders and focused on me. "Here are the basics. We had a tip-off about a murder. It took place in Magenta Vale Woods, only a few miles from here."

"I know those woods. Cole loves to run the tracks around there," I said. "I often walk the trails while he runs."

Olympus nodded. "That's what he told us. He also said he was due to go there for an early run with Reuben Whitehaven."

"That's what I heard, too. Who died?"

"Bram Gregor. His neck was broken. Although there are more tests to complete, it looks like he was shaken and then thrown against a tree."

"Any werewolf bites?" I asked. "If he was bitten, you can match the bite pattern to Cole's teeth. That'll prove he didn't do it."

"Unfortunately, not." Olympus took a long drink of coffee.

"There's more? The eyewitness? Tell me about them." I blinked away tears. I had no time to cry. I had to rescue my fiancé.

Olympus nodded slowly, smiling gratefully at Odessa as she pressed a plate of warm breakfast muffins on him. "We have a credible eyewitness who saw Cole in the area."

"They didn't see Cole kill Bram?" I asked. "That's good! It was a coincidence Cole was in the area at the time the murder happened."

Olympus picked up a muffin but didn't eat it. "I'd agree with you if we didn't have Cole's blood at the scene and the eyewitness swearing blind he watched Cole stalk the victim."

A pain in my gut made me feel as if I'd been punched. "How did Cole's blood get there?"

"That's the puzzle we can't work out," Olympus said. "Cole is saying he's innocent. He doesn't know Mr. Gregor, and he wasn't out at the time of the murder. He was awake, getting ready for his run, but he repeatedly says he wasn't in the woods, so he doesn't know how his blood was at the crime scene."

"Could it be old blood?" Storm asked. "Werewolves are always fighting."

"It was fresh."

"I want to see him," I said.

Olympus shook his head. "Sorry. No visitors at this time."

"He must want to see me."

"Of course. Cole keeps asking for you. He got rough with my guys when they refused him. He had to be sedated."

There was a gentle cough from the kitchen doorway. Reuben stood there. "The front door was open. I hope you don't mind me letting myself in. I overheard what you were saying, and I can help you get to Cole." He lifted his hands, and a wave of magic covered him from head to toe, turning him into a slim tabby cat with a missing ear tip. He strutted around and flicked his ears before reversing the magic.

"Impressively showy, but why should we care that you can turn into a cat?" Storm asked.

"Because, if Luna goes in disguise to visit Cole, she could sneak in without being noticed," Reuben explained.

Olympus took a breath. "I don't want to hear this. If I don't know what laws are being broken, I can't stop it. And I need to leave, anyway, see how things are progressing."

I stared at Reuben then flipped my attention to Olympus. "Are you sure there's nothing else you can tell me?"

"As soon as I have new information, I'll let you know." He touched my arm. "And if it's any help, I believe Cole is innocent. I'll do what I can to clear his name and get him back to you in time for the wedding."

"I'll come with you," Indigo said. She hugged me then hurried off with Olympus.

I focused on Reuben. "Who do you think did this?"

He lifted one shoulder. "Cole's dealt with plenty of unstable packs over the years. He comes from an incredibly powerful family. He's gotten himself a reputation for being a fierce, no-nonsense negotiator, and he's marrying a powerful witch with influence. That'll get you attention from the wrong werewolves."

I stared at the list on the table then flipped it over, not wanting Reuben to see his name on it. "I must see Cole."

"And I've got the way to get you in," Reuben said. "It won't be easy, but we can do it."

I turned to Storm. "Can you help me get a handle on my crazy weather? Since my emotions are all over the place, it won't stop snowing."

"You got it. I'll tackle your anxiety-induced snowstorm." She cracked her knuckles.

"Odessa, I need your scarecrows to distract the Magic Council while I visit Cole," I said.

She grinned and clapped her hands together. "They'll be thrilled to put the scares into some stuffy officials."

I looked at Earl, who sat on the edge of the kitchen table. "And I need you to show me how to be a convincing cat."

Chapter 4

"Sway your butt more from side to side. Your walk is everything when you're a cat." Earl sat on the floor, his critical gaze focused on me. Beside him was Indigo's cat familiar, Nugget. "No! Not like that. Now you look constipated."

"You said more sway!" I was still surprised at how my voice sounded the same, even though I was a tiny fluffy tortoiseshell cat with an adorable heart-shaped patch of white fur on my head.

"Like this. Nugget, show her how to do it," Earl said.

Nugget twitched his whiskers then strolled around the kitchen, giving off an air of nonchalance every cat had mastered since they were a tiny fluffy kitten. "It's all in the rhythm. Put a little bounce into your step while you sway."

I attempted to bounce and sway, and Earl and Nugget keeled over and laughed.

"This isn't funny! If I get this wrong and someone from the Magic Council figures out I'm not a cat, I'll end up behind bars, too. Then I'll be no help to Cole."

"Sorry, sorry. You just look like you're disco dancing from the seventies. It's adorably terrible." Earl staggered to his paws and took a moment to get his laughter under control.

"You're doing great." Odessa leaned against the kitchen counter, with Reuben standing beside her. From the look on his face, he wasn't convinced by my cat performance either.

"How do you make it look so easy?" I asked him.

"Years of practice. When I was a kid, my parents encouraged me to use illusion magic as much as possible. I loved turning into an animal. It was the easiest way to get out of difficult situations. I'm sure Cole has told you our childhood games led to a few scrapes. Turn into a small cat and you can get out of most places in a hurry."

I nodded my furry head. I'd heard tales of their mischievous, youthful activities. "Do you strut and bounce when you walk?"

"Kind of. But it's not so much the rhythm, it's the way you move your front and back paws in alignment. Watch Earl and Nugget walk around a few times then copy them."

"I've been doing that for almost two hours! I'm a terrible cat."

"You're a perfect cat," Odessa said. "And with luck, you and Reuben can sneak into the cells without anyone seeing you. Then they won't notice your strange walk."

I sighed and flopped onto my belly, watching Earl and Nugget wander around and swish their tails.

Indigo and Olympus had been gone for almost two hours, but I'd received no updates about Cole.

Odessa had summoned some of her scarecrows to help on this mission, and they were lurking outside. It worried me she'd had to tell them not to tear any heads off, but right now, I was open to all options if it meant getting Cole free. Storm was outside, still battling my emotion-tainted snow flurries.

While Earl and Nugget dispensed less than helpful advice on how to be a perfect cat, I hopped up and walked over to Reuben. "Do you think our marriage is a good idea?"

His eyebrows rose. "I didn't know you cared."

I jabbed him with a murder mitten. "Me and Cole! Does everyone in the werewolf community think it's a mistake?"

"I don't! Or I wouldn't have agreed to be his best man. We've always been honest with each other. I told him when he met Jade that she was as unstable as an untrained werewolf during a blood moon, and time proved me right."

"Morrigan doesn't approve of me, though, does she? And her opinion matters to Cole. To all werewolves."

Reuben crouched and rested his back against the kitchen cabinet. "You picked up on that, huh? It's not so much that she doesn't like you, but she's always had ambitions for Cole. He's her eldest son, and therefore, there are expectations set on his ridiculously broad shoulders."

"He's talked to me about what his family expects of him, but he loves his work as a negotiator. If he stepped into a role as pack alpha, that would change."

"He'd have to give it up," Reuben said. "And I know he doesn't want that. We love our roles as negotiators. We both lean toward diplomacy and compromise, and Cole only ever uses violence as a last resort, which is more than most other negotiators do."

"Why did you arrange to go for a run so early?" I asked Reuben.

"Cole's been stressed about the wedding. And before you worry, it's got nothing to do with you. But this is a big deal, and his parents are relentless in insisting things are perfect and done the werewolf way."

"I'm aware. Just as my parents are insisting everything is done the baking witch way."

"It's made for some fascinating clashes, but I admire your family. They don't back down, no matter how many werewolves snarl at them." Reuben thumped his head back against the cabinet. "All Cole wants is for you to have the perfect day."

"And that's all I want for him!"

"A long run first thing in the morning is the best way to get rid of excess stress energy," Reuben said. "I figured, if we ran before dawn, Cole could work off the stress, feel more relaxed, and then face your families without wanting to tear their heads off."

"And he could be around to make sure I didn't lose my cool, too?" I glanced at the turbulent sky.

Reuben smiled. "Something like that. I thought I was helping. I had no idea it would lead to this."

My snow globe pinged with an incoming message from Indigo. I leapt up and opened it.

Indigo stared at my unfamiliar furry face. "Um... I'm looking for Luna Brimstone. Did I make a bad connection?"

"It's me! I'm practicing being a cat. What news have you got?"

"Huh! I hope you've practiced enough. Cole's being moved to a more secure location soon. And the Werewolf Council is meeting with the Magic Council to discuss the next move. According to Olympus, this will be a diplomatic nightmare if things go wrong, so tensions are high."

"We need to go to the cells now," I said to Reuben.

"Sure. If you think you're ready."

"You need to be," Indigo said. "And there are extra guards stationed outside Olympus's office. You'll need to remove them before you can get inside."

"Odessa's scarecrows will deal with them," I said. "How much time do I have?"

Although Indigo tried to hide it, she grimaced. "I suggest you hurry."

I hopped off the counter. "Odessa, are your scarecrows ready?"

She lifted a hand. "I'll send my boys now. They'll wait for your signal before unleashing carnage."

"Controlled carnage, right?"

She shrugged. "Most likely. Good luck."

I turned back to Reuben. "Let's go."

After a quick goodbye, I cast a translocation spell that took us to the alleyway behind Olympus's office. It was a small building, with an open office and cells out the back to hold any misbehavers.

Reuben transformed into a cat, and then we slunk to the end of the alleyway.

As Indigo said, there were two guards outside dressed in the familiar Magic Council's black uniform, wearing capes and wide-brimmed hats. They had their chins tucked in to avoid the worst of the snow that pelted down.

"Your backup is over there." Reuben inclined his head toward the other side of the street. Lurking in the shadows of a nearby alleyway were two giant seven-foot scarecrows. If it weren't for the gleam in their eyes, I wouldn't have seen them.

My body quivered. This could be my only chance to see Cole, so I couldn't afford to mess things up.

"You don't have to do this. I can go in on my own," Reuben said.

"I need to see Cole. I must make sure he's okay." I drew in a breath then I stood on my back legs and waggled my two front paws in the air.

Odessa's scarecrows bolted from the alleyway and charged toward the guards. They yelped, but before they cast any defensive spells, they were lifted off their feet and carried away by the scarecrows.

We dashed to the door. I stared at the handle and twitched my nose. How was I supposed to open that with paws?

"I've got this. I need to stand on your back, though, so I'm high enough to reach the handle. That's one thing about turning into a cat. You don't realize how important thumbs are until they're gone," Reuben said.

I got into position and braced myself. Reuben leapt onto my back, and a few seconds later, the door opened with a spark of magic. We ran inside, and Reuben shut the door behind us.

A second later, there was a predatory growl from the corner of the room, and Monty loomed into view.

I squeaked. I'd forgotten about Olympus's leopard familiar being on guard. Monty bared his teeth, and Reuben did the same, his hackles lifting.

"Don't bite us! I'm Luna. Smell me. I'm a friend."

Monty blinked, his hackles still up, then he sniffed the air. "Luna! Why are you disguised as a cat? You're cute, but so small I could have trodden on you if I wasn't paying attention."

"No time to explain. This is my friend, Reuben. We need to sneak in and see Cole."

Monty's eyes widened. "Oh! Of course. He's in so much trouble. It's all people are talking about."

"I wish I had the time to tell you about it, but I have to see him. Is there anyone else here we should be worried about?"

"Just me. Although there are guards outside."

"Not anymore," Reuben said. "Luna, I'll keep watch with Monty and see off any trouble. Go talk to Cole."

I dashed past Olympus's desk, through the small kitchen at the back, and into the cell area. There was only one occupied, and Cole was in it. He sat hunched with his shoulders forward and his head down. My heart raced. He was okay. Behind bars but safe for now.

The second I entered the corridor, his head lifted, and he inhaled deeply. He growled as he looked at me. "Luna?"

"It's me!" I tried to slide between the bars, but I couldn't fit. "Reuben disguised me so I could visit you."

Cole launched himself off the small cot onto his knees and tried to shove a hand through the bars. The magical barrier keeping him inside sparked a warning, and he flinched away and bared his teeth as he rubbed the burn on his wrist.

As much as I longed to hold him, now wasn't the time for sweetness. "I know you're innocent. We're working on getting you out."

Cole snarled. "I'll destroy whoever did this."

"Do you know who framed you?" I asked.

His fingers flexed, his eyes burning brilliant amber. "I'll tear them apart."

"I know you're angry. I am too, but we must focus. It's got to be someone who knows you and wants to ruin things for you. Or someone who has a grudge against our families."

This time, when he growled, his teeth showed sharp and pointed.

"Cole Kellam! If you don't get control of your rage, you'll be no use to me," I snapped. "I've got ideas, but I need your input. And we have little time. We can only distract the guards for so long. And the Werewolf Council is already involved in deciding your fate. Get your anger under control."

His nostrils flared, and he drew in an enormous breath. Although his pointed teeth vanished, his eyes still blazed. "I'm focused."

"Good. Do you know anything about the man who was killed? Bram Gregor."

He shook his head. "The name was meaningless when Olympus told me who it was. You?"

"I don't know him either. Olympus said his neck was broken. There were no bites on him, but your blood was found at the murder scene."

Cole snarled again. "I haven't run that trail for at least a week."

"Was it Reuben's suggestion you run that route?"

"It was."

I flicked an ear, which was the closest thing I could do to arching an eyebrow. "Could he have set you up?"

"No! I trust Reuben with my life. Your life. He'd never betray me."

I sat up straight, my fur fluffing all around me and making me want to scratch. "What about your mother?"

Cole didn't move for almost a minute, his gaze fixed on the wall behind my head. "She is... difficult. But would she go as far as to frame me so this marriage doesn't take place? I... I really don't know."

"We can't rule her out," I said. "I have to find out where she was when Bram was murdered."

Cole grimaced but nodded.

"What about any rivals? Werewolves who have issues with your family? Packs that want to bring you down? Enemies you've made through your negotiations?"

"Most werewolves aren't devious, and they don't launch sneak attacks. They're more direct, preferring to clamp their teeth around your neck so you know who beat you."

"Give it some thought. I have one more name on the suspect list," I said. "Jade."

Cole pressed his fingers against his forehead and closed his eyes for a second. "She is in Witch Haven, and she's even less stable than the last time I saw her."

"I'll figure out where she was, too."

He sighed. "What about the eyewitness? I couldn't get any information when I asked."

"I haven't any details about who they are, but I'll see what I can get from Olympus and speak to them somehow." I got as close to Cole as I could without the magic stinging us. "As for any enemies you've gathered, give me a list as soon as you have one. For now, I'll start with the suspects closest to you."

His eyes flashed amber again. "You're going to interrogate my mother, aren't you?"

Chapter 5

My heart ached as I walked away from Cole, leaving him trapped behind bars and magic, unable to touch him. But I couldn't risk staying any longer. I had a mission to accomplish. I was getting Cole out, and he was putting a ring on my finger. That werewolf was mine.

Monty was back in his enormous fluffy bed, but he jumped up when I appeared. "It's all clear. It's just me. A couple of people came in asking questions, but I chased them away."

"Thanks, Monty."

"Did you get what you needed from Cole?"

"Not as much as I hoped. Where's Reuben?"

Monty swished his gloriously furry tail. "He's stopping the scarecrows from ripping the heads off the Magic Council guards. One of the guards set fire to a scarecrow's arm, and it took offense. Magic was flying all over the place the last time I poked my head out the door. Look! I lost fur from my ear tip." He dipped so I could inspect his injured ear.

"They were only supposed to distract them, not slaughter them!" I dashed to the door and stared at the handle.

"Let me. I've gotten great at escaping. Olympus is always telling me off for doing it, but what's a leopard supposed to do when he gets bored and is hungry?" Monty leapt up and yanked down on the handle.

I nodded a thanks and dashed outside. In the distance, smoke billowed in the air. I raced toward it, stumbling over my unfamiliar paws. I rounded the corner to find the scarecrows sitting on top of the Magic Council guards and smacking their butts. Reuben sat in front of them in cat form, swishing his tail back and forth.

He turned as I approached. "Your timing is perfect. The scarecrows want to play tug-of-war with the guards. Which one shall they start with?"

"No!" I stomped toward the scarecrows. "Bad scarecrows. Remember your orders. No killing!"

"Get these things off of us!" a guard bellowed. "And reveal yourselves. What magic users lurk beneath the fluff?"

"None of your beeswax! Follow me," I said to the scarecrows before fixing my fiercest feline stare on the guards. "And if you have any sense, you'll stay where you are and not track us, or the scarecrows will come back. And if you run, they know where you live."

I turned and trotted away with Reuben beside me. The slight shake of the ground under my paws revealed the scarecrows were following like the good giant killing machines Odessa had trained them to be.

Once we were well out of sight of the guards, I turned to the scarecrows. "Excellent work. Now, return to Odessa and tell her how clever you were."

They grinned, and their eyes flashed red before they turned and shot off.

Reuben checked no one was watching then removed the illusion magic. It washed over me like a cool stream of water, and I had a few seconds of dizziness as I got used to my witchy form again.

Reuben caught hold of my elbow to steady me. "Let's walk. Movement flushes out after-effects from using that spell."

I was grateful for his firm grasp as we hurried along the street. My stomach growled.

He chuckled. "That's another side effect. Maintaining that illusion does strange things to digestion. And it burns through hundreds of calories. Let's stop and get food."

"I don't have time to eat," I said.

"We have five minutes. And neither of us wants to faint." Reuben sighed when I shook my head. "What did Cole tell you?"

"He was reluctant to admit his mother could be involved in framing him, but he didn't rule her out. And I know he has rivals, but he refused to name them."

"Because he doesn't want you getting hurt."

I slid Reuben some serious side-eye. "You're his best friend, so you know the names of the difficult werewolves on his radar. Who wants him out of commission?"

Reuben ran a hand over his shaved head. "We rarely talk about work."

"Don't think you're protecting me by concealing the truth," I said. "I'll find out the information, eventually. In case the crazy weather overhead isn't giving you a clue, I've got my own powers."

"Cole told me all about your magic. In fact, he mainly talks about you, not his work."

That made me smile but only for a second. "Who could have set him up? It must be another werewolf."

Reuben kicked a stone along the street. "There is someone. A big bad jerk of a werewolf you don't want to spend any time with."

"Tell me more."

He stared ahead, his expression pensive. "His name is Gray Hawthorne. He used to be the alpha of the Pine Ridge Pack, but he got involved in shady business practices, mainly smuggling. Another werewolf in his pack challenged him, and there was a fight. Things got messy, and another pack got involved when they smelled weakness. More challenges were thrown down, and Cole was called in to negotiate a deal before too much blood got spilled."

"Gray lost his pack in the negotiation?" I asked.

"He's lucky he didn't lose his life. The guy is scum. He's been in the wind ever since he was kicked out and branded a troublemaker. He blames Cole for what happened to him. But it wasn't Cole's fault. Gray behaved like a reckless jerk and endangered the lives of his werewolves." Reuben glanced at me. "I really hope it was Cole's mother who did this. Morrigan's scary, but she's nothing compared to this guy."

"He won't scare me. I must speak with him."

"Cole won't like it."

"He may not, but there's nothing he can do about it while he's behind bars. And we're running out of time. With the Wolf Council and the Magic Council meeting to discuss Cole's fate, we must act now."

Reuben blew out a breath. "I'll put out feelers and see if I can find out where Gray is lurking."

"You do that. I need to interrogate my mother-in-law-to-be."

Half an hour later, after the effects of the illusion magic had completely worn off, I stood outside Morrigan's hotel room. How could I ask her if she'd set up her own son without ruining what tenuous relationship we already had?

I had to go for the direct approach. Werewolves appreciated that. I drew in a breath and knocked. Morrigan opened the door a few seconds later and peered down her long, straight nose at me. "You must have a death wish, showing up here."

"Just as you had a death wish, accusing me of making Cole kill a man." I pushed past her, not waiting for an introduction. I was stepping into the werewolf's den, but I had to show I was unafraid. And with Cole's freedom on the line, I'd go up against any monster to guarantee he got out.

I turned as Morrigan approached, an amber warning glinting in her eyes.

"I've seen Cole," I said.

Surprise flashed across her face. "How? The Magic Council blocked all my attempts to visit."

"I used a little magic. Sometimes, it's more effective than brute force."

Morrigan bared her teeth then breathed through her nose for several silent seconds. "How was he?"

"Angry. Cole wants to destroy the person who framed him," I said.

"Then he should look closer to home." Her fierce gaze ran from my hairline to my toes and back again. "Who was the victim to you?"

I crossed my arms over my chest, refusing to be intimidated. "A stranger. At least, I don't recognize the name, and I'm certain the Magic Council won't let me see the body to double check if it was a fake name."

Morrigan waggled her fingers in the air, a mocking smile on her face. "Why don't you use some of that magic you were just boasting about?"

"If it comes to it, I will. Whoever framed Cole is close to him. They know his movements, where he likes to run, and somehow got a sample of his blood to plant at the murder scene."

"You're capable of doing all of that," Morrigan said.

I lifted my chin and met her stare dead-on. "So are you."

She growled and stalked toward me, not stopping until the toes of our shoes touched. "You think I did this to my boy?"

"You've never hidden that you hate me. I know you want Cole to marry another werewolf."

Morrigan inhaled and exhaled, her warm breath hitting me in the face. "I don't hate you, Luna. But I won't hide the fact I was disappointed in Cole's choice of partner. We're one of the oldest werewolf families in existence."

"And you want the bloodline to continue. That'll be diluted if we have a family."

"Exactly. I knew you weren't stupid. As the eldest son, Cole has a responsibility to fulfill."

"What if he doesn't want that responsibility?"

She growled in my face. "Sometimes, we have no choice about the responsibilities placed on our shoulders. That's the way things have always been."

"Does it have to be that way? Just because something has always been done a certain way doesn't mean it's the right way or the most efficient way. And you have two other sons. Both of them are dating werewolves."

Morrigan glared at me. "I'm proud of all of my sons, and I want them to be happy."

"I make Cole happy, just as he makes me happy. I know I'm not the daughter-in-law you hoped for, but don't write me off because I can't sprout a tail and fangs." Although not so long ago, that was exactly what I'd done. "I have power that could be at your disposal."

Morrigan flicked a glance at the window. "I'm aware of what you're capable of. I'd never agree to any son of mine marrying someone unworthy." She stepped back, and a thin smile crossed her face. "And I know how you met Cole."

I arched an eyebrow. "And...?"

"You matched him. It's not your power I question."

"I match him in power, but I also match him in the intensity of my feelings," I said. "When Cole declared I was his mate, it terrified me. I'd never met anyone who was so decisive and knew what they wanted from a relationship. But once I got used to it, it made sense. We're perfect for each other."

Morrigan ran her tongue across her top teeth. "I know about your unsavory couplings with other men before meeting my son. You were involved with a sugar daddy before Cole, is that right?"

I blushed. "That was a misunderstanding. But since you've done your background research, you'll also know I struggled with my magic until I knew its source."

"That's another thing that concerns me. Your dubious parentage."

I clenched my fists, and thunder rumbled overhead. "Neither of my parents are dubious. Clovis Brimstone is one of the most in-demand witches in the baking dynasty. She travels the world to serve the whims of royalty and influential leaders. And my father is—"

"Not here." Morrigan strode to the window and looked out. "Your biological father provided you with this." She pointed at the rolling clouds overhead. "The tumultuous power that you have little control over."

"I control it! But when I'm distracted by something like my fiancé being framed for murder, my attention slips."

"I should not like to be around you when you lose total control."

"I assure you, it would be unlikely you'd survive."

Morrigan pivoted on her heeled foot. "You threaten me?"

"I tell the truth. I'm not a werewolf, but I'm strong. And I love your son. I'm determined to find out who framed him and get him free. We will marry, whether you like it or not."

A series of emotions flashed across Morrigan's face then the hardness in her eyes vanished. She walked over and surprised me by embracing me. "Stubborn witch. You'll need that stubbornness when you join the pack. I won't deny I grieve the loss of ever having werewolf cubs from Cole, but as you rightly pointed out, I have two other sons who happily spread their wild oats."

"That's good to know." I wasn't sure what to do with my hands. Morrigan had me pinned so tight, I could barely move them. What was it about werewolves and their bone-bending embraces?

She chuckled into my ear. "And you didn't hear this from me, but there are several unofficial grandbaby cubs already in existence, thanks to my younger boys' wild behavior. When the time comes, the cubs will be allowed into a suitable pack."

"Should I say congratulations?" I wriggled away from her hug.

A rare smile crossed Morrigan's face. "They're adorable. But I'm sure any children you and Cole have will be just as cute. Now, what are you doing to ensure my son's innocence?"

"Questioning suspects," I said. "And therefore, I need to know your alibi."

She bared her teeth again, but her smile remained. "Of course. Looking at me would only be right after the trouble I've caused you."

I nodded and maintained a steely silence.

Morrigan lifted one shoulder. "I was here with Cole's father. He had time off from the silver mines, so he stopped by. We ordered room service. Rare steak, which we ate while I caught him up on the situation."

I blew out a breath, relaxing a fraction. Her alibi would be simple to check. My future mother-in-law wasn't a killer. "So, who do you think framed Cole?"

Morrigan cocked her head. "Have you forgotten the naked picture you received as a wedding gift?"

I stared at her with wide eyes. "How do you know about that?"

She smirked. "Jade is special to me, but she's unable to keep a secret. Even I thought that gift was crass. It's time you confronted the abandoned ex."

Chapter 6

After my bracing confrontation with Morrigan, ruling her out as a suspect after checking with the hotel clerk that she'd been eating steak with Cole's father and they hadn't left the room, I walked out of the hotel and stood on the steps, my eyes closed as I breathed in deeply.

"Luna! There you are. We've been looking for you everywhere. You must be in pieces about Cole."

My eyes snapped open as my mother's high-pitched familiar tone reached me. My father, Galahad, was beside her, his expression anxious and his suit, as always, impeccable.

I walked down the final steps to reach them. My mother embraced me in a chocolate chip-scented hug, while my father patted my arm.

"You're allowed to cry over your loss." My mother peered into my face. "Such a devastation."

"Cole's not dead!" I said. "He's just in jail. And I'm getting him out."

"It's admirable you want to stand by your man," my father said, "but this gives you the perfect opportunity to leave now before it's too late."

I took a step back. "You don't want me to marry Cole?"

My mother tucked a strand of hair behind my ear. "Darling, we want the best for you, and we were excited when you joined with Cole. His family and ours uniting is a fairytale."

I sighed. "Let's not start that again." We'd argued repeatedly over my parents' less-than-subtle nudges about the opportunities the families joining would present them. From being able to provide exclusive baking opportunities to powerful werewolf families, to the exciting press it would garner. None of that interested me, but I knew it mattered to my parents.

"Cole is a polite, charming man, well, werewolf. But I was always worried you were getting in over your head with all the odd wolfy business," my mother said. "And now he's been accused of murder!"

"He may be accused, but he's innocent," I said. "Cole has been framed, and I'm finding out who did it."

"There is another option," my father said.

"Not for me, there isn't."

"Hear me out. We'll leave Witch Haven. You can legitimately break off the engagement. You don't want to be entangled with a family whose reputation has been besmirched by murder."

No one spoke while I inhaled this repellent option. It was a struggle not to yell at them, but I managed. "They're werewolves! Violence runs through their everyday activities. Morrigan will have killed in the name of pack alpha, as has Cole's father. Werewolf punishments are brutal and often lethal to those on the receiving end."

"Exactly! Do you want to associate with that level of disturbingly base behavior?" my mother asked. "I know a dozen eligible, less violent bachelors who'd be thrilled to date you."

I lifted my hands, and an icy wind whirled around us, picking up snow. "My power is as primal and chaotic as werewolf energy. Until I knew how to handle it, I was adrift. I was a mess of a witch who had no idea how I worked. I could barely bake a basic scone and considered myself a blunted magic user. Now I know exactly what I am, and I feel more aligned to the werewolves than I do either of you."

My mother pressed a hand to her silk-covered chest. "Don't say that. We're your family."

"You are!" I caught hold of my dad's hand. "Both of you, no matter how I got here. My powers are different from yours, so they fit better with the werewolves. I fit with Cole."

"What if it turns out he did it?" my father asked. "Would you still want to be with him?"

My mind blanked. I couldn't be with a cold-blooded killer. But that wasn't Cole. He didn't rampage through the woods killing people because his bloodlust was up. He was a responsible werewolf. He was my werewolf.

"We can take you anywhere," my mother said, sensing my hesitation. "We have contacts across the world. If this is too much for you—"

"No! This is where I need to be. I'm staying. Cole is innocent. Someone is out to get him. This has to do with an attack on the Kellam family or an attack on me and Cole to prevent us from getting married."

My parents were silent for a few seconds as they exchanged a concerned look.

"If the latter is true, this won't be the last time this kind of thing happens," my father finally said. "The Kellam family are the apex alphas in the werewolf community. There'll always be a target on them. Someone will always be stalking them to take them down and replace them. When that happens, your life will be at risk."

"Maybe it will, but their enemies' lives will be at risk, too." I flicked my fingers and lightning flashed across the sky. "I'm not afraid of defending the people I love. Whether that's Cole, Morrigan, or you."

My mother embraced me again. "We want what's best for you."

"And if you think this dangerous, power-mad werewolf family is it, then so be it," my father said. "We wanted to ensure you knew what your options were."

"You shouldn't be unhappy I'm marrying into a werewolf pack. They have huge appetites, so your services will always be in demand. You'll make a fortune out of them because they're so greedy."

My father smiled and pinched my cheek. "That's not the only reason we want this union to work."

I raised both eyebrows. "It's a big one, though. We all know that." I held up a hand as my mother began to protest. "And I don't mind. Your careers and family status are important to you, just like they are to the werewolves. That's why you'll get along so well."

"We have one or two things in common," my father said. "But please be careful when investigating what happened to Cole. If whoever framed him knows you're poking about, they could come for you."

"I'll be ready for them if they do," I said.

"We trust you to do the right thing, darling," my mother said. "We'd offer our help, but I'm not sure how whipping up the perfect meringue would assist you in finding the killer."

"You can help me by keeping an eye on the wedding planning. I have no time for it while I'm helping Cole. And the wedding day will be here before I know it."

My mother's face brightened. "We can do that. Morrigan was too heavy-handed and tried to do everything her way. The only time I could get a word in was by stuffing cake into her mouth. With her distracted by her son being behind bars, we'll take the lead."

I narrowed my eyes. "Please don't tell me you both framed Cole so you could be in charge of the wedding."

My father roared with laughter. "I wouldn't put it past your mother, but if we did, there'd be no groom for you to marry, which would rather defeat the point."

"You have substitutes waiting in the wings," I said.

My mother's face was a picture of innocence. "As if we'd do such a thing! Come on, Galahad. We have a wedding to make perfect."

My parents hurried away, talking animatedly, their heads bent together. They were never happier than when they got to take over a lavish event.

They were exasperating to the extreme and so focused on their social standing it made me queasy, but they weren't violent. If they wanted to punish anyone, they'd make them a 'special' cake with an ingredient that would keep them in bed for a month. If I'd discovered Cole doubled over with stomach cramps and sickness, I'd have blamed them, but they weren't the types to stalk a stranger and break his neck against a tree.

No, I was looking for a werewolf. A very blonde, very pretty, extremely curvy one. I took a few steps, and my knees wobbled. The ground tilted, and I staggered.

An arm wrapped around my waist. "You look about ready to fall over." Indigo's welcome voice filled my ears. "When was the last time you ate?"

I sagged onto the bench she led me to, not caring I was sitting on snow. "This morning? Didn't Odessa feed me something? I remember muffins."

"Which means you haven't eaten all day. Get this into you. It was meant for Olympus, but you need it more than he does." She shoved a brown paper bag into my hands.

My fingers shook as I pulled it open. My blood sugar must have crashed. Indigo sat beside me in silence as I ate the tuna mayo sandwich and drank half a takeout cup of coffee.

"Any news from Olympus?" I asked around a mouthful of sandwich, already feeling better now I had food in my stomach.

"Nothing yet. It's still closed doors. Although, we had to deal with two injured guards after some rampaging scarecrows attacked them. Imagine that." Indigo quirked an eyebrow.

"Can't think how that happened." I grinned at her. "Cole is doing okay. He wasn't much help in providing suspects, though."

"Typical. Protecting his mate."

"Reuben gave me a name. Although, I'm not going after him straightaway. And I just had an interesting conversation with Morrigan."

"You faced down the mother-in-law with claws and survived?"

"It was touch and go. But I don't think she hates me as much as I first thought. And she has an alibi, so she's off the suspect list."

Indigo nodded slowly. "You think it's the crazy ex-girlfriend, don't you? I've been hearing about Jade."

I finished the last of the sandwich and pulled out a dark chocolate bar, which I broke in half and handed a piece to Indigo. "It's got to be her. She can't have Cole, so no one else can." Thunder rumbled overhead as my mood soured.

Indigo winced. "I get why you're angry, but Storm is almost on her knees trying to keep your snowmageddon under control."

I huffed out a breath of surprise. "She is? I didn't know. I'm not that bad, am I?"

"If she wasn't fighting your swirling crazy clouds so hard, this village would be under ten feet of snow by now. It would be a winter whiteout."

"Oh! I didn't realize I was that out of control." I bit my bottom lip. "Sorry."

"No worries. You're still growing into your witchy weather magic," Indigo said. "It's no surprise that, when your attention shifts, it misbehaves. But spare a thought for Storm. She'll never tell you, but you're even stronger than she is."

I placed a piece of chocolate in my mouth, closed my eyes, and slowly sucked it. I'd learned breathing techniques to help me handle my power, but they didn't always work. Since I'd never gotten training in weather magic as a child, my power was unpredictable. And an unpredictable elemental witch was a dangerous one. If I let a stray lightning bolt fly, it could destroy a building.

Indigo remained silent while I centered myself. She'd seen me lose control of my abilities many times, so she knew to give me space. I took one final breath and opened my eyes before popping another piece of chocolate into my mouth.

"You need a clear head if you're going to solve this mystery," Indigo said.

"What I need is to find Jade and shake the truth out of her."

"Speak of the devil, and she shall appear." Indigo gestured with her head across the street. Jade strutted past in sky-high heels and skintight black jeans, seeming unconcerned by the snowy conditions.

"Thanks for the food. Gotta go." I shoved the paper bag into Indigo's hand and dashed away. "Jade! Wait up."

She turned on her heel, and her top lip curled. "Shouldn't you be at a dress fitting? Looks like you've gained a few pounds since the last time I saw you."

"You saw me a day ago! Although I should be stress-eating, given what's going on."

"Has Cole left you?" Her eyes widened. "He's come to his senses, and he wants me back. I knew it."

"Something tells me you're off your meds," I said.

She growled softly. "What if I am? Maybe I'm trying an alternative route. Anyway, what do you know about my meds?"

"Lucky guess. What do you know about framing Cole for murder?"

Her jaw dropped open. "Murder? What are you talking about?"

"Do you know where Cole is?"

"Probably still lounging in your bed." She growled out her disgust.

"Jade, he's been arrested on suspicion of murder."

She snorted, and several garbled half-words came out of her mouth. "He'd never do that. He's a teddy bear. The sweetest werewolf I know."

"Cole is sitting in a jail cell awaiting sentencing. There was an eyewitness who saw him do it and evidence at the scene to show he was there."

Jade's genuine shock had me stunned as she shook her head and kept shaking it. "Not my Cole. He may play the big bad wolf in negotiations, but he's a sweetheart. And you know all about that, since you get to snuggle with him these days. He's not a killer."

"Well, he's looking guilty to everyone else."

She lunged forward and clutched my shoulders, concern etched across her pretty face. "You don't believe he did it, do you? It would destroy him if you abandoned him. His wolf would pine to death without his soul mate."

"Of course not! That's why I'm questioning you. You want him back. You hate the fact he's with me."

Jade paused, and she pursed her lips. "I do want him back. Cole's adorable. And I don't like you because you slammed the door on any chance I had to snare him again." She hugged me so tight she squeezed the breath out of my lungs. Werewolf hugs sucked.

"Let me go," I wheezed as I whacked her back and flailed. "Can't breathe."

Jade stepped back but kept hold of my shoulders. "I'm so sorry this is happening. And... I'm sorry for being such a jerk to you."

I blinked several times. "I'm sorry you're such a jerk, too."

"And I feel terrible about the naked picture in your gift box. That was seriously uncool. I'm not usually such a brat."

I nodded sagely. "Do you feel terrible about portraying me as a gnarled old witch with a giant wart on her nose and a hunchback?"

"It's how I see you! At least it is in my nightmares." Jade gave me a crooked smile. "I am jealous of how happy you make Cole. It's something I could never do, no matter how hard I tried. I wanted him for myself, but he was always upfront with me and said we'd never be serious. His fussy, uptight wolf didn't approve of me, but I kept hoping, and I figured his wolf might change his mind or realize what a catch I was. It never happened." Her gaze dipped. "And then he met you, and Cole's wolf went head over heels, howling at the moon madly in love with you. I knew then I didn't stand a chance of winning him back."

"That must have been rough on you," I said. "I didn't realize you cared about him so deeply."

She shrugged. "He's an absolute honey bunny. Being a footloose and fancy-free female werewolf has its issues. Some male werewolves aren't always respectful of my choice to go solo and not be in a pack. And they don't understand the word 'no.' Now, don't worry, I know how to fight if one of them puts his hand in the wrong place while making an assumption something's gonna happen. But if I was under the Kellam pack's protection, I'd never have to worry about that. I wouldn't need to glance over my shoulder for fear I was being stalked. That holds a lot of appeal."

"I see why it would," I said. "And I hope you can also see why I think you may have framed Cole for murder."

"Of course I do, silly!" Jade whacked my arm. "If the roles were reversed, I'd be coming after you just as hard. When did this all happen?"

I rubbed my arm. "In the early hours of the morning. Cole and Reuben were going for a run in Magenta Vale Woods. That's where the Magic Council found the body."

"How awful. And you say there's an eyewitness and evidence to prove it was Cole?"

"That's what the Magic Council tells me. I don't believe them. Where were you at that time?"

"Moi! You can't think I did this."

I cocked my head and waited.

Jade tossed her hair over one shoulder and giggled. "Good for you, not backing down when your man is in trouble. I was in Hollow Cove with Atticus."

"The local alpha?"

"Uh-huh. I was testing the water with his pack. They had a gathering that went on until dawn, so I chatted to a few pack members to see how I'd fit."

"Atticus will confirm you were there?"

A hint of anger lit her eyes then she shrugged. "Naturally. I'm unforgettable."

"What did you do all night?"

"Ate, drank, flirted, hunted. The usual. Feel free to check. I promise I'd never do something so awful as to frame Cole. Once you're married to him, we'll become the best of friends. Well, maybe we'll be more like sisters. Sisters fight a lot, don't they?"

"I look forward to fighting with you." I needed to confirm Jade's alibi, but if it checked out, she couldn't have framed Cole, and I needed to cast my suspect net wider and into deadlier territory.

Chapter 7

"It wasn't Jade." I stood with my back to Reuben as I stared at the moon through my kitchen window. It kept being blotted out by yellow clouds. Snow clouds I was making with my panic. "I got a message from Atticus, who confirmed she was with his pack. He said we could keep her. Too unstable for him to handle, despite a couple of his guys showing an interest."

"I had my doubts she'd be the killer." Reuben walked over and placed a mug in my hands, the warmth doing little to dispel the chill that surrounded me. "Jade's as nutty as a fruitcake, but she's not malicious. She even tried being vegetarian once. You can imagine the stick she got from other werewolves. She doesn't buy into the violent werewolf lifestyle, either. That's why she was attracted to Cole. He'd rather negotiate than bite."

"When I confronted her, she was sassy, but she had no idea what had happened to Cole." I sighed and traced a finger down the condensation on the window. "Which leaves us looking at other suspects. Have you gotten anywhere with contacting Gray?" I turned from the window and took a sip of the coffee Reuben made me.

"Yeah. About that. It's a bad idea."

"But it's an idea I'm pursuing," I said. "Do you know where he is?"

Reuben hesitated. "I do."

"And have you made contact to arrange a meeting?"

He grimaced. "He's unstable. Don't go anywhere near him."

"If Gray is as unstable as you claim, he could have gotten it into his head that it was sensible to frame Cole for murder. I must face him and get answers."

Reuben was quiet for several seconds. "I figured you'd say as much. But if anything goes wrong when you meet him..."

"I'll be responsible for the outcome."

"Nope. Even though Cole's not one for violence, he'd rip my head off if anything bad happened to you."

"Then come with me. You want justice for Cole just as much as I do."

"You bet I do." He flashed me a brief grin. "Which is why I've arranged a meeting for both of us."

I smiled in relief. "Where? When?"

There was a knock on the front door, and a few seconds later, Storm, Indigo, and Odessa strode in with Olympus. They were all wrapped in winter clothing and covered in snow.

I set down my coffee and hurried over to them. "You've got news?"

"Give us a second." Indigo shoved Olympus into a chair. She grabbed a mug and filled it with coffee before handing it to him.

I stepped from foot to foot, impatience coursing through me, but I could see how exhausted Olympus was. His shoulders sagged, and the scruff on his chin showed he hadn't been home to shower or shave. True to his word, he was doing everything he could to get Cole free.

Once everyone was settled in seats, Olympus looked at me. "It's bad news. The Magic Council and the Wolf Council have met. They agree Cole is guilty. They can't fault the evidence presented to them."

I swallowed my cries of protest. There'd be a way out of this. "Who is the eyewitness? They must be lying about what they saw."

Olympus shook his head, but Indigo nudged him.

"His name is Evander Thomas," Olympus finally said.

We all looked at each other. That name wasn't familiar. It wasn't anyone who lived in Witch Haven.

"Is he a werewolf?" I asked.

Olympus drank more coffee. "No. Your average warlock."

"What was he doing out in the early hours of the morning in the woods?" I asked. "Whoever set Cole up must have paid Evander to be there so he could fake being a witness."

"Technically, he wouldn't have needed to be in the woods if he's lying," Storm said.

"We only have his word he was there," Olympus said. "But he gave an accurate description of Cole in human and werewolf form. He said he saw him change as he stalked the victim."

"This stranger's word means nothing," I said. "Did you ask him if he was bribed?"

"Of course. He assured me he was telling the truth. Evander is married with two young children, and one of them has been ill with a stomach bug for the last week. He needed a break from the sick house, so he went for a walk."

"Where does this guy live?" Storm asked. "What does he do for a job?"

"Two villages over and he works at a bar. I checked his background and looked into his financials. There's nothing unusual about him," Olympus said. "He's got no criminal record and no associations to any werewolf packs. I couldn't find any reason he'd lie about what he saw."

"What happens to Cole now?" A ball of ice-cold terror sat in my stomach and refused to budge. I could be about to lose my wolf.

"The councils are still in negotiation," Olympus said. "And they won't make a final decision tonight since it's getting late. It'll most likely be decided by noon tomorrow, though."

I slapped a hand on the table. "Good. That gives me time to follow another avenue."

"Do you have a new suspect?" Odessa asked.

I glanced at Reuben, but he wouldn't meet my gaze. "We've identified a werewolf who has issues with Cole. Cole negotiated a deal between packs, and the losing alpha was forced to leave and become a lone wolf."

"Don't mess with a disaffected werewolf with an attitude," Olympus said. "Give me his details, and I'll approach him through the official channels."

"That'll take too long," I said. "Reuben has already made contact. He's arranged a meeting, haven't you?"

Reuben ran a hand over his head tattoos, his palm rasping against stubble. "Gray's open to talking but don't expect an easy ride. He's an evil son of a gun and will want something in return for any information he provides."

"He'll have to be breathing to make his demands," I growled.

Olympus set his mug down. "Luna, do nothing reckless. I know how important Cole is to you, but if you go to jail too—"

"I won't! But I will get answers. I'll figure out how to make this guy talk."

"I have an idea to get Gray to open up without getting violent with him," Reuben said. "I'll use my illusion magic, so Luna smells like a werewolf."

"And that helps how?" Odessa asked. "If Luna smells like a yummy female werewolf, won't Gray think she's a potential mate?"

"I've already laid the groundwork when I made contact," Reuben said. "I introduced her as a new pack negotiator who's been reviewing Gray's case file and has questions for him." He looked at me. "I can't make you shift into a werewolf. My illusion magic won't change you into anything larger than a small dog, but I can create the illusion of smell. You'll meet Gray, and he'll believe you're a werewolf. So long as he doesn't expect you to shift, the disguise should work."

"Won't he know who Luna is?" Indigo asked. "Everyone knows about the upcoming marriage."

"It's a hot topic of gossip in most packs," Reuben said, "but Gray has been on his own for months, so he's out of the loop."

"It's risky," Olympus said.

"But it could work." Indigo nudged him again. "We can't stop Luna from doing this."

Storm nodded. "And we shouldn't. No offense, Olympus, but the Magic Council moves too slow to be effective in stopping this."

He shrugged. "It's why I'm not putting up a bigger fight. Time isn't our friend."

"We'll need a different name for you," Storm said. "Just in case this guy makes a connection."

Hope lit inside me. "This could work. I'll use Reuben's illusion scent disguise to get close to him. I'll ask questions about Cole, and if Gray refuses to talk, I'll use whatever means I have to, so I get the truth out of him."

"Keep it legal if you can," Olympus said. "Any testimony you get needs to stand up in front of a judge."

"A small amount of violence is permitted, though," Storm said, with a smirk. "And fear is an excellent motivator to make people talk."

I stood and looked down at Reuben. "We go now?"

Reuben nodded. He stood next to me, raised his hands, and moved them around me, from my head down to my toes. His illusion magic shimmered in the air, and although I couldn't smell anything different, my body tingled.

Earl, who'd been curled in a ball on top of the heater, lifted his head and wrinkled his nose. "You smell gross."

"But do I smell like a werewolf?" I twirled for him.

He hissed at me. "Stay away from me until you lose the wet dog whiff. That's nasty."

"It might be to you, but it'll be heaven to other werewolves." I hoped it would, or this mission would end in a no-holds-barred brawl with a bitter werewolf who had nothing to lose.

I said goodbye to the others, and after getting directions from Reuben where we needed to go, I cast a translocation spell over us.

We arrived to find an eerie stillness in the middle of a wooded glen. Moonlight struggled to penetrate the canopy, casting deep shadows that danced upon the frost-covered ground. Leafless branches reached out skeletal fingers, their gnarled silhouettes creating a sinister tapestry against the sky. The air hung heavy with a damp chill, sending shivers down my spine, and silence wrapped around us, broken only by the occasional hoot of an owl or the distant rustle of unseen creatures.

"It's the perfect place for a murder." I resisted a shudder. This was no time to wimp out.

"Gray's got a small base here," Reuben whispered. "He has to keep moving regularly, though, in case the territory alpha sniffs him out. He'll kill him if he does. Atticus Farraday despises Gray, and he's got a solid reputation around here. When he barks orders, other werewolves listen."

We walked in silence for a few minutes until a faint drift of wood smoke reached me.

Reuben caught my eye, his gaze gleaming in the gloom. "I'll stay back and let you talk. If there's any trouble, I'll be right there. Gray won't hurt you. I'll watch his every move."

I nodded my appreciation, pushed my chest out, and lifted my chin, attempting to recreate the strut I'd seen Jade do so expertly. I had to convince this guy I was a werewolf. My future happiness depended on it.

A faint flicker of flame drew me closer, and I discovered a clearing with an open fire, the smell of coffee and roasted meat lingering in the air. Alongside that was the scent of something tart and the unwelcome tang of blood.

A squat, solidly built guy with black hair and a long scar running down one cheek was slumped by the fire. His eyes were closed, one arm wrapped around his ribs, a grimace of pain on his face. In his free hand, he held a glass bottle.

He didn't stir as I got closer, and I froze, tilting my head. Was Gray dead? His face was covered in fresh bruises, and there was dried blood on his shirt.

"What do you want?" His voice was guttural and rusty.

"Gray Hawthorne?"

"And you are?"

I recalled the name Storm had made up for me. "Lacey Bane. You're expecting me."

"You're friends with that smooth-talking jerk, Reuben?" He still had his eyes closed and spoke slowly, as if it was painful to talk.

"That's right. I have questions for you."

"There's not much else I can do but talk right now. Found myself in a little bother when I was hunting."

I stepped closer. "Another werewolf?"

He grunted. "What else? He told me, when my ribs heal, I'll have to move on. Guess I found him on a good day. You're lucky I'm still here."

"I'm one of those lucky wolves." I remained standing, waving away the bottle he held out to me. "I have questions about your former role as the alpha of the Pine Ridge Pack."

"Reuben said you might be able to get me back in."

I drew in a quiet breath. That was how Reuben convinced this guy to give me an audience. "I work with the werewolves to make sure justice is done."

"There was nothing just about me being kicked out of my pack. I was a tough but fair alpha. The weaklings couldn't cope with the discipline. That wasn't my fault." He finally opened his eyes, narrowing them as his nostrils flared. "Reuben didn't tell me you were so cute. You mated?"

"It's not relevant. Give me your opinion of your negotiator, Cole Kellam."

Gray scowled. "He's the reason I'm here. I'm convinced the new alpha paid him off. He wanted my wolves, so he slid a fat wad of cash to that lying pup. Cole collected false evidence against me then presented it to the alphas and the Wolf Council, suggesting I wasn't fit to rule."

"Do you have evidence of that?"

"Gut instinct. That was enough for me."

"So, you don't like him?" I kept my tone level, even though my insides churned. Gray had the perfect motive to want to take Cole down.

"I despise the guy. There's not a day that goes by when I don't think about how to destroy him. Mess up his life just like he did me."

My hands curled into fists. This was my killer. He must have snuck to the trails and set Cole up. And even though he wasn't part of any pack, he must have an ear to the werewolf gossip. He'd learned about our marriage and saw it as the perfect opportunity to strike a blow.

"Why don't you come here and make me feel better?" Gray asked. "Give me something to make my tail wag."

My top lip curled. "When did you last visit Witch Haven?"

"Witch Haven. Why do you ask?"

"Perhaps you traveled through recently? Spent a night in the woods. Maybe near the Magenta Vale running trails."

"What are you going on about? What does this have to do with me getting my pack back?" Gray lifted himself up. His gaze turned amber as it roamed over me. "Are you sure you're a negotiator? They don't usually hire females. Too distracting."

I lifted my chin. "Of course. And I'm the one asking questions. When was the last time you saw Cole?"

Gray grunted. "I see him in my nightmares all the time."

"But in the flesh?"

He shrugged. "I don't remember. A while."

"I don't believe you."

Gray growled softly. "You can believe all you like, sweetheart. That wolf has only ever brought me trouble, and I want nothing to do with him, other than spitting on his worthless grave when the happy day arrives."

My hands flexed, my magic desperate to burst out and give this jerk a much-needed whipping. "You thought you'd repay his kindness?"

His grubby forehead furrowed. "You've lost me. Unless you've found dirt on Cole that'll get me back in my pack, this conversation is over."

I lifted a hand and shot a mini lightning spell at him, whacking him square in the chest with a sizzling hiss.

Gray dropped back to the ground, his eyes wide as his breath wheezed out of him. "You're a freakin' witch! I knew there was something wrong with you."

I advanced, magic sparking on my fingers and thunder growling overhead. "You did it. You despise Cole, so you framed him for murder."

"Are you hexed senseless? Get away from me." Gray scrambled back, his face a mask of pain as he held his ribs.

"You won't stop us from getting married."

"What are you going on about? What marriage?" He cringed as I raised my hand. "Stop! I'm not fighting. I couldn't have done anything to Cole. I can't even fight you off."

"Admit you set Cole up, and I'll stop coming for you."

"I'm admitting to nothing. What did he do? Did he mess up? Kill someone?"

"No! Come with me. You're confessing to the Magic Council." As much as I wanted to blast this jerk into the middle of next year, I needed his confession so Cole would go free.

Gray stilled and stared at me then he lowered his head. "Fine. Whatever. I'll be safer in a cell than out here. I doubt I'll survive the next werewolf attack."

"You'll come with me, just like that?" I stepped back, surprised he'd given in so easily.

His sigh was laced with exhaustion and pain. "I want a place where I can close my eyes and get a decent night's sleep. I'm always having to sleep with one eye open in case some power-hungry jerk slinks out of the woods and wants to make a name for himself by destroying me. The other alphas are still jealous of my achievements."

"And you'll answer the Magic Council's questions about what you did to Cole?"

"I still don't know what you're talking about, but I'll answer any questions they have. And from the sounds of it, someone has made my day if they've messed with that puffed-up wolf and put him out of commission."

I bared my teeth at him. "Get up. I'll take you to the Magic Council."

Gray shot me a lazy salute. "You're the boss, beautiful. Just give me a minute. I don't move so well with busted ribs." He inhaled and grinned. "You had me fooled. You smell just like a werewolf, but I knew they'd never hire such a firecracker. All us boys would howl at the moon every time you stopped by with your questions."

The second I lowered my hand, Gray lunged at me. I dodged back, a lightning bolt flaring on my palm, but a blur of movement pounded into Gray, sending him flying as he yelped his alarm.

It took me a second to figure out what was going on, but then I gasped. A huge bobcat had his fangs wrapped around Gray's throat and was choking him.

Chapter 8

"I'm so sorry, Luna." Reuben stood behind me as we waited in the local hospital for news on Gray. "I thought he was going to kill you. I had to act. I only meant to slow him down, not put him in here."

That must have been the hundredth apology he'd given me since he savaged Gray when he'd turned into a bobcat. The werewolf had been in such bad shape that he hadn't had time to transform and attack before he'd passed out from loss of blood. "I understand why you did it. But I was under no threat. Gray could hardly stand, let alone do me serious harm."

"He still went for you. I thought he'd figured out you knew the truth about him and was playing up how badly injured he was to make you drop your defenses."

I turned and patted his arm. "I'm not angry. You were protecting me because that's what Cole would have done."

Reuben heaved out a sigh. "I may not be a werewolf, but I have a special bond with Cole. We look out for each other, and that includes our families. Cole would never have forgiven me if anything happened to you while you were clearing his name."

I pointed a finger at the snow swirling around outside. "I have skills. You keep forgetting that."

"Don't hate me for saying this, but I know your magic is growing, and you're still learning to finesse it. I didn't want to run the risk that you malfunctioned at a crucial moment. Gray would have exploited that in a second, and then you'd be dead."

The male doctor who'd been treating Gray approached us. "You brought in Gray Hawthorne?"

I nodded. "How is he? Can we see him?"

"He's stable, but I have concerns. What do you know of his background?"

"Gray used to be alpha of the Pine Ridge Pack," Reuben said. "They recently had a disagreement, so he's been out on his own for a few months."

"That would explain the injuries," the doctor said. "But it doesn't explain why he's not healing."

"He's a werewolf. They always heal fast," I said.

"Gray has a couple of busted ribs and injuries from the bobcat attack, and although they're serious, neither should be fatal. But the healing magic we're giving him is having minimal effect. It's as if his werewolf healing abilities are in hibernation, and his wolf doesn't care if he lives or dies."

Reuben sighed and scrubbed at the back of his neck with a hand. "He's given up. It can happen with lone werewolves when they're unaffiliated with a pack. When they lose that connection, they can lose the will to live. I've seen it happen before, and it's not a pretty sight. The wolves descend into violence, madness, and ultimately death."

I gripped his elbow, my stomach pinching in panic. "He needs to heal. We need Gray's confession. Otherwise, all of this would have been for nothing."

"You won't get anything out of him yet," the doctor said. "Even before sedation and strong pain relief, he was unresponsive."

I gulped down my fear. "He'll recover?"

The doctor's mouth twisted. "Maybe. He needs time."

"We don't have time! That man is a killer. We need his confession or an innocent man is getting charged with murder."

The doctor raised his eyebrows. "Gray can do no harm while he's in his current condition. Has the Magic Council been informed he's here? If he's wanted, they'll put a guard in his room."

I shook my head. The last hour had been a blur, and I'd not been thinking straight. "No, I haven't been in touch with them."

"I have," Reuben said. "Olympus will be here soon."

"Can I see Gray?" I asked the doctor.

"No visitors. You'll get nothing out of him, anyway. He hasn't opened his eyes since you brought him in." The doctor's expression grew grimly sad. "If he has any friends or family, inform them to come and say their goodbyes."

As the doctor walked away, I leaned against the wall and closed my eyes. I was convinced he'd framed Cole, but if Gray died, his secrets went with him, and there'd be no way I could get Cole free.

A hand settled on my shoulder, and I opened my eyes to see Reuben standing in front of me, his expression full of sadness. "If it was Gray, we'll get the answers we need."

Anger heated my cheeks. "He was coming with us! You shouldn't have attacked him."

Reuben dropped his gaze. "I panicked. I thought you'd let your guard down, and Gray thought you had too, because that's when he made his move."

I swiped a hand across my face. "I know, I know. Sorry. I didn't mean to snap, but if we lose Gray's confession, then I lose Cole. That's unacceptable."

"I'll lose him too. I don't want that. He's my best friend." Reuben ducked until his gaze was level with mine. "We'll make this work. I don't know how, but we'll figure something out. Cole is getting out of jail, and you will get married."

There was nothing we could do but wait, so while Reuben grabbed hot drinks, I slumped into a plastic seat. I was bone weary, and my head throbbed. I couldn't see a path to getting Cole back. All the times I'd complained about the wedding stress, I'd take it all back and double it to ensure our union went ahead.

"There you are!"

I lifted my head at the sound of Indigo's voice. I raised a weary hand as she sat beside me and looped an arm around my shoulders, pulling me in close. "Did you get the guy who framed Cole?"

"Yes, I think so. But I couldn't get him to confess. I told him I was taking him to the Magic Council, and he agreed to come with me."

"What went wrong? Olympus got a message from Reuben that you were here and you had an injured suspect. Gray didn't want to cooperate?"

I took a few minutes to fill her in on the unsatisfying events in the forest, and Reuben shifting into a bobcat and going all slashy and bitey.

"Why do these guys have to go all alpha and think we can't look after ourselves?" Indigo shook her head and sank back into the seat. "Olympus used to be like that. I've trained most of it out of him, but he still has his moments of puffing out his chest and going all gruff. The guy's not even half as powerful as I am. I could blast him into oblivion in a heartbeat, but it's like they have this gene, and they can't help themselves but rescue the damsel in distress."

My laugh came out tired, but at least it was there. "It's annoying but also adorable. I understand why Reuben reacted the way he did. I get the impression he feels almost as protective of me as Cole does. It's like their friendship bond encompasses me. Cole looks out for Serenity and the girls the same way."

Indigo smirked. "And I expect she finds it just as infuriating."

"She does! We've had more than one argument about it." Reuben returned carrying two mugs. "Sorry, Indigo. Have mine. I didn't know you were coming."

She shook her head and waved away his offer of coffee. "I'm good. I just wanted to check in and see how things were."

"Any updates on Cole?" Reuben settled in the seat on the other side of me.

"Slightly better news than the last time Olympus updated you. He passed on the message you left about having a new suspect. As a result, both councils will hold off from making a formal charge for another forty-eight hours."

A trickle of hope warmed me as I sipped the coffee. "But they still have the evidence that points to Cole, don't they?"

"They do. And that's not going anywhere unless you get Gray to confess that he set this all up," Indigo said. "How helpful has he been?"

"He's in silent mode," I said.

Indigo scowled. "Give me ten minutes alone in a room with him, and I'll get him to change his mind."

I patted her knee. "It's sweet of you to offer, but the doctor said Gray hasn't woken since we brought him here. He's having difficulty healing."

"It may be a shifter problem," Reuben said. "His werewolf side is grief-stricken over losing its pack. It may have decided enough is enough. If his wolf doesn't want to heal, no amount of magic will bring Gray back."

I closed my eyes, partly to stop the tears from falling, but also from sheer exhaustion. I'd been running on adrenaline and caffeine for too long, and I'd just slammed into a wall that refused to budge.

"That's enough." Indigo's voice jerked me awake.

"What is?" I looked around, my eyes bleary.

"For you. That's enough for you. You must be exhausted. And if you're able to fall asleep in one of these hard chairs, it shows the situation is dire." Indigo stood and held out her hands. "Come home with me. You can sleep in my spare room."

"No, I'm good. I want to wait here in case Gray wakes, so I can question him," I said.

"I'll stay," Reuben said. "I've had more sleep than you, and I've got a few spells up my sleeve that'll give me a boost if I get tired. You get some sleep. If anything changes, I'll let you know."

I opened my mouth to protest, but Indigo pressed a finger under my lower jaw and snapped it shut for me. "No debating. You're coming home with me, and I'm putting you to bed."

I was too tired to protest, and there was nothing I could do here, so after a sleepy goodbye to Reuben, we left the hospital. I just needed a few hours of sleep, and then I'd get straight back to it. Once Gray woke and talked, we'd get everything sorted. And by the end of the day, I'd have Cole back where he needed to be—right by my side, stressing over our wedding together.

Chapter 9

I jerked awake with a start, fleeing from the middle of an intense dream that involved Cole standing before the Magic Council and the Wolf Council, receiving a death sentence.

I rubbed my eyes and checked the time as my rapid heartbeat slowed. Twirling broomsticks! It was almost noon! Why had Indigo let me sleep in so long? I'd only wanted a few hours before heading back to the hospital.

After rolling out of bed, I grabbed my clothes and pulled them on. I was heading to the door when raised voices from downstairs reached me. I inched open the bedroom door and poked my head out. I recognized Olympus's voice and Indigo's, but there was an unfamiliar male voice mingled in too.

"Luna won't know anything about this." Indigo's tone was sharp, and the snap of her words hinted she was close to losing her temper.

"It's crucial I talk to her," the unfamiliar male voice said.

"She's been here all night," Indigo said. "Before that, she was doing your job by chasing the actual suspects in this murder investigation."

"Gideon, Indigo's right," Olympus said. "Luna won't have anything to tell you. And she needs to rest."

"As much as I respect your position in the Magic Council, Olympus, you're married to one of Luna's best friends."

"You're saying you don't trust us?" There was a harsh edge to Olympus's words.

I crept to the top of the stairs, holding my breath as I continued to listen. Whoever this Gideon was, it sounded like he'd brought up accusations that involved me and my friends.

"I'm saying you're not impartial in this investigation. There have been rumors you may have helped," Gideon said.

"Take that back! My husband is always on the right side of the law. He wouldn't help a criminal escape," Indigo said.

"So why is Cole's cell empty?" Gideon asked.

The air whooshed from my lips. Cole had escaped? I descended the stairs then stopped. Where was he? If he'd gotten free, he'd find me. He must be hiding close by.

"Be careful what you say next," Olympus growled out. "And if you want to make this an official complaint, go through the proper channels rather than throwing out veiled threats and turning up here uninvited and making demands."

"You'd do the same if you were in charge of this investigation," Gideon said. "Luna must know something about the escape. Cole's a werewolf, and she's his mate. He'd come for her before fleeing the village. Werewolves never abandon their mates."

My heart thundered loudly. I pressed a hand against it, worried it would give me away. Gideon was right. If Cole had gotten out of his cell, he wouldn't leave me behind.

As the arguing continued, I tiptoed down the rest of the stairs. I crept along the hallway to the back door, grateful to find it unlocked. I opened it swiftly, eased it closed behind me, and took in a deep breath of icy air. Then I sniffed hard.

Spending most of my time with a werewolf meant I'd picked up odd habits, one of which was using my sense of smell more often. Cole was always sniffing things out. At first, I'd found it weird—that guy loved nothing more than burying his nose into my hair and sniffing. But smell tells you a lot about a person. Right now, all I wanted to do was pick up Cole's scent.

But I picked up nothing. And in front of me, a thick layer of snow, which must have been falling while I slept, covered any tracks.

In the distance, storm clouds piled one on top of the other, representing my chaotic mood as I kept sniffing.

"Where are you? You'd never leave me. Show yourself." I whispered his name several times. Werewolves had great hearing, and if Cole was looking for me, he'd find me.

I glanced over my shoulder, aware I was short on time. With the Magic Council wanting answers as to where Cole had gone, Olympus and Indigo would only be able to hold Gideon off for so long.

Action was needed. I hurried away from the house but slowed as movement in nearby trees caught my eye. It was Cole! I broke into a run, joy firing through me. I barely noticed how cold it was without my coat on as I flung myself into his arms. We held each other, not speaking, as he gently moved me back into the trees and out of sight of the house.

"I knew you'd come for me," I finally said, looking up at him with tears in my eyes.

"Of course. I'd never leave you." His body radiated with tension as his gaze darted around. His voice sounded rough, suggesting he'd been yelling. Most likely arguing with members of the Magic Council.

"Why did you run? The Magic Council is at Indigo's house, looking for answers. As soon as I heard what happened, I left."

"I figured you would," he said. "That's why I've been watching the house."

"So? How did you break out of the cell? Olympus didn't help you, did he?"

Cole shook his head. "I did it on my own. I waited until the right moment and broke through the magic."

I furrowed my brow. "You didn't have any help?"

"There's no time to explain. No one listened when I told them I was innocent. They've already made up their minds. If I'd stayed in that cell, my life would have been over."

"Mine, too. So, what do we do? Do you know who framed you?" Cole's hands were cold on my skin, and his usually delicious scent was absent. Spending all that time in the cell hadn't done him any good.

"I know who's behind this," Cole growled out. "We're going to get the truth out of him."

Relief whacked into me, and I sagged against him. "How did you work it out?"

"I'll tell you later. Let's go. I'll carry you."

"Wait! This is going too fast. I need answers."

"We can talk while I run. We have little time. Like you said, the Magic Council is already on my back. I hoped they wouldn't notice me gone so quickly, but they must have shown up to move me somewhere more secure. Which means only one thing."

"What?"

"They're ready to pass sentence. We have to act now."

I gulped down horror at the thought of Cole being charged with murder. "I'll translocate us. That'll be quicker."

"No, I need to move. You know how tetchy I get when I've been trapped inside. Too much energy." He rubbed his forehead. "I don't feel so good after being in a cell."

"You sound like you're getting a cold." I nodded slowly. When Cole was penned up for too long, he got super grumpy. "How far are we going?"

"To the next village." Cole scooped me into his arms and took off. He ran at a slower pace than usual, his grip on me a little too tight to be comfortable.

"It's okay. I know this is a stressful situation, but we'll work this out. Once we get this guy, we'll make him confess, and everything will go back to normal. The only stress we'll have to deal with is wedding stress."

Cole grunted. "Let's hope it's that simple."

I was silent for a moment, trying to relax now I was back with Cole, but I couldn't settle into his arms like I usually did. "Are you going to tell me who it is?"

"You don't need the details."

"I want them. Please, Cole. We're in this together. You don't need to protect me from the truth."

He was quiet for a long time as we made our way through the trees. "Zodiac Black."

"The guy who gifted us the knife set you hated?"

"Zodiac has serious issues over werewolf ranks. He's wanted his family at the top for decades."

"Why him?"

"It's his style. He's a sly werewolf. And we tussled recently."

"You never told me."

"It was nothing. Typical werewolf bluff. He surprised me, and we fought. That must have been when he got my blood to plant at the murder scene."

I sighed. "Cole, we promised each other no more secrets. After everything that happened when we first met, we agreed total honesty was the only way our relationship could work."

"Sure, I remember, but the fight meant nothing. At least, I didn't think it did. But then I didn't know the guy was getting evidence to frame me and ruin my life."

"You're sure it was Zodiac?"

"It's got to be him. Thanks to you and Reuben looking into suspects, everyone else has been ruled out."

I jolted in Cole's arms and had to cling to his neck as he leaped over a fallen tree. "Have you spoken to Reuben? Does he know what you're planning?"

"No, and the fewer people who know I've escaped, the better. Olympus kept me up-to-date with the investigation, though. I know about what happened when you confronted Gray. That was risky. The guy is unstable."

"I really thought it was him," I said. "When we found him and he was so angry, I put the pieces together, and they showed me Gray framed you. How did I get it so wrong?" I asked.

"I doubt you'll ever know. From what I heard, Gray's not waking up anytime soon."

"Reuben acted rashly. I wish he hadn't attacked Gray."

Cole slowed his pace and shifted his hold on me. "He regrets it, but I support him. We look out for each other. We're brothers in all but blood."

"I know."

"He's been taking good care of you?"

"Yes. He's been helpful," I said. "You should get him involved in what we're doing. He could be useful."

"If I had the time to spare, I'd get more support, but I don't want the Magic Council stomping over everything, and Zodiac fleeing before I've confronted him." Cole's breathing was labored, and his throat sounded scratchy.

"Are you okay? You must have taken a whack from the magic when you escaped from your cell. If you need to take a break, I don't mind."

"I reckon I did. And they didn't exactly give me werewolf-sized rations when I was in there." His smile was strained.

We were in the middle of the woods, so there was nothing I could do about feeding Cole. I usually carried jerky and granola bars to keep my greedy werewolf fiancé from getting hangry, but I'd left the house with nothing in my pockets. "Stop. Put me down. You need to rest."

"Just for a minute." Cole dropped me to my feet and then leaned over, taking in a few deep breaths, his hands on his knees.

"Are you sure you're not injured?" I peered at him with concern. The only time I'd ever seen Cole so weak was after I'd accidentally broken his leg when he'd chased me around the Witch Haven Library and an enormous wooden bookcase had fallen on him.

He waved away my concern. "I'm good."

I let him rest for a few minutes while I shivered, leaning against a dead tree. "My idea to elope sounds appealing right about now, huh? We wouldn't have been in Witch Haven at the time of the murder."

"Elope! Morrigan would rip out our hearts if we even thought about it."

I arched an eyebrow. "So much for you being prepared to do anything as long as it made me happy."

Cole stood and stared at me for several seconds. "Sorry, of course. We should have eloped. Then we wouldn't be in this mess."

"I don't mind being in the middle of this mess, as long as I'm with you."

"It'll be over soon." Cole took hold of my hand. "Maybe we could use some of your magic. We need to go to East Wicken West. You know the place?"

"Sure. I'll get us there." I stood on my tiptoes and kissed him. "You don't always have to be the one looking after me."

He grumbled to himself. "That's my job."

"It's our job to take care of each other. Hold on tight." I swirled a translocation spell around us. Instead of feeling Cole's usual strength and determination mingling with my power, I sensed his exhaustion and a hint of fear. Zodiac Black must be a monster if Cole was concerned about confronting him.

We arrived in East Wicken West, and I took in our surroundings. We were on a quiet, straight road, with large yards and detached dwellings on either side. Snow covered the ground, and only a single set of prints marred the pristine white.

"That's the place." Cole pointed out a house set back from the road, surrounded by hedging, so it was impossible to see if anyone was looking at us from inside.

I squeezed his hand, my pulse pounding with a determined thrum. "Let's finish this, and then we're getting married."

Chapter 10

We walked quietly but with purpose toward the house. Daylight was already fading, partly because of the storm clouds whirling overhead.

"There are no lights on inside," I murmured. "Maybe no one's home."

"I don't see any vehicles. Let's take a closer look," Cole said.

"Maybe Zodiac knows you're coming for him. He could have heard you'd escaped from the Magic Council. He must realize you'd confront him the second you could."

"I wouldn't put it past him to have a mole inside the Magic Council," Cole said. "He's made a lot of money by deceiving people and exploiting their secrets. He has to get that information from somewhere."

"That's how you came to know him?" I asked. "You negotiated a dispute he was involved in?"

"Something like that. But I always keep an eye on the werewolves who don't play by the rules. They're the ones who cause the most trouble for other packs. Zodiac has been on my radar for a long time, and when I learned I'd been framed for murder, his name was at the top of the list of wolves who could have done it."

"Why didn't you tell me when I came to see you? I could have worked with Olympus and Reuben to get a confession out of Zodiac."

"That's not how he operates. And if we'd played by the rules, Zodiac would have been long gone. The first hint of trouble and he flees. He never stays and fights. He wins by stealth and trickery. There's nothing worse than a sneaky werewolf."

"That must make him unpopular."

"He's trodden on plenty of paws over the decades. And he's always resented my family for playing fair and staying at the top." Cole was squeezing my hand so hard that my fingers were losing feeling, but I kept my grip tight in a show of support.

Unease swirled through me as we drew close to the house. It was huge. There could be dozens of werewolves hiding inside. "Let's call in backup. I can get Indigo, Storm, and Odessa here. They know how to bend the rules when necessary."

"We won't need them. As long as we're together, nothing can mess with us." Cole stopped walking and turned to me. "I'll go in alone. I want you to stay out of sight."

"No! You need me. Zodiac could have his entire pack in there." I stared at the gloomy windows that could hide any number of attackers.

"Zodiac moves between packs, and he has few close allies. The only help he'll have is hired thugs."

"Now I'm worried! He doesn't sound stupid, so he won't want to face you alone."

"Luna, please. Do as I tell you. I don't want you getting injured."

I huffed out my frustration. "I can look after myself."

"But you don't have to because you've got me. Now, behave." Cole growled softly. "I'm serious. You're my weakness. If he grabs you, there'll be nothing I can do. I may as well have stayed in that cell and accepted my fate."

My brow furrowed. "You've never called me your weakness before. We're a team. We help each other. We make each other stronger. And if Zodiac messes with me, I'll slam a lightning bolt his way."

Cole sighed. "Just do this for me. This one time. If you're not there to distract me, it won't be a problem. I'll make this right. I know I can."

I glared at him for several silent seconds, and if it weren't for the hint of desperation in his voice, I'd have kept arguing. It wasn't the first time we'd had this argument about him being overprotective, and I doubted it would be the last, but now wasn't the time to bring that up. "I'll stay outside. But in five minutes, I'm coming in."

"Give me at least ten." Cole pressed a quick kiss to my cheek then ran around the side of the house and out of sight.

My gut churned. This felt wrong. What was the point of bringing me here if I couldn't help Cole take down the guy who'd framed him for murder and almost ruined our wedding?

I had to follow him and make sure he did nothing reckless. I crept out from behind the bush we'd been using as cover and tiptoed around the edge of the house. I needed to be careful. If Cole heard me, he'd send me right back.

I was just in time to see him go through an unlocked back entrance. I dashed to the door then followed his path as he passed windows, heading further into the house and into a single-story extension at the back. Two windows along, I froze. A tall, dark-skinned guy, solidly built and muscled, stood with his back to the window behind a desk. Cole stood in the doorway, facing him. I ducked, hoping he hadn't seen me.

Despite the freezing conditions, the window was open a crack. You had to love werewolves and their desire for fresh air. I lifted as high as I could without revealing myself and strained to listen.

"You're looking good," Zodiac said. "And I didn't expect to see you so soon. You must be eager to get the job done." He sounded remarkably calm for someone who must realize he was facing a world of hurt if he didn't answer for what he'd done to Cole.

"I would have been here sooner, but I got delayed."

I lifted my eyebrows. Delayed! I'd hardly call it that.

"Care for a drink?" Zodiac asked.

There was no reply, but then I heard the crack of two beer bottles being opened. "Take it. It won't kill you."

"I didn't come here to celebrate." Cole's tone was sharp. "You know what I want."

"One beer. For old times' sake. This has been a long time coming, so surely, I deserve it," Zodiac said.

His last beer as a free man. I gritted my teeth. I so wanted to be beside Cole, staring this guy in the face and telling him exactly what I thought of him.

There were a few seconds of silence then a beer bottle slammed down.

"Is there something you want to tell me?" Zodiac asked. "Your thunderous expression suggests a problem. Changed your mind about coming here?"

"I need your assurances. I have to know they're safe before anything else happens."

My stomach flipped. What were they talking about? Why wasn't Cole confronting Zodiac and forcing a confession out of him? And Zodiac didn't seem the least bit surprised Cole was standing in his study.

"You have my word," Zodiac said.

"That's not enough," Cole growled. "I know the kind of deals you make. You double and triple-cross people within the blink of an eye if it serves you."

I risked a glance through the window. Zodiac had moved to the end of his desk, and Cole stood at the other side. They were facing each other, legs apart and chests out, werewolf posturing.

Zodiac took a sip from his beer bottle. "Sometimes, I bend the rules to get what I desire. We both know werewolves can be tricky. Some of the packs follow the old ways. Some have modernized, some are a hybrid mix, and some of them get strange ideas in their heads about marrying witches. What a blow to the Kellam bloodline."

"Luna's an incredible witch."

I nodded. I was more than willing to zap Zodiac with a spell to knock sense into him and stop him from making dumb comments. And he must have a death wish, insulting me in front of Cole.

"I have nothing against witches. Live and let live. If Luna is a perfect match, then my blessing is given," Zodiac said. "My point was, I've had to adapt to thrive in the werewolf community."

Cole picked up his beer and slugged some back. He slammed it down again. I stared at him then refocused on Zodiac. There was something unsettling about this situation. Something about this whole thing that twisted my gut.

"Tell me where they are," Cole said.

"It wounds me that my word isn't enough for you." Zodiac pulled a phone from the back pocket of his jeans, scrolled through it, and then handed it to Cole.

He stared at it, flicking through what must be messages or images.

"They were taken an hour ago. As you can see, everyone is well," Zodiac said.

"Are they here? On the premises?"

Who was Cole talking about? Why wasn't he talking about the murder?

"I'm not stupid enough to keep them that close. They're safe, warm, and well-guarded. We can make the trade as soon as you like," Zodiac said.

Cole grabbed the bottle again. And that was when it hit me. He was using his right hand. Cole was one of the most left-handed people I knew. He was left dominant in everything, from his eyes to his feet. I gulped as the realization hit me harder than an ice shard in the heart.

Cole's sharpness toward me when I tried to help, his lack of familiar scent, his odd-sounding voice, and his unusually formal affection. When we were together, Cole couldn't keep his hands off me.

And the final clue. When we'd reunited, Cole hadn't sniffed me once.

I stared with an open mouth through the window. Why was Reuben pretending to be Cole?

Chapter 11

Seconds passed, and I was too shocked even to breathe. Reuben was behind this. He'd deceived us all. But why? I knew how steadfast he was. Cole trusted him with everything. He even trusted me with him. Reuben was one of the few men Cole didn't mind me spending time with because he knew how loyal he was.

I shuffled down and hunched against the wall, barely noticing the cold biting into me. What had gone wrong? Why was Reuben doing a deal with Zodiac? What were they making a deal about?

My thoughts were so scrambled that my body had a hard time functioning. I hadn't taken a breath for almost a minute, and I was dizzy with panic and fear. If Reuben was impersonating Cole, did that mean he'd killed Cole? Cole would have been vulnerable, trapped in a cell.

I shook my head. No, the magic barrier surrounding Cole's cell was strong. It would be hard for anyone to injure him. But not impossible. Reuben could have gotten in to see Cole, maybe convinced Olympus that he should talk to him, and then killed him.

My hand went to my eyes, and I struck away a rogue tear. My bond with Cole ran deep. He wasn't dead. I'd feel it if he was gone. Our souls were entwined. If one of us broke, so would the other.

"Let's get something to eat before we make the final plans." Zodiac's voice sounded far away from the window.

"I'm here to make a deal, not break bread with you."

"Your stomach just growled. I know how much energy you burn through using your illusion magic," Zodiac said.

Even though I needed no more evidence, that confirmed my suspicions. Zodiac knew this wasn't Cole he was talking to.

"Ten minutes! Or don't you think your little witch will behave herself that long?" Zodiac asked.

"Don't underestimate Luna."

"I never would. That's why she's a part of this deal." Zodiac chuckled. "Just think how Cole will react when he knows she's mine."

I clenched my fists. There was no way in the seven seals of hell I'd have anything to do with this treacherous werewolf. When I was done with him, I was taking down Reuben, too. Zodiac must have offered him one heck of a deal to betray his oldest friend, and that was unforgivable.

My calves strained from crouching as I looked back in the window. Zodiac had led the fake Cole to the door and had an arm slung around his shoulders. He opened the door and gestured for Reuben to walk through.

After a moment of hesitation, Reuben complied and walked out. Zodiac chuckled again and followed him.

I did the same, sneaking along and checking in windows to see which direction they were going. I reached the back of the house and crouched again, inching along until I arrived at the kitchen. There they were. Reuben remained standing while Zodiac looked in the fridge. They were talking, but with no windows open, I couldn't hear their conversation.

My heart pounded, a frantic rhythm matching the chaos in my mind. Reuben had deceived us all. The realization hit me like a thrashing dragon's tail. How could I have been so blind?

Fear surged through my veins, a wild current threatening to consume me. Images of Cole, vulnerable and trapped, flashed before my eyes. I couldn't bear the thought of him in danger, alone and defenseless. Panic surged within me, urging me to act, to find him, to save him. My hands trembled uncontrollably as I fought to steady myself. Every instinct screamed at me to confront Zodiac and Reuben, to unleash my fury upon them.

But amidst the turmoil, a glimmer of rationality urged caution. I had to be strategic, gather my allies, and plan the next move carefully. Cole's fate and our happily ever after rested on the choices I was about to make.

The air heated around me, and Earl plopped into the snow, making a grunt of disgust as he landed. He looked up at me and flicked snow off one paw. "What's the problem?"

I stared at him then glanced back at the house. "How did you know I was here?"

He rolled his eyes. "You're still terrible at this witch familiar bond thing we've got going on. But in case you've forgotten, when you're in trouble, my fine feline senses trigger."

"I know they do! But you usually ignore those pings and leave me to muddle through."

"Yeah, well, we've both been going through changes. What is this place?" Earl flicked more snow off his ears and looked at the house. "Stinks like werewolves."

I was glad he was here. After so many years of having a distorted familiar bond with Earl because of my magic struggles, I still forgot I had a solid, ride-or-die ally by my side if ever I needed one. And did I need one now.

"I know who framed Cole," I said. "And he's inside this house."

Earl jumped onto the window ledge, making me gasp. "Relax. If they notice me, they'll just see your average cat doing what cats love to do."

"Zodiac Black is in there, along with Reuben."

"I see some muscled dude. That's Zodiac?"

I nodded.

"He's talking to Cole! How did he get here?"

"That's not Cole," I hissed. "That's Reuben disguising himself as Cole. He set this whole thing up."

"Are you sure that's not Cole? I heard he escaped."

"I don't think he escaped. Reuben did something to Cole and is now disguised as him. He's working with Zodiac."

Earl twitched his whiskers. "What are you gonna do about that?"

The shock of the situation still made my heart pound unsteadily, but I pushed the feelings to one side. "I need you to go back to Witch Haven and tell the others to look for Cole. The real Cole. Reuben won't have been able to move him far, but I have to make sure he's okay."

"I can do that. What about you? You're confronting this werewolf and Reuben alone?"

"No. After you've done that, I need you to come back and help me."

"Got it. Do nothing dumb while I'm gone." Earl hopped off the window ledge and vanished mid-jump.

While I waited for him, I closed my eyes and opened my magic. I touched the silver wolf I always wore around my neck. It was the first gift Cole had ever given me, and it would help me locate him using a spell.

I had no map as a reference point, so I used my hands, pointing to where Witch Haven was on my left index finger and then situating Zodiac's house on my other palm below my middle finger. That would give me an idea of where Cole was.

The spell bounced around, a tiny bright dot zooming around my palms. It stopped on top of Zodiac's house then pinged back to Witch Haven. This ping-ponging continued, the spell muddled by Reuben's powerful illusion magic.

I snapped my hands shut. Reuben was the most powerful mage I'd ever met, so my magic was confused because his illusion was so effective. But it wasn't effective enough to fool me.

A vicious wind wrapped around me, sending a shiver down to my bones. I peeked through the window. Zodiac was finishing a sandwich while Reuben drank his beer.

Earl reappeared in a flash of magic and landed in my lap. "Olympus has gone to check the cells for any signs of a fight, and Indigo, Storm, and Odessa are hunting Witch Haven. They tried a location spell but couldn't get a fix on Cole. There's something in the village that links to him, though. They're going there first to check it out. And I brought back-up."

I looked around. "Who'd you bring?"

"Nugget, Russell, and Hilda are waiting in the wings. Indigo super-sized them before sending them your way. If you need help when you confront Zodiac and Reuben, they'll be there."

"There's no time like the present to confront these asshats." I primed my magic, sparks of lightning shooting from my fingertips. Earl hopped onto my shoulder as I strode to the back door. This situation called for a flare of dramatics to knock the werewolf and his subservient illusion mage down a peg or two. I thrust out my hands and blasted the door with a spell, causing it to slam open.

Zodiac froze, a beer bottle half raised to his lips.

Reuben stared at me. "Luna! What are you doing? I told you to wait outside."

"Don't speak to me like we're friends." I stamped into the kitchen, ensuring they saw my magic was ready to fly if they made a move I didn't like the look of.

Zodiac recovered quickly. He sipped on his beer then set it down. "You're welcome to join us. It's time I got to know you better, anyway."

"There's nothing you need to know about me. I know you're behind this. You framed Cole for murder."

Reuben rushed over and tried to grab hold of my elbow, but I dodged away from him. "I know this is stressful, but I've got a handle on things."

I snarled at him. "I know who you are. Your illusion magic is good, but you can't deceive me."

A roll of thunder made the glasses in the cabinet chink together, and a flurry of snow slammed against the windows.

"The game's up." Zodiac's tone was infuriatingly smug. "It was fun while it lasted."

"No! The deal is still on," Reuben said. "Luna, you can't interfere. I won't allow it."

"It's that kind of talk that convinced me there was no way you could be Cole," I said. "He never orders me around. He has a healthy respect for women."

"I respect women. Especially ones as pretty as you," Zodiac said. "You're not a werewolf, but you'll be the perfect fit in my new pack."

A crack of lightning hit a chimney stack, and the building shook.

"Get control of your woman," Zodiac snarled. "She doesn't know her place."

I snarled back. "I know your place is behind bars."

My heart raced as Zodiac lunged at me. Earl launched off my shoulder, and I shot magic at him, causing him to super-size as he smashed into Zodiac. They fell to the floor in a bundle of flying fur and snarls as Zodiac shifted into a werewolf.

I swiftly raised my hands and turned on Reuben, summoning a swirling vortex of wind. The gusts howled around us, and my eyes blazed with determination as I focused my magic on Cole's betrayer.

Reuben had a spell swirling in his palms, his eyes full of regret. "Luna, I'm sorry."

"So am I." Dark clouds materialized above us, crackling with thunder. With a flick of my wrist, lightning streaked toward Reuben. He dodged the bolts with uncanny agility.

Earl screeched, his sharp fangs glinting as he lunged at Zodiac, claws slashing through the air. Zodiac fought back fiercely, teeth gnashing, but Earl's ferocity matched him, even though he was half his size.

Reuben unleashed an illusion at me, casting deceptive images and mirages that danced around the kitchen. Shadows contorted, confusing my senses. Summoning my power, I commanded the elements, conjuring a torrential rainstorm within the kitchen, water cascading from the ceiling and forming a protective shield around me. The room became a temper, with water swirling and lightning flashing within its confines.

With a primal howl, Zodiac broke through the storm defense, his vicious claws scoring my arm. Pain surged through me, but I retaliated with a blast of heat, causing the water around Zodiac to boil and scald. His agonized howls echoed through the kitchen, growing when Earl jumped on his back and took him down again.

My spells collided with Reuben's illusions, shattering his power and sending shockwaves through the room.

"Luna! Stop. This deal could work out in your favor. Let me explain." Reuben staggered back, his face sweaty and his eyes wide. "You've had doubts about marrying Cole. There are other options. Other packs who'd take you."

I slammed a fierce blast of icy rain at him. "Liar! And I'd never choose to join with an insane, murderous werewolf like Zodiac!"

"I had to do this." He blasted out the illusion of a dragon, smoke swirling around and blinding me.

I channeled the full force of my weather magic, summoning a mighty tornado, its furious winds tearing through the kitchen, uprooting furniture and shattering windows.

Reuben yelped, dropped to the floor, his illusions fading as he held his head.

As the storm subsided and the kitchen fell silent, I marched to Reuben and pinned him to the ground with a shimmering bolt of light. "What does Zodiac have on you to make you turn on Cole?"

Reuben stared at Zodiac, his jaw wobbling and tears in his eyes.

Zodiac shifted back into human form. "Don't say a word," he snarled at Reuben from his prone position on the floor. Earl's fangs were wrapped around his throat, and his giant murder mittens pinned Zodiac's arms. "You know what'll happen if you do."

Reuben's panicked gaze widened. "You gave me your word."

Zodiac smirked. "And as you so adeptly put it, my word means nothing."

I kept a firm grip on Reuben, checking Earl still had Zodiac trapped. "I overheard you. Has Zodiac got someone you care about?"

"Don't do it, man," Zodiac said. "One word from me, and this will all be over. You'll never see them again. And you'll go crazy wondering what we did to them."

I sucked in a breath. "He's taken Serenity, hasn't he? That's why she was a no-show with the girls at the wedding prep."

Reuben closed his eyes and nodded. "A pack of unruly werewolves grabbed her. They busted into our home and took Serenity and our daughters. I had no choice but to help Zodiac, or he'd have killed them."

"The second I get free, they're dead." Zodiac's tone was ice-laced. "And so are you. Both of you."

A tear trickled out of the side of Reuben's eye. "I'm sorry, Luna. I had no choice but to betray Cole. I'd do anything to keep my family safe."

"You should have trusted Cole enough to tell him what was going on. We could have worked together to figure out how to defeat Zodiac and keep your family safe."

"I panicked! Zodiac gave me a deadline and said I was being watched. I couldn't risk anyone finding out I'd confided in Cole."

Although I was sorry Reuben was going through this, I couldn't forgive him for what he'd done. "Get on your feet. You make any sudden moves, and I'll knock you into next week." I eased off Reuben and pulled back my magic. He sagged forward, the fight gone from him. I trapped his hands so he couldn't cast more illusion magic then turned to Zodiac. "It's time you confessed."

"Reuben has already heard my confession." Zodiac smirked. "He knows what'll happen to his family now he's proven himself unreliable."

"Serenity and the children will be safe." I took a step toward Zodiac. "You killed someone to ruin our lives."

"It was no less than Cole deserved." Zodiac's top lip curled. "He ruined me when he favored another werewolf in a deal, and I'm sure he had no sleepless nights over it. It's unfortunate you got in the way, but since you're his mate, there was no option but to involve you. You're a handy bargaining chip to add to the arrangement."

I cocked my head. "This trade you arranged with Reuben involved me?"

"It's hard to ignore such potential. I'm gathering a new pack, but I needed something unique. Something to make me stand out and stop anyone from making a power grab. With a powerful elemental witch to do my bidding, every wolf would have thought twice before making a move."

"You'd never have convinced me to join you," I said.

Zodiac sucked air through his teeth. "Maybe you'd have been broken enough by your mate's loss to let loose that witch power for me to use however I liked. You'd have been convinced Cole was a disloyal, cold-blooded killer. Your heart would shatter, and you'd have been lost."

"Not lost enough to join you. You're coming with me to the Magic Council, and I'm telling them everything."

"That's not how this will work." Zodiac tipped back his head and howled. The bone-shuddering noise echoed around the kitchen, followed a few seconds later by heavy paw thuds. Six werewolves piled into the room, their amber eyes flashing and their teeth bared.

"Now, tell your creature to let me go, unless he wants to become my pack's next meal," Zodiac said.

Earl's hackles lifted, and he growled menacingly, but one giant familiar was no match against a pack of fierce werewolves.

"Let Zodiac go," I said to Earl.

Earl hissed, but after a few seconds of eyeballing Zodiac, he backed off and slunk over to join me.

Zodiac slid away and stood. He checked his injuries then shrugged. He looked at me, but his gaze settled on Reuben. "Shame. We had something good going, but you blew it because you couldn't keep your dumb mouth shut."

A strangled sob came out of Reuben as he cowered on the floor. "Please, I'll do anything. Don't kill my family. They're my whole world."

"Then it's time you broadened your horizons." Zodiac pulled out his phone. "Say goodbye to your family."

I blasted a lightning bolt that smashed the phone from his hand, and it shattered on the floor.

Zodiac growled at me. "Stupid witch. You can't beat me. Not on your own. You keep fighting me, and you'll only make things worse for yourself."

"I never expected to beat you on my own." I looked at Earl and winked. He tipped back his head and let out an impressive cat wail, besting the werewolf howls, the noise full of summoning magic.

Zodiac smirked. "Is that supposed to scare me?"

I glanced out the window and grinned sharply. "No, but this will."

Hilda exploded through the glass in her giant, hairy, fangtastic spider form, and landed on Zodiac's head.

Chapter 12

Sparks flew and magic crackled in the air as a battle erupted within the kitchen. Zodiac howled his rage as Hilda sank her fangs into his arm.

A werewolf lunged, his feral form towering over me. I conjured a blast of lightning to deflect his attack, narrowly evading his razor-sharp claws.

In the whirlwind of chaos, Nugget appeared in the window. His enormous black-furred form descended upon the other werewolves, his fangs and murder mittens primed for attack. The room trembled as the werewolves howled their protests and bounced off walls to avoid his magically enhanced blows.

Earl leaped into the fray, his claws slashing at the werewolves' vulnerable underbellies. With every swift movement, he left deep gashes in their fur as he tag-teamed with Nugget to maximize confusion and hit the wolves where it hurt.

Russell swooped in next, his sharp beak pecking at the werewolves and zooming around Reuben, who stayed in one corner, his eyes wide with horror.

I flung spells, whacking into the wolves whenever they threatened any of the familiars, but these awesome, wonderful creatures were fearless and not afraid to tackle these overgrown pups with bad attitudes.

Hilda's squeal had me wheeling, and I turned to see her hit the wall. Zodiac reared up. He snarled at me and then shifted into his werewolf form.

Earl leaped onto his back, his claws digging deep into the werewolf's thick fur. Zodiac wailed in pain, attempting to shake off the determined feline, but Earl clung on, refusing to let go.

Zodiac, fueled by fury, roared at his werewolves to destroy us, but the combined efforts of my magic and the familiars' blistering attack meant they were outmaneuvered at every turn. My magic pulsated with raw elemental energy, every spell striking a direct hit and slowing them down, making them pause before striking another blow.

Two of the werewolves turned tail and dashed from the kitchen, helping to even the numbers. I channeled the chaotic power within me, harnessing the elements to their full extent. An explosive surge of magic burst out of me, engulfing the kitchen in a dazzling display. Fire, water, wind, and earth spiraled around me, knocking aside all attacks and flattening our enemy.

The remaining werewolves cowered, their strength sapped, while Reuben was curled into a ball on the floor, his illusions shattered, revealing his true form.

With a heaving breath, I surveyed the aftermath. The once tidy kitchen bore the scars of the fierce clash, its walls scorched and singed, the atmosphere heavy with the remnants of magic and bloodlust. I looked around, relieved to see Earl, Nugget, Russell, and Hilda all in one piece as they guarded the werewolves and Reuben.

"Luna!" A familiar and welcome voice pierced through me. Cole staggered through the back door, bloody and bruised.

My heart flipped at the sight of him. "Earl, hold Zodiac. If he makes a move, bite him. Hard."

Earl grabbed the barely conscious Zodiac by the throat and pinned him to the ground before sitting on his head.

I ran to Cole and wrapped my arms around him. His wonderfully familiar scent filled my nose, and relief flooded my senses. "I knew you were alive."

"Barely," he wheezed out. "I don't feel so good."

I pulled back and stared into his eyes. His pupils were scarily dilated, and his breathing labored. "What did you do to him?" I snapped at Zodiac.

Zodiac shifted back into human form. "I didn't touch him. It was his best friend who got him out of the cell. Isn't that right, Reuben?"

Reuben lifted his head, and the sadness in his gaze would have broken my heart at any other time. "I had to. Zodiac has Serenity and the girls. And you won't die. I gave you a potion to slow you down. Once it's out of your system, you'll be fine. No lasting damage."

Cole growled softly as he held me to his side. "I remember you coming to my cell. You gave me something to drink. That's the last thing I recall."

"You used your illusion magic to convince the guards to open the cell?" I asked Reuben.

He lowered his gaze. "They were easy to fool, but I had some trouble with that big cat. He recognized my scent, but I distracted him with his toys. I got Cole out, and we hid him while I came for my girls."

"How did you get so beaten up?" I asked Cole.

He shook his head. "I woke like this. Your friends found me locked in a shed."

"I had help from Zodiac's werewolves," Reuben said. "They'd been told to teach Cole a lesson. They hit him while he was unconscious."

"Cowards," I spat at the werewolves. I turned back to Cole. "I know what happened. Zodiac is behind this. He forced Reuben to work for him."

"It's true that Zodiac has your family?" Cole asked Reuben, the pain of betrayal shimmering in his eyes.

Reuben nodded. "I'd never have done this if he hadn't taken what was most precious to me. You must understand. If this happened to Luna, you'd have moved heaven and earth to get her back and betray anyone you had to."

Cole rested his forehead against mine. "He's right, but I still don't like it."

"Neither do I. But Serenity and the girls are safe. I stopped Zodiac from making a call to whoever has them."

"I may not have made the call, but we're on a deadline. If they don't hear from me soon, it'll be game over." Zodiac chuckled darkly. "Reuben will have lost everything and gained nothing. He's lost his family, his best friend, and all credibility when word gets out that he can't be trusted. And the Magic Council and Werewolf Council will still come for you, Cole, since my eyewitness saw you kill. And then there's your blood at the scene. You're a guilty werewolf."

"If I'm going to lose everything, then I may as well tell the truth about the witness and the planted evidence," Reuben said.

Zodiac snarled at him. "Do it, and I'll hunt you down and destroy you."

"I'd welcome it. If you take everything I love, you'll leave me with nothing to fight for. The only thing I'll have left is to tell the world the truth. I imagine no werewolf will join a pack run by an alpha who can't be trusted and who breaks his word. An alpha who slaughters women and children. Let's reveal the monster you truly are."

Although Reuben had done Cole and me a great wrong, I admired him. He was close to losing everything he loved, but he was standing up to this vicious bully. I couldn't forgive him now, but maybe in time, I would.

Earl howled and flailed as Zodiac slammed a hand against his side. Russell shot toward Zodiac, but he couldn't catch him as he flung himself at Reuben, his jaw distorted, sharp fangs aimed at his head.

I spun away from Cole, flinging my arms out and sending an epic blast of magic through the kitchen. Everyone was flipped off their feet, including me, but my spell's power focused on Zodiac, smashing him into the wall before he could savage Reuben.

I kept him pinned as I dashed to Reuben, who lay stunned on his back. "Anything broken?"

He blinked twice. "No. He didn't get me. Thanks, Luna."

"Thank me later once we get your family back." My gaze flashed around the room. "Earl?"

He groaned as he rolled out from under the shattered kitchen table. "I'll live. Maybe. You do your thing while I silently die."

"Don't be so dramatic." Nugget crawled over to him. "There's barely a scratch on you."

Hilda spun down from the ceiling on a giant string of shimmering webbing. "We'll keep him safe."

I turned and glared at Zodiac. I had dozens of reasons to destroy this werewolf, but as much as I longed to end his life, he'd live, so he could pay for the crimes he'd committed. And I needed him alive so he would confess and clear Cole's name.

Cole rested a warm, safe hand on my shoulder. "That's my girl. My fierce, brilliant, perfect mate."

I drew in a breath, the hurricane of rage and revenge inside me fading. Everyone and everything I loved was safe once more.

"You need a helping paw to deal with that jerk?" Earl limped over and head-butted my calf.

"Always. And I know I've got it with you." I looked at Cole then kissed his bruised cheek. "You, too."

Earl winked at me as he shook his head. "The crazy things we do for love."

I stood in front of the full-length mirror in my bedroom and smiled. My dress was exactly how I dreamed it would be. Cream silk, simple lines, the hem sweeping the floor, and my favorite silver necklace with my wolf on it around my neck.

Earl rolled over on my bed, crumpling the cream silk bowtie I'd taken twenty minutes to convince him to wear. "I like it. My fur will show up on the silk, though. And if I get a claw snagged—"

"Keep those murder mittens tucked away," I grumbled. "Although I don't mind the fur."

"Looking good, Brimstone." Storm leaned against the open door, a smile on her face.

I caught her eye in the mirror and returned the smile. "I could say the same for you. Do you approve of the pantsuit?"

"Even if you'd shoved me in an over-the-top frilly dress with a plunging neckline and covered in scratchy lace, I'd have worn it. After all, you only get married once." Storm looked stunning in a deep purple pantsuit with a flared leg and velvet collar.

"Are you ready?" Odessa dashed in, carrying my bridal bouquet. She wore a silk ruched dress in the same deep purple as Storm's pantsuit, which accentuated her ample curves. "Oh! That dress is divine."

"Given how extravagant today's going to be, I wondered if it was too simple." I gently smoothed my hands down the soft fabric.

"I like it." Indigo ambled in next. She'd chosen a pantsuit just like Storm but set it off with a trilby hat and dramatic dark makeup.

"So long as we all feel good about what we're wearing, that's the only opinion that matters." I turned to my friends, and we group hugged. "How's it looking out there?"

"Everyone's waiting. Cole looks unbelievably handsome and nervous," Indigo said. "Don't worry, Olympus is doing a sound job as a stand-in best man and calming his nerves."

After Reuben's revelations, he had no option but to stand down from his best man duties, and I was grateful to Olympus when he willingly accepted Cole's request to be his new best man.

"Are Serenity and the girls here?" We'd found them locked in a concealed barn in the backyard of Zodiac's home. There'd been a brief struggle as the werewolves guarding them had protested when we got them out, but when they realized Zodiac had been caught, they gave up. Reuben's family had been scared but unharmed, although distraught when they learned of his involvement in framing Cole.

"They're here," Odessa said. "We'll look after them. Serenity seems shaky, but she'll be good. She's not sure if she'll stand by her man, though."

"I hope they work things out, but whatever she decides, it'll be right for her and her family," I said.

A lot had happened over the last week in the lead-up to the wedding, but my parents had been true to their word, and I'd barely had to think about the last-minute details. I was so grateful they'd taken care of everything.

"Olympus went to the Magic Council headquarters before today's events got too distracting," Indigo said. "Zodiac has been charged with half a dozen crimes, including kidnapping, extortion, and murder."

"And he admitted to bribing the eyewitness," Storm added.

"Only because the fake eyewitness handed over the money Zodiac gave him to lie. He said he had no idea what Zodiac planned to do. Zodiac told him he wanted to frame an out-of-control werewolf, who was randomly attacking people, so he thought he was helping, not putting an innocent werewolf behind bars," Indigo said.

"And Reuben?" I asked.

"They're holding him. He'll be punished for his part in the crime," Indigo said.

"Cole was stunned by his betrayal, but Reuben was pushed into a corner and felt he had no choice but to protect his family. Still, I'm not sure Cole will ever forgive him. Maybe, in time, they can talk. See if they can't work something out," I said.

"That's enough murder and betrayal talk," Odessa said brightly. "Today is all about new beginnings and cementing forever bonds with the person you love the most."

"Luna needs to focus on how she'll handle her terrifying mother-in-law when this is all official." Storm smirked.

"I'm interested in finding that out too." Morrigan appeared in the doorway, looking stunning in a form-fitting moss green dress, the bodice adorned with shimmering sequins. Completing her outfit, she wore a pair of green stiletto heels that elongated her already statuesque figure.

Storm shrugged, her expression unrepentant. "I'm only telling it like it is. You're hard work."

"I'd expect nothing less from Luna's closest friends. Ladies, if I may have a minute with my almost-daughter-in-law," Morrigan said.

My friends turned to me, waiting to see if I was willing to have alone time with Morrigan. I nodded, signaling them to go, and they headed out, closing the door, all of them giving me a discrete thumbs-up.

Earl remained on the bed, watching the interaction with interest.

Morrigan strode over and hugged me tight. I squeaked, her embrace as painful as always. She stepped back, still holding onto my shoulders. "I know I've said it before, but thank you. You saved my son, and you never doubted him, even when the evidence proved his guilt."

I stared up at her in surprise. She'd given me a single curt thank you after I'd brought Cole home. I'd never seen her this emotional. "I'll always look out for Cole, just as he'll look out for me. We truly love each other. I know you have your doubts about this union, but—"

"No! Not anymore. You're a true alpha's mate." Her eyes glinted amber. "You're an alpha, too. You'd be welcome to join my pack. We're unique and wonderful. No males allowed. Of course, we enjoy ourselves with the men from time to time, but my ladies look after themselves and look out for each other. We're fierce, loyal, and true. Those are the markings of all great alpha females. And I'm honored and deeply proud to have you join our family."

I smiled, choked up by this surprising show of feeling. "I'm looking forward to being a part of your family."

Morrigan pulled me into her embrace again, and I was glad for the distraction so I could blink away tears. "Now, grab your wrap and let's get you married to my son."

We made the short journey in a decorated horse-drawn carriage through the peaceful snowy lanes to a stunning listed barn on the edge of Witch Haven. Earl rode with me, tucked under my thick, silky cream cape, purring softly against my belly. Although we didn't speak, Morrigan held my hand the whole way, her grip warm and comforting.

My mother and father met me. My father opened the door and helped me out. "You look beautiful, darling."

Earl hopped down then jumped from paw to paw as snow lodged between his toe beans. I should have gotten him cute booties to go with his bowtie.

My mother embraced me, her voice low and close to my ear. "I hope Morrigan didn't cause you too much trouble. She insisted she collect you despite me arguing with her. She wouldn't budge. These werewolves are so stubborn. Are you sure you know what you're getting yourself into?"

I kissed her cheek and laughed. "I couldn't be any surer. And just so you know, werewolves have excellent hearing."

My mother flushed and had the grace to duck her head as she glanced at Morrigan.

"No more fighting between us," Morrigan said. "Today is all about Luna and Cole. Shall we?" She swept away to take her seat.

"It'll be a miracle if that woman doesn't fight me today," my mother said. "I wanted to collect you so I could share tips on how to have a long, happy marriage."

I stepped back, one eyebrow arched to its fullest extent. My parents' marriage had been far from happy, and I was the product of that unhappiness thanks to my mother's dalliance with another man.

"My dear, you can share your knowledge after the ceremony." My father tried to lead her away, but she resisted. He shook his head. "Expect a few hurdles, and you won't be too shocked with what married life throws at you."

"That's perfect advice." I laughed as I caught hold of their hands. "And I'm so grateful for what you've done. Everything looks amazing."

My mother sighed, finally realizing that today wasn't about her. "So long as you're happy, darling."

"I am. Now, go take a seat." I nodded at her.

She pressed her lips together, gave another resigned sigh, kissed me, and hurried away.

My father took my arm and led me toward the entrance but then turned and took me around the building.

"Aren't we going in through the main entrance?" I asked. "Everyone is inside."

He smiled, a warm glint of humor in his eyes. "I know you think we don't listen, but an outdoor wedding was always important to you and Cole. We talked you out of it because we were concerned about the cold. But... we changed a few things and moved everything outside. Your friends have been casting spells, so everyone stays warm."

My heart lodged in my throat as we walked along a snow cleared path to an enchanting forest clearing, illuminated by softly glowing lanterns hanging from branches. The ethereal light cast soft shadows that danced amidst the evergreen foliage and illuminated sigils etched into the trees. An altar took center stage, adorned with winter blooms, crystals, and cascading vines, symbolizing the harmonious union of werewolf and witch.

"Do you like it?" he asked. "Not too earthy? Your mother kept saying it was earthy, but I think it's exactly what you really wanted. Not all the pomp we kept forcing on you."

I couldn't speak, so I nodded. It was just as I'd pictured but better. I opened my eyes wide to stop the tears from falling.

Soft, encouraging whispers of incantations from the witch guests created an otherworldly soundtrack as I walked, and the werewolves grumbled their approval and nodded at me as I passed them.

My steps faltered when I saw Serenity and her daughters. She caught my eye and nodded, her gaze full of sadness and understanding. This must be so hard for her, but I was glad she was here.

As I drew closer to the altar, the air was infused with a bewitching medley of scents. The sweet aroma of blooming winter flowers and herbs mingled with the earthy scent of moss-covered trees. A subtle hint of smoky incense lingered in the air, carrying the essence of ancient rituals and magical blessings.

Cole took my attention. My handsome, perfect, wonderful mate. His suit was dove gray with a red cravat, his usually messy dark hair swept back from his face. But it was his smile that captivated me and made my heart swell. It was full of love and the promise of a wonderful future together.

My father stopped by Cole, his expression serious. "I'm trusting you with my only daughter."

Cole tore his attention from me. "It's a trust I'll never break, sir. You have my word."

He nodded then gently released me from his grip. My heart raced in anticipation. Ever since our worlds had collided during our first meeting when we'd chased a bad guy, I knew my life would never be the same, and I could hardly contain the joy that filled me.

Our elderly werewolf celebrant, Tiberius, his wise eyes gleaming with warmth, began the sacred words that would bind our lives together. His voice, deep and soothing, resonated through the forest.

"Luna and Cole, you stand here today, under the watchful eyes of the sun, moon, stars, and the elemental power of nature, ready to embark on a journey. From different realms you have come, united by a love that knows no boundaries."

I held Cole's hands, and we looked into each other's eyes.

"Luna, as the moon guides the tides, so shall you guide Cole with your unwavering love and compassionate spirit. And Cole, as the strength of the wolf protects the pack, so shall you protect and cherish Luna with your fierce devotion. Today, you pledge yourselves to each other, and may your love be an eternal flame that illuminates the path you walk together."

I smiled at Cole. Every moment we'd shared, every laugh and tear, every near-death experience flooded my mind, reaffirming my love for him. It was time to exchange our vows, to bare our souls before each other and our friends and family.

"Luna, you may speak your words first," Tiberius said.

"Cole," I began, my voice quivering with emotion, "from the day I first laid eyes on you, I knew my life would be changed forever. You captured my heart, awakened my spirit, and showed me a love that transcends all realms. I've found solace and strength to be exactly the witch I need to be. Today, I vow to be your partner in all things, to support and encourage you as we navigate our life together. I promise to honor our differences and celebrate our similarities. I'll love you unconditionally for all eternity."

The werewolf guests gently howled their approval.

Tears shimmered in Cole's eyes. "Luna, you're my guiding light and the source of my joy. In your presence, I've found a love so pure and powerful that it defies logic. You've seen the darkest corners of my soul and you love me, anyway. Today, I pledge my heart and my life to you. I promise to be your protector, your confidant, and your biggest supporter. I will cherish you, respect you, and stand by your side through every twist and turn life may bring. With you, Luna, I've found my forever."

The witches swirled their spells around us in a show of support, enveloping us in their warm affection.

As our vows hung in the air, a silence enveloped us. It was as if time held its breath, acknowledging the sacredness of this moment. And then, with a gentle smile, the celebrant spoke once more.

"We will now begin the elemental blessing, followed by the shapeshifting ritual."

"You don't have to take part in the shapeshifting," Cole whispered against my ear. "I figure you've had enough of illusion magic to last a lifetime."

"I don't need to be a werewolf to run with you and the rest of the wolves. Storm's got my trainers tucked under a chair. I'm coming with you."

He chuckled. "I'd be honored if you'd join us. I know you can keep up."

And so, the elaborate rituals began, and I loved every second of them. The witch blessings, the werewolves shifting and dashing through the snow-covered trees with me beside them with Earl riding on my shoulder, and the gift of a delicious twinning cake from Uncle Albert to bless the union with sweetness, which the werewolves fell on with greedy abandon. It was perfection.

By the time it was over, I was exhausted, pink-cheeked, and deliriously happy as we settled back at the altar. My gown was torn, my flowers long lost, but my happiness more than compensated. Life with the werewolves was messily amazing.

Tiberius nodded at us. "The traditions have been completed and sanctioned, which leaves me to say, by the power vested in the spirits that surround us and the elements that protect us, I now pronounce you forever mates. May your union be blessed with harmony, passion, and everlasting love."

The werewolves let rip with a chorus of joy-filled howls, the witches danced, and the familiars dodged and weaved through the guests, sparking confetti everywhere and showering the snow in colorful sparkles.

I tensed when Jade appeared, wearing a stunning red gown with a slit up the thigh. She crushed me in a hug before stepping back. "Congrats, beautiful! Wow, what a ceremony. And you can run fast. Using a little of that witchy stuff I expect to keep up with us."

"Luna will always outpace me." Cole held my hand tight.

I shook my head. "I'll always be by your side. Just like you are mine."

"Oh! You two are to die for." Jade covered her mouth for a second. "Oops! Bad choice of words. I'm glad you're not dead, Cole, or in prison. I knew my girl would fix things." She punched me in the arm.

I grimaced then nudged Cole. "Didn't you have something you wanted to say to Jade?"

He sighed. "Luna thinks—"

"Uh-uh. We both think you should try again with Atticus and his pack in Hollow Cove. Cole met with him and explained what an asset you'd be."

"He did? You think I'm an asset?" Jade's eyes widened as she stared at Cole.

Cole shuffled his feet and shrugged. "Luna is all about giving people second chances."

Laughter burst out of Jade. "In my case, it's about fifty more chances. OMG! Are you for real? You've put in a good word for me?"

I nodded. "Cole did the hard work. And Atticus likes you, but maybe tone it down a bit, so he can get to know the real you. The kind side you showed me when you realized Cole was in so much trouble."

She chewed on her bottom lip. "I don't do vanilla, but I can try to be a bit more zen. Atticus is here, isn't he?"

"He is. Spend some time together and you might find a home with him. It could be fun," I said. "Maybe even better than being a footloose and fancy-free werewolf. No more checking over your shoulder."

Jade grabbed me and spun me until I felt dizzy. "You're an angel. A witch angel!" She smacked a kiss on my lips and then dashed over to a group of werewolves, Atticus in the center.

I chuckled. "Atticus is about to get his paws full. But once Jade relaxes, she should fit in."

"I don't know how you stay polite around her." Cole took my hand again.

"We're all complicated and trying to find our place, the group we fit in and the special people we're meant to be with." I squeezed his hand. "I found you and my family in Witch Haven. Maybe Jade can do the same in Hollow Cove." I caught Earl as he jumped at me and settled him on my shoulder.

"Have I ever told you how amazingly wonderful you are?" Cole leaned close to kiss me, but Earl shoved his tail in between us.

"It's not the honeymoon yet. Hold off on the PDA. You have guests to entertain. And I'm hungry."

I laughed as I walked down the aisle with my new mate, basking in the glow of our union. The future lay before us, brimming with possibilities, and with each step, my heart soared with gratitude.

Cole looked down at me, his grin wide. "Happy we didn't elope?"

"And miss this? The thought never entered my head."

"If you'd eloped, I wouldn't have to compete with those greedy hounds for food." Earl curled his tail around my neck. "Did you see what they did to the cake?"

"It's why Uncle Albert made three more cakes," I said. "And get used to it. These furballs are your family, too."

"I'll have to take you hunting sometime," Cole said. "That's if you can keep up with the wolves."

Earl puffed out his chest. "Anytime. Although I prefer my food to come out of the fridge. You got me salmon at the meal, didn't you?"

I continued smiling as my two best guys good-naturedly bickered over food. Witch Haven was safe again. Cole was free, the killer in jail, and order restored. My gaze swept over my amazing best friends who surrounded Serenity and her daughters with love while keeping an eye on the excitable werewolves to ensure they didn't steer the wedding party too close to chaos.

Life as an elemental witch who'd married into werewolf royalty would always come with a few twists and turns, but with my family, friends, and familiar by my side, I knew I'd found my forever home and eternal happiness.

About the Author

K.E. O'Connor (Karen) is a mystery author living in the beautiful British countryside. She loves all things mystery, animals, and cake. If you want to practice spells, solve a few murders, and spend time with amazing witches and their talking familiars, join her weekly newsletter.

Sign up today.

Newsletter: https://BookHip.com/GXDVFRA
Website: www.keoconnor.com
Facebook: www.facebook.com/keoconnorauthor

Also By

Witch Haven: Welcome to Witch Haven, where nothing is what it seems. Meet four fabulous witches as they struggle with their destinies, deal with misfiring magic, murder, and the Magic Council.

Crypt Witches: Meet Tempest Crypt, a witch who swallows demons, and Wiggles, her mini-talking hellhound, while you enjoy magical murder and intrigue.

Lorna Shadow: A cozy mystery series set in the fun world of a personal assistant who sees ghosts. Meet Lorna, her ditzy sidekick, Helen, and Flipper, the dog who senses ghosts, as they solve crimes and save the day.

Holly Holmes: An adorable cozy culinary mystery series set in the beautiful village of Audley St. Mary. Each book is full of treats, murder, and twists. Join Holly and Meatball, her clue-hunting dog, as they solve murders and eat cake.

www.ingramcontent.com/pod-product-compliance
Lightning Source LLC
Chambersburg PA
CBHW030808200726
48285CB00015B/1868